Something SO SWEET

Breakaway Book One

A novel by

Meika Usher

Something So Sweet

Meika Usher

Copyright © 2017 by Meika Usher

First edition

www.meikausher.com

Cover design by germancreative

Edited by Jessica Snyder, Keyanna Butler

Distribution by Pronoun

ISBN: 978-0-9991180-0-9

For all you dreamers out there:

Make that shit happen.

—

1: Punch Bowl Massacre

You ever see those movies where the heroine enters a room and it goes dead silent? Everyone is staring like she's the dog that got caught stealing the Christmas ham?

Yeah, that.

Only, I'd take a belly full of ham over a shoe full of fruit punch any day.

As if my place as June Lake's favorite pariah weren't already secured, I'd managed to kill the music *and* deplete the beverage supply within thirty seconds of my arrival.

Easing into the backyard, I shook the unplugged extension cord from my foot and stepped over the mess I'd created.

I lifted my hand in a half-wave as I looked up and found the backyard full of people staring. "Hi," I said, trying for a smile. A few people waved back, but mostly they just stared.

Was it too late to slip back out through the gate?

"Are you all right, pumpkin patch?" Dad ambled forward, donning a Kiss the Cook apron and a concerned expression.

Yep. Too late.

"Oh, I'm fine." I shook the punch from the gift bag clutched in my hand and held it toward him. "Happy birthday!"

Dad took the bag and wiped it on his apron. "Thank you. And thanks for that spectacular entrance." His eyes, the same green eyes he'd passed on to me, twinkled with laughter, and *maybe* a beer or two. "I was worried people were getting bored." He dropped a kiss on my forehead and I caught a whiff of Budweiser. Yep. Definitely a beer or two.

"Tierney! There you are!" my mother hollered from across the yard—as if I needed any more attention. "I was beginning to think you'd gotten lost."

"No, not lost." I glanced at the punch bowl massacre at my feet. "Just…thirsty, apparently."

Her eyes followed mine and she shrugged. "There's plenty more punch inside." She put her arm around me and steered me away from the mess. "Go towel off and grab another jug from the fridge." Someone called her name and she gave my shoulder a squeeze before wandering off.

Stares and whispers followed behind me. My skin prickled. Why had I let Mom talk—no, *guilt*—me into coming to this thing? Sure, it was a milestone birthday, and sure, I loved my father, but dammit. I'd stayed away from events like this for a reason.

My eyes grazed the swarm of people and I let out a slow breath of relief. So far, so good.

Glancing back at Dad, who was now lost in conversation with a couple friends, I turned and started for the house. Maybe I'd just stay there for the rest of the party.

Really? Twenty-nine years old, and you're really going to hide inside like a coward?

I ignored the voice. I'd gladly take the coward's way if it meant I didn't have to see—

A pair of blue Converse stepped into view. I skidded to a stop, dread settling over me. Slowly, my eyes followed a pair of dark blue jeans to a white t-shirt with a skull and crossbones across the front, only the crossbones were kitchen utensils. Finally, I reached a grinning face.

The dread eased. *Not him.*

This guy had dark hair, just long enough to curl at the ends, just short enough to avoid complete chaos. His blue eyes gleamed with unadulterated amusement. Huh. Cute.

"Thirsty?" He held out a cup of punch, and his lips twitched.

Well, cute until the smartass came out to play.

3

"Oh, I get it." I pushed passed him. "Because of the whole punch bowl thing. You're funny."

"I think so." He moved in front of me. I didn't slow my pace, so he had to walk backward or be run over. "I don't know about everyone else, but I thought that was one hell of an entrance. I mean, nothing says 'I have arrived,' better than a flying punch bowl. Maybe it's just me. I do have a thing for cute brunettes that know how to make an entrance."

"Maybe I didn't want to make an entrance." I looked over his shoulder to the open back door. Almost there.

"Aw, come on. Why not? Who doesn't like to be the center of attention?" He grinned and continued walking backward.

My eyes fell on the single step up to the patio. "Hey, watch—" I started, but it was too late.

He hit the step, stumbled backward, and landed on the patio with a thump, fruit punch spilling all over his once-white shirt.

The look of pure shock on his face had me laughing before I thought to ask if he was okay. "Dude." I moved forward to offer him a hand. "Watch your step."

He took my hand and got to his feet, brushing at the bright red stain. "A little late with the warning, doll," he said, though he didn't sound angry.

"My apologies." I glanced around to see people staring and laughing. "How about we get you a towel?" I slid open the screen door and he motioned for me to go in first.

"You're welcome, by the way," he said as he closed the door behind him.

"For what?"

"Well, my public display of awkwardness took everyone's attention from you."

I crossed the kitchen and opened a drawer. "That was very kind of you. I am forever in your debt." I handed him a towel. Squinting, I tried to place how I knew him. An image of a scrawny blue-eyed teen ran through my head. A ha! "You're Wes's little cousin, right? John? James?"

"Jack." He glanced up and grimaced. "And I'm not Wes's *little* anything. We're the same age."

"Okay," I said slowly. "My bad. You just...seemed younger."

"Plus, I'm taller," he grumbled, handing back the towel. "Better looking, too."

"And oh-so full of yourself."

"Please," he shot back, leaning against the counter right next to me. "You think I'm a little cute."

I shook my head, heat creeping into my face. "Not even a little bit, buddy," I stared at a spot on the counter, avoiding his grin. "I like my guys less cocky."

"Fair enough." He leaned an elbow on the counter. "I'll try to tone down the cocky."

"Please do." I glanced up in time to catch him running a hand through his hair. My eyes lingered on his bicep. Huh. He'd certainly grown up nice, hadn't he? No sign of the gawky teen that'd helped me run the dunk tank at Spring Thing eons ago. Maybe I really *could* spend the rest of the party inside.

"So," he interrupted before I could ogle him further. Something about the spark in his blue eyes made me forget all about the mob just beyond the glass door. "How have you been?"

"Oh, you know." I searched my mind for a suitable answer. Really, what I'd been up to was a whole lot of nothing. Working at Pencil Pusher Publishing for the last six years, biding my time until something better came along. Going out on bad dates and girls' nights with my best friend, Cat. Watching too many TV shows about teenage vampires. "I'm doing all right," I finally said, wishing I had a more interesting answer. "How about you?"

"That was a cop out if I ever heard one." Jack's eyes lit with laughter. "But I'll let you get away with it." He paused, his lips tilting. "For now." His gaze lingered on my face, promising more effective interrogation tactics to come.

"Oh, really," I started, leaning in just a touch. "How do you—"

"Tierney?"

A voice, warm as a memory, filled the kitchen. I turned and everything inside me frosted over. There he was. The reason I'd avoided June Lake for nine years. The reason why, when I did come home, I never stayed long. The reason I didn't want to come tonight.

His eyes met mine and just like that, I went back. I could smell the rain-soaked breeze, hear the sound of breaking hearts. I could feel my footsteps as I walked away.

I exhaled, his name catching on my breath.

"Wes."

2: History Repeats

I could feel it happening. Sweaty palms, palpitating heart, dry mouth. I was reverting. Soon, I'd fully transform into the awkward, anxious girl I'd been in high school. In five, four, three, two...

Wes smiled, his golden hazel eyes warming. A squeak slipped passed my lips.

And there she is.

I cleared my throat and smiled back. "H-hey."

"And on that note." Jack's voice yanked my attention away from Wes. I looked his way in time to see him ambling toward the exit. "Nice seeing you again, Tierney," he added as he slid the screen door open.

I opened my mouth to stop him, acutely aware that he was about to leave me alone with Wes, but before I could eke out a syllable, Wes stepped back into my line of vision.

"It's been a while." He leaned against the counter I straightened my shoulders. *Get it together, Tierney.* "You look good."

I glanced at the simple green dress I wore and wished I'd put a little more effort into my appearance. Brushing my reckless waves from my face, I said, "Thanks. You, too."

I willed my lungs to fill with oxygen as my eyes traced over him. His blond hair had been forced into cooperation with scissors and a comb and now sat neatly over his ever-appealing eyes. His smile, that perfect, beautiful smile, remained the same, though. It still sent my heart bouncing around like a Ping-Pong ball gone awry.

How was it possible that he looked even better *now?*

"How have you been?"

His question broke through the static in my brain and I nodded. "Yeah. Good. Me, too." Wincing, I tried again. "I've been doing well."

"I'm glad."

Silence crept over us. I grabbed a dishtowel from the counter and twisted it in my hands. Just beyond Wes, half a dozen sets of curious eyes peered through the patio door. *Go away,* I thought, turning my attention back to Wes. *This is not a live-action soap opera for your entertainment.*

Except that, in a town like June Lake, it kind of was.

Tossing the towel back on the counter, I took a breath. "Rumor has it you took over the veterinary clinic when your dad retired." I swallowed around a sudden lump in my throat. "Just what you always wanted."

He tilted his head. "The rumors are true."

"That's..." My throat burned with *congratulations* that wouldn't come. I urged the word to tumble from my tongue, but it refused. I was happy for him—really. But here he was, making all his dreams come true, while I...well, I wasn't.

"So listen," he said, glancing behind him. Our group of spies scattered like cockroaches. "I've got to get going, but maybe we can grab lunch tomorrow? Catch up?" He gave me a hopeful look and my angst was forgotten.

"Yeah, okay." The words spilled out before I could stop them. Eyes widening, I tried to pull them back. "Actually—"

"Great. Noon at the Backdoor Diner?" He moved passed me before I could answer. A whiff of something warm and spicy hit my nose, sabotaging any last attempt at declining I had on my lips.

And then he was gone.

I sagged against the counter and rubbed my hands over my face. I just agreed to meet Wes. For lunch. Tomorrow.

Why had I done that? I was leaving tonight.

Letting out a groan, I pushed away from the counter. I couldn't go. It was that simple. I needed to get back to Port Agnes, I needed to get back to work, I needed to get away from—

Wait.

Did…did Wes just ask me on a *date?*

Why would he do that? He—

He *did* seem happy to see me. And he'd said I looked good. Maybe…

I glanced out the window at the party still in full swing. As my father held up a platter piled high with food, Jack reached up and poached a hot dog, grinning in victory as Wes eased behind him, headed toward the gate.

As if he could feel my eyes on him, Wes glanced back, a smile just for me on his lips. Heat flooded my cheeks and I smiled back.

Yep.

I was definitely going on a date with my ex-fiancé.

***

As soon as I'd returned to the party, I was greeted with daggered looks and questions ahoy. It seemed Wes and I had stolen the show.

I'd been in town for barely two hours and I'd already greased the gossip mill.

I let my eyes scan the yard as I headed back toward my father, looking for a head of messy hair and a stained t-shirt. I hadn't gotten to properly thank Jack for his rescue earlier. Looked like I wouldn't get my chance tonight.

I squelched the disappointment as Mom sailed out the back door, birthday cake in hand. A rousing rendition of "Happy Birthday" filled the yard, and I looped my arm through my dad's as the blazing pastry arrived. Directly across from me, my brother, Stephen, stood—five-year-old daughter in his arms, wife at his side. He caught my eye and smiled, prompting my niece to wave excitedly. I waved back and, in that moment, I was glad I came.

Half an hour later, I sneaked back into the house, a paper plate piled with cake in one hand, fork in the other. "Ahh, cake," I murmured as I stuck my fork into the delicious concoction. I turned the corner, heading for the living room. Far, far away from the crowd. "You've always been there for me."

One could only take so many *How are you's* and *It's good to see you's*. No matter how well-intended.

And, let's be real, they weren't *that* well-intended.

The people here, they didn't like me much.

Eyes glued to the cake, I crossed the room to the couch. I'd missed this couch, with its soft cushions that hugged you like—

"What the—" My butt hit a seat too stiff and unforgiving to be my mom's couch. Leaning forward, I turned to investigate. Sure enough, this was not the poufy, delicious sofa that had been in the family room for years. This monstrosity was electric blue and not poufy in the least. Pretty sure my derriere would bruise from just sitting there.

I stood and rubbed my rear, my eyes moving around the room for the first time. I'd been so focused on the cake that I didn't notice that I walked into a parallel universe.

It looked like someone had loaded a canon with the highlights reel from an HGTV show, then shot it all over the room. The walls had a weird texture in a shade of blue lighter than the couch, yet somehow more eyeball-searing. The fireplace, once a perfectly pretty red brick, had been redone in glaring white subway tile. The mantel was covered with Buddha statues of all shapes and sizes. Well, all sizes. There was really only one Buddha shape.

Since when had my parents converted to Buddhism?

Putting down my cake, I ventured further into the room. From furry rugs to shiny curtains, everything had changed. Fear for the rest of the house overtook me. Cake forgotten, I wandered into the dining room, wincing at the modern, sharp-edged black furniture and absurd zebra-print rug. *How* long had I been away? I mentally calculated. My last visit was for Christmas, so…four months?

Did my mother launch headfirst into a midlife crisis in that short amount of time?

As I reached the stairs, something occurred to me. If the lower level had managed to change so drastically, what did that mean for the rest of the house? Was my childhood bedroom transformed into a modernistic torture chamber? I was almost afraid to find out.

"Oh, you *are* still here." Mom popped around the corner with an armful of beers for the still-partying guests. "I thought maybe you'd hit the road."

"Without saying goodbye? What kind of daughter would I be?" I crossed the floor and took a few beers from her. "I may not come visit as often as you'd like, but give me some credit, woman. Also," I continued, sweeping my free hand across the room. "What's up with all *this*?"

"I've been taking interior decorating classes at Brightwell Community College. Do you like it?" Mom's eyes lit with pride and I didn't want to tell her I was afraid the army of Buddhas might kill me in my sleep.

"Yeah, it's...great." I hoped my grimace passed for a smile. "I particularly like the, uh...spaghetti and meatballs painting in the dining room."

"Thank you, sweetheart." Mom took my words at face value, admiring the abstract atrocity from afar.

"So," I said. "I think I'm gonna crash here tonight, if that's all right."

Mom's eyes widened. "You're staying the night? We could go shopping tomorrow! Oh, we'll have so much fun."

"I've actually got lunch plans," I said, hesitant to be specific.

"Oh, yeah. I saw you talking to Jack earlier." Mom said it with a smile that told me that she wasn't the only one who'd noticed.

"What? No." I brushed her off with a hand. "Just an old friend. But maybe we can go shopping after." I threw in the last part to keep her from asking who the 'old friend' was. I didn't need word getting around town that Wes's barracuda ex-fiancée had reeled back in. That might prompt the gathering of an angry mob outside the Backdoor Diner. And I hadn't brought my running shoes.

"Sounds good." Mom whirled back to the kitchen. "Oh, and when you're ready for bed, come find me. We'll have to put sheets on the futon."

Well, that didn't sound good. Glancing into the kitchen, then up the stairs, I sighed. Where did I put that cake?

3: Burgers & Temptation

Mistakes were made.

I tugged my cardigan over my chest and grimaced. When Mom had offered up her closet this morning, I didn't take into account our...uh, size differences.

This dress, a black and white floral number, may have looked good on my mother, but on me...well, let's just say the extra cup size wasn't helping. Just what I needed. To show up in the crowded diner dressed like a Sunday school teacher with a naughty streak.

But show up to the diner, I did. Because what choice did I have? I couldn't stand the guy up, could I? Especially considering my track record.

Plus, I had to admit, part of me was looking forward to seeing Wes again.

Last night, as I laid awake on the uncomfortable futon in the corner of what used to be my bedroom, I kept reliving the six years Wes and I were together. I had considered myself the luckiest girl in all of June Lake—make that all of Michigan—because Wes had chosen me. Quiet, shy, awkward me. Out of all the girls he could have had—and there were a lot of them—he'd picked me. He'd loved me.

Until I dumped him.

Sighing, I sank back against the vinyl booth and eyed the door. Maybe Wes was going to stand *me* up. A small, petty little way to get back at the girl who'd broken his heart.

I picked up a packet of artificial sweetener and began shaking it. Around me, the stares were obvious. In the corner, Dottie Daniels, founding member of the Blue-Haired Biddies, sipped her tea and sent poisonous looks my way. For a nice old lady, she sure did have the evil eye down.

From the counter, Dorothy Anderson stared my way. She'd been over here once already, asking for my order, and I'd told her I was waiting for someone. Her dark eyes narrowed as if she were trying to read my mind. Then, she just nodded and walked away.

Weird how you could spend your whole life in a place, then suddenly become a stranger. Not just a stranger, either. A full-blown villainess.

The bell above the entrance jingled. I looked up in time to see Wes enter, and just like that, all else faded away.

17

He caught sight of me and smiled, lifting his hand in a wave. I sat up straighter, tugged at my cardigan and wrung my hands in my lap. Was I smiling? It sort of *felt* like a smile.

"Sorry I'm late," he said as he sat across from me. I tried not to notice how the springtime sun caught glints of gold in his hair. "Tim Richards' cow went into labor last night, and there were complications."

I nodded, swallowing passed the lump in my throat. "It's okay. I...um...haven't been here long." Twenty minutes wasn't really that long, right? "Everything turn out okay? With the cow?"

Wes nodded. "Calf was up and walking when I left." His smile was sheepish. "Almost makes me feel guilty for the burger I'm about to order."

I laughed as he raised his hand to get Dorothy's attention. "But sometimes you just gotta give in to temptation." His eyes lingered on mine.

Clearing my throat, I glanced down at my wringing hands. "Yeah, well. Burgers, man," was all I managed to say. *Me no word so good.*

"Yeah, burgers," he repeated as Dorothy arrived.

"Afternoon, Handsome." She flashed her pearly whites at Wes. "How's your day going?"

"Oh, you know." Wes treated her to his own trademark smile. "Birthing cows, saving lives. The family business."

Dorothy laughed and swatted Wes on the arm. "That's my boy," she said, whipping her pen and pad from her apron. "I do have to say," she continued, turning to me, "that I'm feeling like I've stepped back in time. Seeing you two kids together, it takes me back." She smiled and my eyes darted to Wes.

He waved Dorothy off. "I can guarantee you haven't."

"Thank the Lord." Dorothy laughed. "I couldn't live without my Netflix." She paused, chewing on the end of her pen. "What I wouldn't give to have my waistline back, though."

"You and me both," I said, hoping to break through the awkwardness.

"Please, the only weight you've gained is peeking out of your sweater." She raised her eyebrows toward my chest.

I pulled the cardigan closed again, feeling my face heat. From the corner of my eye, I saw Wes smirk.

"You're looking good, though," Dorothy added, her face softening. "Haven't seen you in a while."

I nodded, relieved that Dorothy didn't seem to have any simmering hostility toward me. "Yeah, I've been busy." Guilt gnawed at my gut. I'd spent two summers working at the Backdoor, and she'd been a great boss. I should have known Dorothy better than to assume she'd jump on the anti-Tierney bandwagon.

"I hear you're making it big in the city." She smiled and there was a glimmer of pride in her eyes.

"I wouldn't call it making it big." I pictured my cubicle at Pencil Pushers and fought back a grimace. An associate editor with a small-scale publishing house wasn't exactly what I thought I'd be doing with my life. "But I'm doing all right."

Dorothy nodded and then poised her pen over her paper. "What can I get for you two?"

Once she took our orders, she walked off, leaving Wes and I alone. I picked up my roll of silverware and unwrapped it, twisting the napkin in my hand. "So...how's the family?"

Wes stretched his arm over the back of his booth and the sunlight caught the sprinkling of hair on his forearm. He wore a pale blue button-down, the sleeves rolled up, and it was easy to imagine him in a white coat, doctoring up all the animals in June Lake.

Easy and nice.

"The family's good," he said and I forced my eyes back to his face. Oh, yeah. I'd asked a question. "Darcy's graduating college this year. Mom's sort of a wreck over it. Hell, *I'm* sort of a wreck over it. That's my baby sister, you know? And she's not a baby anymore." He looked at me, his eyes wide. "Makes me feel old."

"Ugh." I shook my head. "That makes *me* feel old. How old was she when we first...um, I mean. She had to be like seven or so, right?"

Wes nodded, graciously ignoring my allusion to our history. "Eight, actually. You'd hardly recognize her now." He smiled and the pride he had in his little sister was evident.

"Wow." I pictured the little blond girl who followed me everywhere for the first two years of my relationship with Wes. She'd become like a kid sister to me, but once I left for college, we rarely saw each other. "I can't believe she's graduating from college."

"Time flies, huh?" Wes's eyes found mine.

The restaurant full of people faded away. "Yeah, it does."

***

The rest of lunch passed in a blur. We talked and laughed and reminisced about the past until Dorothy brought us our checks. Wes insisted on paying for my burger, and as we headed outside, a pleasant warmth radiated through me.

"This was nice," I said as we stood on the sidewalk, getting around to goodbye. I didn't know what to do with my hands and so I tugged at my sweater for the one-hundredth time.

Wes smiled, holding my eyes with his. Something deep inside the golden-hazel depths flashed bright, and the ground shifted beneath my feet. "It was good seeing you," he said, oblivious to the mini-earthquake. "Don't be a stranger."

I nodded, thinking that this didn't feel like strangers. This felt like picking up where we left off. This felt like—

No.

I tore my gaze away. I couldn't afford to think like that. The absolute last thing I needed was to go down that road again.

But it'd been such a good road for so long...

I lifted my eyes to find Wes still looking at me, his eyes warm with memory.

My heart thudded crookedly as I tumbled headfirst down Reminiscent Road. Detours from First Kiss Lane to Proposal Park had me stepping forward before logic could stop me. "I—"

"Tierney?" A shrill voice halted me in my tracks. I turned just as a talon-like hand closed around my forearm. "It *is* you!"

A pair of colossal blue eyes blinked at me and I instantly willed the sky to open up and strike me with lightning.

If the universe was trying to tell me Wes was a bad idea, I'd call this move a win.

"Lola, hey." I rustled up a smile, and peeled her hand from my arm. "How are you?"

Lola "Crazy Eyes" Sparks, head cheerleader, Prom Queen, Wes's ex-girlfriend, stood in front of me, as beautiful and unhinged as ever. "Oh, just fantastic!" She tossed her cascade of dark hair over her shoulder. Her gaze flitted to Wes. With a lifted brow, she continued. "I'm not interrupting, am I?"

"What? No." Wes waved her off with a level of dismissiveness that I would have found insulting if it weren't for the uncomfortable number of stares we'd accumulated. If I looked behind me, I bet I'd find the noses of everyone inside the Backdoor pressed against the window.

There's no place like home, I thought, willing myself to disappear. What I wouldn't give for the anonymity of Port Agnes right now.

"Tierney's in town for her dad's birthday," Wes continued as Lola crossed her arms over her chest and stared. "We were catching up."

She pursed her lips and tapped the toe of one of her high heel shoes. "I bet you were."

A stare-off ensued. Tension clouded the air around us. What in Hitchcock's name had I walked into?

The two stared at each other for an uncomfortable number of seconds before I tapped out. "Okay, well." Pushing between them, I started up the walk. "It was good to see you, Wes. You, too, Lola. But I really must be goi—"

"Oh!" Lola sparked to life, her talons reaching for my arm again. "I almost forgot to tell you!"

"Ahh, uh..." I spun away from her grasp. That manicure was lethal. "Yes?"

"I'm engaged!" She held out her hand to show off a chunky, sparkling diamond.

So, *that* was it. Wes and Lola must have...

Wes heard my question before I asked it. The subtle shake of his head and frantic widening of his eyes gave me my answer. Relief whooshed over me. Stupid, sweet relief.

Shoving all fuzzy, nostalgic *what-if* feelings deep, deep down, I flashed Lola a smile. "Congratulations!"

"Thank you!" She waved her hand in the air, sunlight glinting off a rock the size of Pluto. "I don't know how I got so lucky."

"Oh, I'm sure he's the lucky one." I took an ever-so-subtle step back. *Lucky if he manages to survive.*

"You're too sweet." She reached out and squeezed my arm, preventing my escape. Again. "Oh! And hey!"

"Y-yes?" I tensed, like a mouse when a hawk flies overhead. She was going to eat me alive. I just knew it.

"My engagement party is tonight!" she said, as if it had anything to do with...well, anything.

"Okay. Have fun." I tried moving again, but her grip was firm. If I looked down, I'd probably find blood pooling at my feet. Like a scene from *Psycho* or something.

"You should come!" Her eyes were like two jumbo marbles inside her unnervingly pretty face. "Everyone will be there." She glanced at Wes before adding, "Lots of time to *catch up.*"

My brain tingled, suspicion like a thousand bitey spiders. I eyed Lola. Why would she invite me to her engagement party? To say we were *frienemies* was an exaggeration. She straight-up hated me. Had from the moment Wes asked me out.

"You know you want to," she sang, batting her fake lashes. "Music, dancing, free booze…it'll be a blast!"

I looked from Lola to Wes. "I'm sure everyone would love to see you," he said in the most unhelpful way possible.

No. No. Say no, my brain screamed, even as my mouth gave in to peer pressure. "Sure!"

As soon as I said it, I wanted to slap myself across the face. No good could possibly come of this.

But, hey, at least the booze would be free.

4: Embrace the Cheese

Lakeside Gardens was already full of people buzzing around with drinks in their hands and manic smiles on their faces. Events like this always brought out the party animals in even June Lake's most stand-up citizens. It wasn't every day they had an excuse to get drunk and dance. Not twenty minutes in, and there were pinkened cheeks and bright eyes galore.

A lot of familiar faces bobbed in of the sea of people. A lot of faces I'd wondered about after I left. Mike Galloway from the school paper. Annette Ramsey, star of the girls' softball team. David MacArthur, captain of the debate team. If it weren't for the drinks in their hands and significant others on their arms, I would have thought I was back in high school.

That illusion was complete when I caught sight of Winn Porter, against the wall, surveying the crowd in true wallflower fashion.

My stomach twisted. Winn had been my best friend for years, until we drifted apart. Right about the time I started dating Wes.

Would it be weird to say hi? Or would it be weirder to avoid her?

Locating the bar, I ordered a martini and took a sip, steeling my spine. Would she even speak to me? I was a douche to her back then. Then again, it'd been years. She had to be over it by now, right?

Rolling my eyes at my indecisiveness, I pushed away from the bar and weaved through the crowd.

Winn looked up when I reached her. Recognition flickered in her wide gray eyes and her lips curved tentatively. "I heard you were in town."

I took the empty space beside her. "The punch bowl incident?"

She glanced my way, amusement lighting her face. "Nobody cared about the punch bowl." Pulling at the cuff of her long sleeve white shirt, she raised her eyebrows. "People are placing bets on how long it takes you and Wes to get back together."

"What?" Heat flooded my cheeks. "That's not—"

Winn leveled me with a stare, shutting me up. "Come on, really?" She shook a wisp of blond hair away from her face. "You grew up here. You know it doesn't take much to get these people talking."

I started to dispute it, to tell her that I'd done nothing to encourage the rumors, but a flash of people staring just this morning as Wes and I stood outside the Backdoor shut me up. "Dammit."

Her lips twisted. "Uh huh." She crossed her arms over her chest and turned back to the crowd. I joined her, the familiarity of the situation not lost on me. Most of our friendship looked a lot like this.

After about a minutes' worth of quiet, I turned back to her. "I'm sorry about—" I started just as she said, "It's really good to see you."

Once my half-apology sunk in, Winn waved a hand. "Kid stuff," she said. "It was a million years ago, and I'd have probably done the same thing."

I studied her face, looking for a hint of duplicity. Her light eyes were clear. "But I was such a jerk."

"You were. And I was pissed for a while, but I got over it." She grinned. "Besides, I felt a little vindicated when you dumped Mr. Perfect a few years later."

A surprised laugh tumbled from my lips. "Something tells me you're the only one who felt that way."

"Eh." Winn shrugged. "Anyone who knew you would've seen it coming."

"What—" I started, only to be interrupted by the star of the evening.

"Tierney!" Lola said as she zoomed toward me on shoes that more closely resembled stilts. "You *did* make it!"

Beside me, Winn took a subtle step back. *Abandoner,* I thought, turning to Lola with a wide smile. *Had that coming.*

"I'm so glad!" Lola continued before I could speak. "You look so pretty! Love that dress! Is that a martini? Have you met Bart?" The machine-gun pace she fired the questions left my head whirling. I blinked at the tall, wide-eyed man beside her. He sported bright red hair, a meticulously shaped goatee, and an expression that said, *help me. Help me, please.*

Bart raised his hand in a wave and I smiled, moving forward to extend my hand. "Nice to meet you, Bart. Congratulations."

"Thank you," he said, a tense smile on his lips as he took my hand.

Lola's vice-grip tightened on his arm and she gave him a pull. "Baby," she cooed, batting her extra long fake lashes up at him. "My mother wants us for pictures. We should get going." Her giant blue eyes fluttered back to me, and she reminded me of a Doberman growling over a bone. *Relax, sweetie,* I wanted to say. *I don't want your chew toy.*

"We really are glad you could make it," she continued, dragging Bart back into the crowd. "Hope you have fun!"

I nodded and smiled. "You, too," I said to their disappearing forms. "Poor dude."

Winn chuckled, reclaiming the space next to me. "I have to say, considering your history with the bride-to-be, this is a weird place to run into you."

"Right?" I glanced over. "I think Lola invited me just to rub her happiness in my face." I found the betrothed couple on the far side of the room and shuddered. "Little does she know, goatees creep me out."

Winn snickered and I looked her way. "So. How have you been?"

"Oh, you know. Living the dream." Her voice was wry, her gaze fixed straight ahead. "But my life is nowhere near as glamorous as yours."

A laugh escaped me before I could stop it. "Is that what people are saying?"

She turned her head, an eyebrow raised. "Pretty much. It's not true?"

"I mean, if mountains of paperwork all day, followed by nights of junk food and Netflix is glamorous, then yeah. It's totally true."

"Sounds good to me." She reached up and tightened her ponytail. "I'd kill for a night of Netflix and junk food."

As she spoke, another familiar face caught my eye. Lifting my hand, I waved to Jack. He smiled and started toward us.

"Ooh," Winn said once she saw Jack coming our way. "Wes might not come out on top this time, huh?"

"What?" I looked her way.

She grinned. "That's ten bucks I'll be happy to lose."

Her meaning sunk in just as Jack reached us. He graced us with a smile. "Hey, ladies. How's it going?"

"Oh, you know." Winn turned and grabbed a tray of appetizers from the table beside us. "I'm a regular party animal." Her lips pressed together in a wry smile, heat filling her cheeks as she lifted the tray over her head and slid between Jack and me. "He's hotter anyway," she whispered in my ear before she disappeared.

I watched her weave through the crowd, mind churning. Waitressing was an honorable job, but of all the things Winn talked about doing when we were kids, this was not one of them.

How did she...

"You're still here," Jack said, pulling my attention back to him.

"Yep."

"And you don't look thrilled about it."

I pulled the tiny plastic sword out of my martini and bit into an olive. My eyes brushed over him, from his shiny black shoes to his crisp white shirt and loosened tie. His blue eyes glittered like he'd heard a good joke he couldn't wait to share, and I found myself wanting in on it. My shoulder lifted. "*Thrilled* is definitely not the word I'd go with."

The corners of his mouth twitched with a smile. "Well, we can't have that, can we?" he said, taking my drink from my hand.

"What are you doing?" I looked from him to the drink he'd sat on the table beside me, then back to him. "How am I supposed to survive the night without the assistance of alcohol?"

"Easy." Jack pulled me toward the horde of townsfolk. "You dance."

"Wait a minute, pal." I pulled back and planted my feet on the ground. "I don't dance."

"You cannot expect me to just stand by and watch a pretty girl die of boredom," Jack said as he continued to pull me. My shoes gave no traction at all, so it was an easy task. "That's gotta be a crime in at least three states."

A tiny thrill ran through me at the word *pretty*. I ignored it. "Please. Please do let the boredom take me."

"Not a chance." We reached the middle of the floor just as the music for "Macarena" started. Jack dropped my hand and began doing the moves right along with the music.

I covered my face in embarrassment. "Of *course* you know 'Macarena."

"Hey, darlin'." He grinned as he flipped his hands. "If there's one thing I learned from living in this town, it's that you don't question the cheese. You just go with it." Then, he cocked his eyebrow, giving me a stern look. "Embrace the cheese, Tierney."

He was right. We were surrounded by people enthusiastically clapping and jumping. By default, *I* looked like the weirdo. With a sigh, I lifted my hands.

"There you go." Jack raised his voice over the music.

I laughed, shocked to realize that I was enjoying myself. Huh. Weird.

"Macarena" became "The Chicken Dance," and then something by the Bee Gees. As the last song melted into some gooey love ballad, Jack looped his arm through mine and we headed back to the bar.

"I can't believe I remembered that dance," I said, climbing onto one of the barstools. My face was warm and my cheeks ached from smiling.

Jack took the stool next to me and angled his body my way. "I can't believe you knew it better than I did."

"Please. Did you see yourself? You're a pro." I ran my hands through my hair, pulling it off my neck. "I haven't danced like that in years." Waving a hand at my face to cool my overheated skin, I closed my eyes and sighed.

Jack shifted closer to me and my eyes fluttered as a gentle gust of air brush over the exposed skin at the nape of my neck. Something deep inside me twisted, hot and jolting, and I shivered. I looked over just as Jack moved away, sheepish.

"Sorry." His lips tilted in half a smile. "You looked hot."

"Don't be sorry," I murmured, my gaze catching his. I watched as his eyes flickered over my face, my pulse quickening. My hand released my hair and it fell over my shoulder, brushing my cheek. Jack tucked a strand behind my ear, letting his fingertips linger over my jawline. My blood heated. He wanted to kiss me. I could see it in those ridiculously blue eyes of his.

Before I could decide whether or not I'd let him, the stool behind me scraped across the floor, jarring us apart.

"You two really had the moves out there, didn't you?"

I turned to find Wes leaning an arm on the bar. "I don't think I've ever seen you anywhere near a dance floor." He kept his eyes on me as he lifted a hand to flag the bartender.

"Yeah, well." Jack rested his arm on the back of my chair. "You've got to know how to charm the ladies."

Wes looked at Jack, a tight grin on his face and Jack responded with an easy grin of his own. "Where'd Sam take off to?"

Wes frowned. Giving the bartender a nod of thanks as he slid a beer across the counter, he cradled the bottle in his hands. "She's around here somewhere," he replied, his eyes searching the crowd. "Probably wherever Lola's at."

Sam, I thought. Did I know a Sam? I squinted, trying to place the name with a face. A former classmate, maybe? A relative of Wes?

"Don't you think you should go find her?" Jack pulled me from my mental Rolodex.

"She'll find me." Wes lifted the beer to his lips. "Always does."

As if on cue, a pixie of a woman emerged from the crowd, made of straight-up sunshine and rainbows in her sugar-pink dress and bright blond hair. "There you are!" She looped her arm through Wes's, jostling his beer. "I was beginning to think you left without me!"

I narrowed my eyes on her face, coming up empty. She only looked familiar in that she resembled Tinkerbell.

Wes smiled—not his usual smile—and extricated his arm from her grasp. "I'm still here," His tone was wry. "And so are you."

"Of course I am, silly! I'm the Maid of Honor. I can't just *leave!*" She slapped his arm and giggled, her perkiness so palpable I felt it wrap its sticky hands around my neck.

Clearing my throat, I looked at Jack. Amusement flitted over his features.

"Are you going to introduce me to your friend?" Cupcake Barbie's Hershey's kiss eyes landed on me. "Sweetie, don't be rude!"

Sweetie?

"Right. Sorry." Wes cleared his throat and tilted his beer toward me. "This is Tierney. Tierney, this is Sam. My—"

"Girlfriend!" Sam filled in, stepping forward. She extended a hand and I took it, noting her sparkly pink nail polish. "I'm his girlfriend."

The flicker in her eyes told me that she knew who I was. I wouldn't doubt she knew who I was before traipsing over here. Hell, if she was Lola's Maid of Honor, no doubt she got the entire backstory.

"Girlfriend, huh?" I repeated, looking to Wes. *That would've been nice to know this afternoon.* "Nice to meet you."

"Oh, you, too!" Sam dropped my hand and whirled to face Jack. "I can't believe your dad owns this place!"

Jack's jaw clenched. "My dad owns most of Michigan. It's not that impressive."

"Oh, I don't know." Sam slipped her arm through Wes's. "Seems like it'd be pretty great!" Then, she turned back to Wes. "Now, what do you say you take me out on that dance floor?"

As she said it, she took the beer from his hand and sat it on the bar. The decision made for him, Wes allowed her to steer him off.

As they turned away, Wes cast one last glance in my direction, something like apology simmering in his coppery eyes. I lifted my hand, then turned back to Jack, ignoring the snap and pop in my veins.

Maybe I felt something, sitting across from him in that diner. And maybe my mind began to wander into *what if* territory. But I was single. I didn't have some boyfriend hidden away while I traipsed down Memory Lane with my ex-fiancé.

Forget about Wes, I thought, turning back to Jack with a smile. "Well, that was awkward."

He slid a fresh martini toward me, transformed back into his charming self. "It's only awkward if you make it awkward." He took a swig of his beer. "Don't make it awkward, Tierney."

I laughed and picked up my drink, letting my eyes graze over him. Had he always been this cute?

As he sat there, looking at me with those baby blues, a shadow of a smile on his lips, my mind began to wander. He liked me. He made me laugh. I'd been having a good time with him. Who said the fun had to end?

Leaning closer, I treated him to my best smile and said the most un-Tierney-like thing I'd ever said:

"You want to get out of here?"

5: In the Swing of Things

"Wait, wait, wait!" I said an hour later, waving a half-empty bottle of beer in the air. "You got kicked out of school for *what*?"

We ended up at the playground, which was only about three blocks away from Lakeside Gardens. On our way out the door, Jack had smuggled a few beers from the bar, and now we sat on the swings, in the middle of a very serious conversation.

Jack leaned back in his swing. "I put the giant bronze bull from the front of the school into the gymnasium," he said as if it were the most logical thing in the world.

"But...how? Bronze is heavy. And I remember you at that age. You were *scrawny*!"

"Hey, now. That's hurtful," he said, even as he grinned. The only light came from the parking lot and the moon, but it was enough to catch the glint in his eyes.

"Please." I kicked my heels off to bury my toes in the sand beneath the swings. "You can't deny it."

"I may have *looked* scrawny," he said, twisting the chains of the swing so he could turn and look at me. "But I was strong. Plus, you know, I had help."

"I knew it!" I shouted, pointing a finger at him. "I knew you had accomplices."

"Yeah, well. No man is an island."

"Huh." I leaned forward to reach for a fresh bottle. "So, that's how you ended up in June Lake senior year."

"Nothing gets you shipped off to Small Town, USA faster than expulsion from private school." He took a swig of beer. "Good ole Pops didn't know what else to do with me, so he sent me to live with Aunt Bonnie. Couldn't have me tarnishing his oh-so-perfect reputation." He said it with a tinge of bitterness in his voice and I leaned forward on my swing to get a closer look.

"Somebody has daddy issues," I sang, just before losing my balance. "Whoops!" I laughed, gripping the chains tighter.

Jack reached over and took my beer. "Haven't talked to the guy in about three years, so yeah. I'd say we have issues."

"That's a bummer." I reached for my beer, but Jack held it just out of reach. "I wasn't done with that."

His laugh filled the empty playground. "Sweetheart, I think you've had more than enough." He sat the bottle on the ground.

I pushed out my bottom lip in a pout but I knew he was right. I'd always been a lightweight, and the martini-and-a-half I'd had before we left was usually more than enough to knock me on my ass. Add two beers to that and...well, I felt pretty darn good.

"So, what have you been up to since you smashed my cousin's heart and disappeared?" Jack posed the question with a deadpan face, and I winced.

Well, I *was* feeling pretty good.

"Geez, you don't pull any punches, do you?" I ignored the twist in my gut, focusing on the spinning scenery around me.

Jack shrugged and I sighed, pushing the swing backward and letting it go. "It wasn't my intention to 'smash his heart.'" I closed my eyes as the swing shot forward. "Anyway, he seems to have moved on just fine."

"Do I sense some jealousy?"

I dug my feet into the sand, bringing my swing to a full stop. "What?" My voice echoed in the stillness. "It's been, like, nine years, dude." I looked over at Jack. "Why would I be jealous?"

"You two were together for a long time." He shrugged. "A little jealousy is probably normal."

I twisted my swing till I faced him. "I had a brief— *very* brief—*what if* moment, but—"

"But then you met his girlfriend?" Jack's voice was dry, disbelieving.

Yes, I thought, immediately discarding it. I leaned forward, squinting to see his face. "But then I remembered that I left for a reason."

The moon caught the glint of doubt in Jack's eyes and it sparked defiance in me. Pushing from my swing, I whirled to stand in front of him. I grabbed the chains of his swing and leaned down. My heart slammed loud in my head as I met his eye. "I don't give a damn about Wes or his girlfriend." My limbs buzzing with boldness and booze. I let the rest of the words fall out before I changed my mind. "All I can think about is your lips."

And then I closed my eyes and moved closer, pressing my mouth to his.

Jack's hands came up to cup either side of my face, and I braced myself for his kiss. But instead of kissing me back, he chuckled. Tucking a piece of hair behind my ear, he murmured, "Rain check."

Embarrassment spilled over me like a bucket of icy water. I spun away, avoiding his eye.

The swing creaked as Jack stood. When he reached me, his hand was gentle on my arm. He turned me toward him, but I wouldn't—couldn't—look at him. "You have no idea how much I want to kiss you."

"Doesn't matter." I scoffed, dragging my eyes to his. "I didn't want to kiss you, anyway."

His eyes flashed with heat. "Really? Because I've been thinking of kissing you all night." He took a step closer and I backed up until I reached the base of the swing set "But I'm still not convinced this doesn't have anything to do with Wes."

"It doesn't—"

His thumb brushed over my bottom lip, stilling my words. "And you're a little drunk." Tilting my chin upward, he waited until I met his eye to continue. "When you kiss me again, I want you to remember it."

"What makes you think I'm going to kiss you again?" I steeled myself against the swing's frame to keep my knees from shaking.

Jack looked at me, the ever-present laughter in his eyes dissipating into something darker, hotter. I gripped the swing set tighter and tried to swallow as he simply said, "You will."

A tiny sound escaped the back of my throat as my eyes helplessly dropped to his lips. "I...um...there you go being cocky again." I squeezed my eyes closed and willed the blood to rush back to my brain.

Jack laughed, the sound pulling at something deep inside me. I wanted to reach up and push my fingers through his disheveled hair. I wanted to grab his tie, pull him closer, crush my lips to his. I wanted to...

"You looking at me like that is making the whole 'waiting to kiss you' thing very difficult." Jack cut off the dangerous path my thoughts were taking. "Come on," he continued, pushing away from the swing set. "Let's get you home."

6: Pre-Party Party

The next morning, I woke up with a blinding headache and a mouth full of sand. Oh, and with my mother flapping over me like a hummingbird from hell.

"Get up, lazy bones. We're going to be late!" she said.

I peeked out from under the blanket and groaned. "Late for what?

"The pre-party party." Her tone implied that I should have known this already.

The warm fingers of sleep beckoned me and I closed my eyes. "The what?"

"The pre-party. Party." She said it again, slower this time. "We talked about it last night. You don't remember?"

Last night...last night...

I searched my fogged-up, achy brain for remnants of the night, but the only thing that came back to me was a pair of blue eyes and the promise of a kiss.

Who…?

I bolted upright, the blanket falling away. Instantly, the sunlight had me hissing like a vampire. Or was that the memories?

The party. Wes. Sam. Booze. Jack.

Jack.

I'd kissed him. And he had rejected me. Mortification ripped through me.

This is why I shouldn't drink.

"Up, up, up!" Mom patted my leg with her hand. "We've got to be there in twenty minutes." She whirled on her heels and left the room, closing the door just as I chucked a pillow in her direction.

Swinging my legs over the side of the bed, I shoved my hair out of my face and squeezed my eyes shut. Home was a bad idea. I should have left right after Dad's party, like I'd originally planned. That way, I wouldn't have stirred up all sorts of weird feelings about Wes. I wouldn't have met his new girlfriend. I wouldn't have kissed Jack.

"Tick tock, sweetie," Mom called from the hall. I stuck my tongue out at the closed door and stood up. "If you need something to wear, feel free to raid my closet."

I froze, visions of too-clingy dresses and cardigans that refused to stay buttoned swimming in my head. Nope. No way. Not happening again. Grabbing the dress I'd worn my first night in town, I shook it out. A blue smudge caught my eye. Upon closer inspection, I realized it was frosting.

"How could you betray me like this, cake?" I tossed the dress aside. The one I'd worn last night was a no-go since I was still wearing it. Sighing, I gazed around the room, my eyes landing on my closet. Maybe...

As I pulled open the closet door, I crossed my fingers that Mom hadn't gotten rid of my old clothes. There had to be *something* that still fit.

***

Careful what you wish for would be etched on my tombstone.

As we pulled into a driveway, I tugged at the snug Journey t-shirt and sighed. "You could have told me the 'pre-party party' was at the Nolan's'." I pulled my sunglasses up long enough to glare at Mom. Bonnie Nolan barely tolerated me when Wes and I were engaged.

"If I had told you, you wouldn't have come. And we need all the extra help we can get." She flashed a smile and turned off the car. "Besides, we're all adults. I'm sure Bonnie's put everything behind her."

"Uh huh." I put my shades back on and unbuckled my seatbelt. "So, what exactly is a 'pre-party party?'"

Mom opened her car door and started to get out. "Well, you know we've got Julie's baby shower to prepare for. And Lola's bridal shower. So, a bunch of us thought it was a good idea to have a party to make all the decorations for the other parties! So, a pre-party party!" She grinned and climbed out.

I pushed open my own door. "Pretty sure there are labor laws for something like this." As I climbed out, I tried not to feel like a shit for completely forgetting that my brother and his wife, Julie, were having a baby shower for their second child.

"You're so funny." Mom slapped me on the arm then started up the walk. "Come on. We're already late."

I straightened my shoulders and braced myself for the hours of total awkwardness ahead of me.

"Charla, there you are!" Bonnie greeted us as soon as we entered her well-kept Tudor house. The moment she caught sight of me, her smile slipped. She recovered quickly, though, pasting on an even wider smile. "And you brought company! How have you been, dear?"

Oh, you don't fool me, I thought, returning my almost mother-in-law's smile with one just as fake as hers. "I've been great," I said. "And you?"

Her eyes flicked over me. "Just lovely." In that moment, she looked just like Kathleen Turner's character from *Serial Mom.* I really hoped she wasn't serving lamb at this party…

Every eye hit me as I entered the room. I reached up, adjusted my sunglasses, and gave them a smile. "How is everyone this lovely morning?" I weaved through the maze of tables, loaded down with various craft fixings. Without looking, I plopped down in the first empty seat.

"So, what are we working on?" I picked up a glass vase.

"We're, um, making centerpieces."

I looked over to find a strawberry blonde holding up a glue gun. "For Lola's bridal shower." She pointed to indicate a completed vase, with glitter hearts on either side.

"Got it." Why couldn't I have chosen a Team Julie table? "Hit me with the gun."

The two women at the table passed looks before obeying. I took the glue gun in one hand and a fresh vase in another. As I went to work making a sloppy heart, I said, "So, Melanie and Andrea, right? How've you been?" I glanced at them from behind my sunglasses, enjoying their discomfort. They'd been Lola's right-hand ladies in high school, founding members of the popular kids. I'd flown under their radar for years, until Wes set his eye on me. Then...well, high school girls were *mean*.

"We've been great," Melanie, the strawberry blonde, said. She smiled her perky, co-captain of the cheerleaders, smile. "How have *you* been?"

I let out a short laugh and reached for a shaker filled with glitter. "Well, I'm inside and yet I'm still wearing my sunglasses, if that tells you anything."

Andrea laid a sympathetic hand on my arm. "Party too hard last night?" she said. "We've all been there."

I slid a half-smile her way then began shaking glitter onto my vase with more vigor than necessary.

About an hour later, I'd had my fill of chit-chat and craftsies. My eyes traveled the room to find my mother. She sat at a table with Julie and her mother, awash in smiles and centerpieces. I was a prisoner in Martha Stewart hell.

"I've got to say, I'm digging the whole stripper vibe."

I yanked my eyes away from my mom to find Jack standing at the table, freshly showered and chipper. My hand tightened around the hot glue gun and I wondered if it'd qualify as assault if I gave him a glitter-stache.

"What are you talking about?" I grumbled, telling my suddenly slamming heart to shut the hell up. The memories returned like a badly spliced home movie.

I've been thinking about kissing you all night.

Tearing my eyes from him, I refocused on the vase in my hand.

"The messy, hungover look, combined with all the glitter—it's kinda working for me." Jack reached out a hand and ran his thumb along my cheekbone, coming away with sparkling silver glitter.

I swatted his hand, gritting my teeth at the heat shooting straight to my core. "Jackass."

He smiled and turned his attention to Andrea and Melanie. "Either of you have 'Pour Some Sugar On Me' on your phones?"

The two women snickered.

"Could you go annoy someone else? Please?"

"Now, why would I do that?" He eyed the vase in my hand. "Is…that a butt?"

I looked down, studied the crooked blob of glitter I'd been working on. "It's a heart."

"Oh. That's a terrible heart. Nice ass, though."

I peered at him over the rim of my sunglasses. "Classy. Go away."

"Now is that any way to talk to your knight in shining armor?"

"You don't look like any knight I've ever seen. Where's your helmet? Your sword?" I pushed my sunglasses back up. "Also, stalking is *very* un-knight-like."

"I usually wait till at least the third date before I whip out the sword." He grinned. "And I'm not stalking you. Your dad told me you were here. I'm here to take you to your car. You know, the car you abandoned last night in favor of a swing set and a few beers?"

I glanced over. Melanie and Andrea were clearly pretending not to listen. Super. Lots of fodder for the gossips. I wondered if they'd started another betting pool yet. "Oh, well in that case," I said, suddenly more than ready to flee this joint. "Let's get going."

"Now we're talking."

He put his arm around my shoulder as we headed toward the door. Looks and whispers followed us and I did not miss the poison oozing from Bonnie Nolan's eyes.

First my son, now my nephew. I could read her thoughts from clear across the room. *Why didn't you just stay away?*

Well, no worries, I wanted to say. Jack was just taking me to my car. Then, I was getting the hell out of this place. Maybe next Christmas, I'd make my family come to Port Agnes instead.

A silver Prius pulled into the driveway as Jack and I started down the walk. Wes climbed out of the driver's seat, then went around to the passenger side to open Sam's door.

"Hey, cuz." Jack pulled me tighter against him as they approached. "How's it going?"

I stiffened and cast a questioning look in his direction. He didn't look back.

Wes's glance fell to Jack's arm on my shoulder and lingered for half a second longer than it should have. Beside him, Sam slithered her arm around his waist. "We're late, aren't we?" Angling her head up to look at Wes, she added, "I told you we'd be late!"

Wes's face contorted into a grin-grimace hybrid. "You were right." He steered her forward. "We should get ins—"

"You know, he just couldn't keep his hands to himself," Sam continued, craning her neck to look my way. "I told him we would be late, but he just didn't—"

"Sam." Wes's voice was taut. "Let's go."

"Sorry, sorry!" She giggled. "It was nice to see you again." Waving her fingers, she allowed Wes to lead her up the walk.

Once they disappeared into the house, Jack dropped his arm from my shoulder and headed toward the truck.

"What the hell was that?" I demanded as we reached his truck.

"I'm sorry." Jack opened the passenger side door and waited for me to get in. "That was stupid. I don't know why—"

"Do me a favor." I climbed into the truck and met him eye-to-eye. "Next time you want to make Wes jealous, don't use me to do it."

7: Ballerina Blackmail

Jack dropped me off at my car with a tight smile and a *have a safe trip home.* My cheeks burned as I drove to my parents', but I couldn't pinpoint the reason. Anger? Embarrassment? Residual hangover side effect?

Hell. I knew what it was.

Disappointment.

I'd spent the weekend thinking this cute, funny guy was into me. Turned out, I'd gotten stuck right in the middle of some weird-ass family rivalry.

Well, no thanks. Putting my car in park, I got out and headed up the walk. I couldn't wait to put the miles between June Lake and me.

I dropped by bag by the front door and followed the voices till I found my dad and brother in the kitchen.

"Hey, sis," Stephen said as I reached the table. "Nice shirt."

I tossed my sunglasses and keys onto the counter and made a face. "Shut it."

"No, really. I feel like we're back in high school. Dad, can I borrow the car tonight? I've got a really hot date."

Dad laughed and shook his head. "You hungry, pumpkin?" he asked. "Waffles on the counter."

They'd toasted a heaping pile of frozen waffles. Beside it, sat a plate of microwave sausage and a few juice boxes. The smell teased at my nose and for the first time today, my stomach roared with something other than hangover homicide.

"You don't have to ask me twice." I grabbed a plate, helping myself to the smorgasbord of dude breakfast. As I slathered butter on my waffles, a tiny pair of arms encircled my legs.

"Aunt Tee-Tee!" I looked down at the dark chocolate eyes of my five-year-old niece, Rory, blinking up at me. She hadn't mastered my name yet, but I secretly hoped she never did. It was so stinking cute.

"Hey, shortcake." I sat my plate aside and scooped her up, smoothing her curls away from her face. "You're getting so big!"

She grinned and I was struck by how much she looked like her mom, all soft brown skin and dark, wild hair. "Grandpa's waffles are not very good," she announced. "Daddy had to put lots of syrup on mine."

My father chuckled and I grabbed my plate with my free hand, heading for the table. I sat her back on her feet and took a seat. "Thanks for the heads up."

"You're welcome," Rory said with a twirl, her bright blue tutu flouncing as she ran away.

I laughed and turned to Stephen. "How did you make such a cute kid?"

"She's all Julie," Stephen said as he picked up his coffee mug. "Except for those dance moves. Those are definitely me." He tilted his head to indicate Rory, who had begun doing a strange combination of pliés and crab walks across the room.

I took a bite of waffle. "I can see that."

Stephen grinned. "Julie put her in ballet classes. Hence the tutu. Her first recital is next Saturday."

Uh oh. *All aboard the guilt trip train.*

"You should come. She'd love that."

To my left, Dad cleared his throat, clearly stifling a laugh. He knew my routine: visit for major holidays only, and keep my stays short. Well, I'd already trashed that routine this weekend, and I regretted the hell out of it. I wouldn't survive another weekend in June Lake.

"Aunt Tee-Tee," Rory sang, skipping back into the kitchen. "Did you see me dance?"

"I did, sweetheart." I smiled, trying not to look directly in her eyes. If I did, there would be no getting out of it. I'd be front row center next weekend, watching a bunch of kids in tutus. "It was beautiful."

"It will be even more beautiful when the whole class dances on stage, huh, Rory?" Stephen said, and I wanted to throw my too-crispy waffle right at his smiling face.

Rory's eyes widened. "Yeah!" She jumped up and down. "You should come! Please?" She pushed out her bottom lip and batted her doe eyes.

I shot Stephen an evil look, but it slid off him like Teflon. *I hate you,* I mouthed before turning back to Rory. "I'd love to come," I said. And as she began twirling in a celebratory dance, I found it very hard to be mad about it.

***

Monday morning.

I plopped down at my desk and stared intently into my coffee mug. I still hadn't recovered from two days of small town purgatory, and I certainly wasn't ready to face the mountain of work ahead of me.

"Hey, Tierney. How was your weekend?" Emily Fitzpatrick sailed passed my desk, her cloud of bright curls rustling as she moved.

"Super." I stretched my face into something like a smile. "You?"

"Oh, you know. Went to a fabulous art show on Saturday, and spent the night in with my wonderful fiancé last night." She paused in her journey to her desk and smiled. "I am just the luckiest, you know?"

I nodded, tamping down the instant annoyance niggling at me. Emily was recently engaged to my boss's son, Ron Jr. "You lucky girl." I picked up a pen and looked at my planner. "Nice chat, Ems. I'll catch you later."

She lingered for a few more seconds, maybe hoping for more chit-chat? Well, she'd have to look elsewhere. Maybe Myra, the Senior Editor, would indulge in a little girl talk.

Once she was gone, I chewed on the end of my pen. If I'd known all it would take to secure my place with the company was to shack up with Ron, Jr., I would have seduced weasel-y little man a long time ago.

A shudder ripped through me at the mere thought as I pictured his squinty eyes and perpetually greasy hair. Scratch that. Not in a million years.

"Morning, Tierney." My boss's voice, jerked me back to the moment. I looked up to find Squinty Eyes, Sr. standing over my desk. "Did you see my notes on the Needermyer manuscript?"

A hefty envelope with a bright blue sticky note on it. My stomach clenched. A single sticky note. That couldn't be good. I held it up. "Just did."

"Sorry. Still not quite up to snuff. You'll let her know, won't you?" Ron gave an almost-sincere smile before heading to his office.

I dropped the manuscript on my desk with a thump and sighed. Joy Needermeyer, author of a fantastic sci-fi novel, was a sixty-eight-year-old woman from a teensy little town not far from June Lake. I'd been pushing for Ron to take her on for months, and he kept brushing me off.

Sighing, I thrust my hands into my hair and rested my elbows on my desk. Of course he'd want *me* to tell this sweet, talented lady that her life's dream of publication would require even more edits. My morning bagel turned to rocks in my stomach. Winn's words drifted through my head: *My life is nowhere near as glamorous as yours.*

My eyes scanned the clutter on my desk. I'd spend the morning with a manuscript on corn crops in Michigan.

Oh, yeah. Real glamorous.

***

A few hours later, my best friend Cat popped her head around the corner. "Hey there, stranger."

I looked up to find her brown eyes on my face.

"How was your weekend in the boonies?"

Tossing my pen down, I pushed my chair away from my desk. I ignored her jab at my small town beginnings and rubbed my neck. "Lunch time already?"

"Yep. Let's go." She turned, her cascade of red hair fanning out behind her.

I stood and followed her, ready for thirty minutes of catch up over a sandwich.

We headed downstairs to Lou's Deli, our regular lunch place and sat at a table. "How are things upstairs?" I asked as Cat picked up the menu and licked her lips.

"Eh. Same shit, day in day out," she said. "But, hey. They pay me pretty well to make perfect models look even more perfect. Let 'em have their rabbit food. More chili cheese fries for me."

Cat worked as a graphic designer at the Midwestern office of Eliza, the country's most popular women's magazines. The office was two floors up from Pencil Pushers. We'd met one day six years ago and bonded over the building's lack of good vending machine grub. We'd been best friends ever since. Nothing soul-bonded you like a love of chocolate covered donuts and sour gummy worms.

"So, you look all kinds of refreshed and energized after your weekend away," Cat said once we'd placed our orders. Sarcasm sparked in her eyes and I sat back in my seat and crossed my arms over my chest.

"Dude, worst weekend ever," I said. "In a matter of two days, I managed to make an ass of myself in front of most of the town, get roped into the engagement party of my high school nemesis, and get very, very drunk. Not to mention, I had lunch with my ex-fiancé, thought we were hitting it off, only to meet his new girlfriend." I threw my hands up and smiled. "How was *your* weekend?"

"Who'd you get drunk with?" Cat leaned an elbow on the table and rested her chin in her hand. Cat had a hot guy radar like no one I'd ever met.

I filled her in. Just as I finished the long version of my story, the waiter brought us our food. I dug into my steaming bowl of mac and cheese, sure that carbs were the solution to all my problems.

Cat shoved a chili-covered fry into her mouth. "I can't leave you alone for even a single weekend, can I?" she said around her food. "If you ask me, you should never, ever go back there. That's just asking for trouble."

"I'm going back this weekend."

Instead of a lecture or a look, she simply shook her head and shoved more fries into her mouth. "Two hot guys, both into you. You sure you don't want to trade me places?"

"I would if I could." I dropped my fork. Even the thought of crossing that city limit line on Saturday had my stomach doing flips. "What are the odds you could pass for me?"

Cat laughed and motioned to herself. "I'd need about five inches in height and two more cup sizes. Then, *maybe*."

"That's it." I sank back in my seat. "I'm going to start screening my friends based on how much we look alike. Just for situations like this."

8: *Boy Germs*

"Repeat after me," Cat said Saturday morning as we stood outside our apartment building. "No alcohol and no kissing cute boys to make other cute boys jealous."

I nodded my head. "Definitely no alcohol. And no kissing. No hugging. No touching of any kind. In fact, I think I should avoid the male gender altogether."

"That's a wise decision." Cat laid a hand on my shoulder. "Go now, young one. Make good choices." She spun on her six-inch stilettos. "See you later!"

If the universe was on my side at all, this recital would pass quickly and Wes-free. Get in, watch Rory dance her little butt off, get out. I'd be home in time to watch *My Boyfriend the Vampire* with Cat tonight.

Oh, and lunch with Mom. Which was why I'd hit the road so early.

Ninety minutes later, I pulled into my parents' driveway to find Stephen and Julie's SUV already there. I turned off my car and got out. Where were my parents?

Stephen held Rory in his arms, following his very pregnant wife down the walk to my car. Julie moved surprisingly fast for someone who was about to pop at any second.

"Tierney!" She rushed toward me and I backed against the car, putting my hands up in surrender. I'd heard horror stories about pregnancy hormones bringing chicks to the brink of insanity, and good ole Jules definitely had a flash in her eye I didn't recognize. "You have to help!"

"Okay..." Stephen seemed considerably less frantic, which led me to the conclusion that this wasn't a serious situation. "What can I help with?"

"Rory lost her tutu we have to run to Brightwell and buy her a new one because she can't be a buttercup without it and your parents aren't here and I can't handle this right now."

"So, what I'm gathering," I said, piecing together the tirade of information that rushed over me. "Is that you need me to watch the munchkin while you two take care of a tutu emergency?"

Stephen smiled and handed Rory off to me. "That'd be great, sis."

"You are amazing. I love you. We won't be gone long. Rory already had lunch but she might be ready for a nap so if you read to her she'll probably fall asleep but if she doesn't there are plenty of toys in the family room and did I say you are amazing and thank you? Your hair looks fabulous by the way. See you in a few hours!" And then Julie waddled to the car.

I swiveled my head back to Stephen. "Wow, um…that's intense."

"Welcome to the last few weeks of my life." In spite of his hurricane of a wife, there was a warmth in his eyes that showed just how happy he was. "Thank you so much for doing this. You're a lifesaver." He leaned in and kissed Rory on the cheek. "Love you, bug. Be good for Aunt Tee-Tee."

Rory wiped away his kiss. "Ew, Daddy! You got your boy germs on me."

Stephen laughed and headed toward his car. "Be back soon."

Rory and I waved as her parents backed out of the driveway and zoomed away. "All right, shortcake." I dug the spare key out from behind a clay pot of marigolds. "What do you say we head inside and I'll read you a story?"

"Okay, but you have to do the voices like Daddy or else the story people get mad."

"Oh, no. Well, in that case, there will be *many* voices." I sat her down and closed the door behind us. Rory took my hand and led me into the den, in all its Buddha-tastic glory. Together, we picked out a book—Dr. Seuss—then settled on the couch that cavemen made.

Julie was wrong. About halfway through *Green Eggs and Ham*, Rory hopped up and declared it was time to play Hide and Seek. There was no sign of a nap in the near future, so I decided to take her to the park.

Usually, the beginning of May was hit or miss in Michigan, weather-wise. One day, it could be sunny and seventy-five, and snowing the next. Luckily, today was on the sunny side of that spectrum. As we walked, I tilted my face up, soaking in the rays.

The playground was the place to be this lovely Saturday afternoon. Kids ran amok while parents sat on the sidelines. I caught sight of Winn on a bench at the far end of the park, surrounded by a few other women. It occurred to me with a jolt that she probably had a kid or two of her own by now. My eyes scanned the park and I wondered which ones were hers.

What a weird thought, people I went to school with reproducing. I glanced down at Rory, who was itching to get to the swings. Not *that* weird, I supposed. My brother was reproducing like a rabbit.

I lifted Rory up and settled her onto the wee people swing. "You ready?" I asked, pulling her back.

"Yes, but not too high, please. Just a little high." She hit me with eyes wider than the silver dollars my dad used to give me when I was a kid.

"Just a little high," I repeated as I let the swing go. She gripped the chains with both hands but let out a squeal of laughter.

"Maybe a little higher," she said as I caught the swing. "But only this much, okay?" She held up her hand, her little thumb and forefinger half an inch apart.

"You got it." I pulled her back and when I let her go, I yelled, "This is Sparta!"

Maybe I had watched *300* a few dozen times too many if something about pushing a five-year-old on a swing made me think ancient Romans battling to the death...

"What is Sparta?" Rory asked when she swung back to me.

Dammit.

"Uh." I reached for something less violent than the real answer. "It's just something I yell when I give a really good push."

Rory turned to look at me, her poufy ponytail tickling my nose. "You're weird. Push me again. Please."

About ten minutes and four more *only this much highers* later, Rory had her fill of the swings. "I want to play with Parker now," she announced, pointing to a blond little boy weaving in and out of the miniature pirate ship. When I was a kid, a simple set of monkey bars stood there. I would have pirated the shit out of that thing at Rory's age.

"All right." I lifted her out of the swing. "Off you go."

She skipped across the grass, leaping right in front of her unsuspecting buddy.

"Does that kid *walk* anywhere?"

Number two on the list of people I didn't want to see sidled up next to me, lips tilted in a charming grin.

"Haven't seen it yet." Squashing the instant smile that tried started to mirror his, I gave him what I hoped was a cool look. "She's hopped, skipped, danced, and crawled, though."

Jack's smile widened and I lost the battle. "I approve," he said. "Kid's got pizazz."

Before I could reply, something nudged me from behind. I gasped, giving Jack an outraged look. He lifted both hands in the air. "Not me. Meet Mousse." He tilted his head down to indicate a sleekly muscled brown and white pit bull at the end of a leash. "Like the dessert, not the animal." He reached down to pet the dog. "Apparently, he's forgotten his manners. Mousse, what did I tell you about greeting the ladies that way?"

Mousse, picking up on Jack's tone, drooped his head and sat. He looked so sorry that I knelt down and held out my hand for him to sniff. "Nice to meet you, Mousse." He extended his paw and I rewarded him with a scratch behind his ear.

Standing, I turned to check on Rory. She'd given up on patronizing Parker and now stood at the base of the ship, practicing her sweet dance moves. "That girl has the coordination of a drunken penguin, but dammit she tries."

Jack laughed and my insides warmed, instantly followed with a wash of irritation. "Wait. I'm mad at you."

"I know. I was a jerk." Jack kicked at the dirt like a boy who'd just been chastised. "You should let me take you to dinner tonight to make up for it."

"I...what?"

He lifted his shoulder. "Really, it's the least I can do. One lousy meal and all will be forgiven. Until the next time I'm a jerk, of course." As he finished, he grinned and I looked away, focusing my eyes on my niece.

"Why do you want to go out with me?" I hadn't meant to ask the question, but there it was. I didn't want to look at him as he answered, so I stared harder at Rory. Was she doing the Running Man?

Jack's answer was quick and simple. "Because I like you."

I looked over, caught off guard. Something sparked in his eyes. Mischief and amusement. "Right."

"Well, that and you've got a great rack," he added with a tilt of his head toward my chest. His smile widened as I crossed my arms. "And if I buy you dinner, maybe I'll get to touch said rack."

Despite the ever-growing flames in my cheeks, I laughed. "Good luck with that, buddy. Besides, I can't. I've got to go watch Rory show off those epic dance moves at a recital. You didn't think I came all the way to town to see you, did you?"

"Well, yeah. Kind of." He put on an adorably pitiful face. "Now that you've crushed my dreams, I guess I'll be going." He walked away, Mousse following behind him.

"I mean, you could probably tag along."

The words fell from my lips before I thought them through. But then Jack flashed a smile rivaling the sunshine and it was pretty damn hard to regret them.

"I'll be there."

I watched the duo till they turned a corner, then turned back to the park. Directly across from me, Winn caught my eye. She flashed me a knowing smile and I shrugged. No words were necessary—the group of chatty moms next to Winn would do all the talking.

Man, I hated small towns.

9: Build Me Up, Buttercup

"Come on, Charla! We're going to be late," my dad called up the stairs a few hours later.

My parents had returned from their impromptu trip to Hope Falls for whitefish at their favorite restaurant. They got home a few minutes after Stephen and Julie picked up Rory, utterly shocked to hear that they'd offered to babysit.

My joke about old age getting the best of them hadn't gone over well.

Now, we stood at the bottom of the stairs waiting on my mother. The recital started in twenty minutes and ten of that would be spent driving to the community center.

"I'm almost ready!" Mom called back. "I'm just looking for my other shoe."

With a sigh, I plopped down on the couch. "Does she have to conjure the little elves to build her a new one?" I asked Dad just as the doorbell chimed.

With a shake of his head, he went to answer it. A few seconds later, Jack walked into the room.

"This fella seems to think he's got a date with you," Dad said, following behind him.

"I...ah, yeah." I stood, smoothing the skirt of my simple black wrap dress.

At least twenty-three times from the moment he walked away earlier to just five minutes ago, I'd thought about canceling. It couldn't be a good idea to date my ex-fiancé's cousin. Especially since, clearly, people hadn't forgotten the history there.

But Jack looked downright delicious in his navy blue suit and white button-down. He didn't wear a tie, so the top couple buttons were undone, and his hair still bordered on unruly. Did he even own a comb? I thought as my fingers itched to volunteer for the job.

Well, maybe just *one* date...

"All right, Pops." I patted him on the belly. "If he tries to get handsy, I'll treat him to that move you taught me when I was fifteen."

Once Jack and I left the house, he turned to me with wide eyes. "What's the move he taught you?"

"Let's just say it involves my knee and some very sensitive parts of your body." I raised my brows as we reached his truck. "You've been warned."

Jack opened the door for me. I started to climb inside, but a box sat in my seat.

"Sorry about that." He reached in to grab the box. As he pulled it out, a few things toppled onto the seat.

"Wait." I grabbed a rogue object. "Here's your..." Squinting, I turned it over in my hand and ran the silicon bristles over my palm. "Paint brush?"

Jack took it from me, his fingers brushing over mine. "What kind of paint brushes are *you* using? It's a pastry brush." A smile tugged at his lips. "I bake."

He leaned into the truck to grab the remaining items. He was so close to me that I could feel his body heat. So close that I caught a whiff of his shampoo. So close that I could...

As if of its own accord, my hand moved to that unruly hair.

Jack turned his head just as I touched a curl. His lips tilted and I pulled my hand away. "I...ah...something. In your hair. Fuzz or lint or...I don't know."

The sun caught the glimmer of laughter in his eyes. "Uh huh. Did you get it?"

My heart picked up pace till it sounded like the drummer of a marching band. "I...don't think so." I lifted my hand. "Let me..."

I trailed off as my fingers got their wish, combing through his hair. Jack's eyes held mine, amusement giving way to something fervent, urgent.

Fire, fierce and fast, roared to life deep in my belly. His gaze slid from my eyes to my lips. My breath quickened. It would be so easy to lean in, close the space between us, press my mouth to his.

Would he taste like the blaze burning in the blue of his eyes?

I took a breath, about to pull him close, when the front door of the house flew open and my parents started down the walk. Jack backed up abruptly, taking all the heat with him. I shivered and pulled on my seatbelt as he closed the door and rounded the truck, depositing the box in the back on his way.

"I was right," he said as he got inside.

I looked over, wishing the damn sun would set already. My face burned so hot it could probably be spotted from outer space. "What?"

"You're going to kiss me again." He glanced over as he started the truck. I tore my eyes away to stare straight ahead.

"Keep dreaming, bucko." My voice wobbled, but I maintained my flimsy façade of aloofness.

"I saw it in your eyes."

I could feel him looking at me, but I crossed my arms over my chest. "You saw nothing."

"Bullshit."

"Could you drive?" I stared hard through the windshield so he couldn't see how right he was. "We're going to be late."

***

Parents of all makes and models milled about the auditorium. From overbearing to adoring, they were loaded down with cameras and cell phones to document this momentous occasion in their children's lives.

Stephen blended right in, overpriced camera hanging from his neck, anxious smile on his face as he watched for his tardy family members. I motioned toward him, avoiding Jack's eye. I couldn't look at him and not think about the kiss that almost was, and I needed to *not* be all blushy and flustered right now.

"Hey, Tier," Stephen said as we reached him. "Where are the parentals?"

"They were right behind us." Jack caught up to me, stopping at my side. Stephen looked his way, brows lifting in question. "This dude has been stalking me ever since I left the house."

"Don't let her fool you." Jack put his arm over my shoulder. "She practically groped me in my truck."

Stephen's lips twitched with a smile. Not the response I expected. History had proven him to be protective of his little sis. In fact, Wes had nearly taken a fist to the chin the first time he came to Sunday dinner.

"Don't you know anything, Tier?" Stephen was clearly trying not to laugh. "Men are easy. You show 'em a little attention, they'll follow you everywhere. Just ask Julie."

"Great." I ducked out from under Jack's arm and plopped down in one of the empty seats. Either Stephen liked this guy or he'd stopped the protective big brother act a long time ago.

But what if Jack was a weirdo who wanted to wear my skin as an overcoat? I had no way of knowing! What were big brothers for if not to warn you against such people?

Jack took the seat next to me, intentionally leaning my way. I ignored him—or tried to. The heat of his arm against mine made it a tad difficult. Clearing my throat, I looked to Stephen. "Where's Julie?"

"Backstage, giving our little ballerina a pep talk. Turns out, she's got a bit of stage fright." He took the seat on my other side. "Can't say I blame her. Do you remember Alice in Wonderland in the fifth grade?" He shuddered.

"The poor front row had no idea what hit them. Well, they knew *what* hit them. They just weren't expecting it."

"I really shouldn't have eaten so many nachos."

Jack peered around me at Stephen. "You didn't."

"Oh, I did. Half the town couldn't eat Mexican food for months."

"You don't have to sound so proud." I elbowed him in the rib. "I still can't watch *Alice in Wonderland* without feeling nauseated."

"Then my job is complete." Stephen sat back in his seat, a smug look on his face. "Let's just hope my girl didn't get *that* gene from me."

"What are we talking about?" Julie took the seat next to Stephen, a huge sigh leaving her lips. "Sitting is the *best.*"

"*Alice in Wonderland.*" Stephen pushed the curls away from her face and she closed her eyes, leaning into his touch.

"Ugh. You better hope none of our kids get *that* from you. Might be grounds for a divorce."

My parents cut off Stephen's response, slipping between the rows to take their seats. A few minutes later, the lights dimmed and the music started. A smattering of tiny tots tiptoed onto the stage and stared at the crowd with wide eyes. At their teacher's urging, they raised their arms over their heads. Three and a half minutes later, we'd witnessed a handful of twirls, a couple kicks, and one full-blown tantrum. Teaching toddlers to dance, it seemed, was about as effective as teaching cats to roll over.

Rory's class was second. As the curtain rose, we were treated to the sight of eight tiny ballerinas, decked out in bright yellow tutus with matching flowers in their hair.

Rory stood on the very end, looking unbearably cute with her afro puffs and giant grin. She spotted us immediately and began to wave. We all waved back as the rest of the troupe began performing a clumsy yet adorable routine to "Build Me Up Buttercup."

The little girl next to Rory remained still, though, staring out into the audience with wide eyes, twisting the ends of her blond braids.

"Uh oh," Jack whispered into my ear. "We may have a puker."

"Shh." I shot him a look then tried to focus on Rory.

He was right, though. That little girl did not look well.

She finally managed to tear her eyes from the audience, choosing instead to focus on Rory. She turned toward my niece, who was dancing with much enthusiasm—and *definitely* doing the Running Man. She was flailing her arms and bumped into the other girl. Stepping away, she tried again, but Blondie was relentless in her disregard for personal space, easing in closer and closer.

Beside me, Jack began to laugh. I shushed him again, fighting off a giggle of my own. Rory transitioned into a series of twirls, doing her best to concentrate. To the right of the stage, things appeared normal. Well, as normal as could be expected when trying to organize a group of five-year-olds. There were twirls and kicks galore, all out of time with the music. But, dammit, they were trying.

The left side of the stage, though...that was where the real show was going down. With each step Rory took away from the other girl, her frustration grew.

"How long before she snaps?" Jack whispered. "Are we placing bets?"

"Shut up." I choked on a laugh.

"Five bucks says they won't make it to the end of the song."

"You're on." I shook his hand and sent vibes of patience to my darling niece. "You got this, Shortcakes. Ignore the Personal Space Invader."

Jack heard my mutter and chuckled. I put a hand over my mouth to keep my own laughter contained.

"What's that girl's problem?" I heard Stephen whisper as Blondie took another step closer.

There were only a few bars of music left and Rory had successfully evaded Little Miss Up in Your Biz. She went into a final series of twirls just as the girl stepped forward once more, knocking Rory off balance. She caught herself before she fell, but she was clearly not happy.

"5, 4, 3, 2," Jack began to count, and I knew I'd lost the bet.

The moment that Rory snapped would forever go down in history.

In slow motion, we watched as Rory stuck her tiny index finger in her nose then turned to the little girl, wiping a booger right on her cheery yellow costume.

The little girl backed up in shock, tripping over her own feet. She landed on her tutu'd bum and started to cry just as Rory turned toward the audience, throwing her arms up in victory.

"*This. Is. Sparta!*"

10: Zip it Up

"You jackass," I said the moment we broke through the doors of the community center. Rory's victory yell had brought the entire recital to a halt. Between the looks Julie and Stephen gave me, and Jack's head on my shoulder as he collapsed into laughter, I had not been able to contain myself. Time to make our exit.

Now, we stood outside, the cool night breeze welcome on my over-heated cheeks. "I was *thisclose* to holding it together." I held my thumb and forefinger a centimeter apart and thrust my hand in Jack's face.

Jack leaned over, his shoulders shaking. "Oh, my God. That was the best damn thing I've ever seen."

"No, no. It's terrible!" My sides ached and tears blurred my vision as I tried to focus on my partner in crime. "I corrupted my five-year-old niece. Stephen and Julie will never forgive me!"

"Please. They'll be telling this story for years." Jack straightened, wiping a tear from his eyes. "This is Sparta," he said through the laughter, shaking his head. "Awesome."

Still giggling, I leaned against the cool brick of the building. Jack leaned in next to me, his shoulder just millimeters from mine. I rested my head on the wall and closed my eyes, breathing through my nose as I tried to pull it together. The heat coming from Jack's closeness served as the perfect distraction. What if I leaned in just a little…?

"It's still early." Jack's voice jarred me. "You want to grab dinner?" He lifted his brows. "I promise not to wipe a booger on you."

***

We ended up at Jupiter's, June Lake's middle-of-the-road eatery. It wasn't as fancy as Lakeside Gardens, with its crystal chandeliers and gleaming wood floors and views of the beautifully designed golf course. On the other hand, it was nicer than the Backdoor. Instead of vinyl booths and black-and-white checkered floors, Jupiter's boasted warm golden walls and an interesting array of movie posters and art prints from the last sixty years.

The hostess led us to a table in the back, right below a *Funny Face* poster. As we waited for our waitress to arrive, I glanced up at Audrey Hepburn, her arms thrown up in mid-dance. A snort escaped my lips as I imagined her yelling, "This is Sparta!" for all of Paris to hear.

I pointed to the poster. Looking up, he was quick to catch my drift. Our waitress arrived just as we lost our composure.

I sat up and took a deep breath. "Sorry." I put a hand up to block my view of Jack, who still hadn't managed to pull it together. I looked at our waitress and smiled. "Winn, hi!"

Winn's lips thinned and a flush crept over her cheeks. "Hey, I didn't know you were back in town."

"Yeah, Stephen guilted me into going to Rory's recital." I shrugged. "I'm sure you'll be hearing all about it."

"I'm surprised you haven't yet," Jack added.

"You mean the Sparta Booger incident?" Winn smiled. "My boy was in the recital. Called me on my break to tell me all about it." She tapped her pencil on her pad. "Should've guessed you were involved."

I thought she was talking to me and so I started to protest. Her eyes were on Jack, though.

Jack splayed his hands in front of him. "Not me, Winn. I wish."

Winn laughed and looked at me, her face open. "All you then?" she asked, amusement in her gray eyes.

I nodded. "I really shouldn't be allowed around the young and impressionable."

"Note to self: keep my kid away from Tierney." She grinned.

I wanted to ask the questions flitting through my mind: How old was her son? Was the father still in the picture? Why didn't she leave June Lake? But I sensed I'd be intruding, so I smiled instead. "Probably a good idea."

"So," she said, back to business. "What can I get you two?"

"How about pizza?" Jack sat the menu aside. "You like pizza, right?"

I nodded, my brain crowding with thoughts. The more time I spent in June Lake, the more nine years seemed like an eternity. Long enough for my former best friend to have a baby. I hadn't even known before tonight. I'd wondered about her. Of course I had. But life had a way of moving so fast that every time she crossed my mind, something else snatched my attention away before I could reach out to her.

Now, I really wish I'd hit the brakes enough to try.

"Anchovies, onions and pickles?" Jack continued and I started to nod again before his words sank in.

"Wait, pickles?"

"Just seeing if you were paying attention." Jack lifted his brows. "Pepperoni good?"

"Yes, please."

Winn jotted down our order, then turned on her heel, her long, blond ponytail swinging. I watched her walk away and shook my head. "I can't believe she has a kid."

"His name's Riley," Jack said as he unwrapped his straw. "He's six. Funny little dude."

"Huh. Wow. Weird." I picked up my own straw and tore the wrapper off.

Before I got the straw in my drink, something thwacked me in the chest. "What the...?" I pulled a rolled up piece of paper from my cleavage.

Jack sat across from me, straw in hand, self-satisfied grin on his face.

"Did you...did you shoot me with a *spitball*?"

"No," he said, as he loaded another wad of paper into the straw. "Why would I do something like that?" Before I could blink, it came sailing across the table.

"Dude, no! It's in my hair!" I sat up and shook out my hair. "What are you, twelve?"

"Hey, man. I couldn't have you sitting there all glum on our first date. That doesn't bode well for the rest of the night." He dropped the straw and rested his elbows on the table, eyes on me. "After all, I'm still hoping to get to second base."

He wriggled his brows suggestively and I fought back a laugh. "You just assaulted me with spitballs. I don't think that's the best strategy to get you all up in this." I motioned toward my chest.

"What *is* the best strategy?"

"There are a few." I met his eye and grabbed my beer bottle. "I'm sure every one of them involves you a lot closer," I said before taking a sip.

Jack's eyes darkened as my tongue darted out to lick the droplets that clung to my bottom lip. "I...uh, oh yeah?" he managed.

I smiled. "Ahh, what's it like to be the flustered one for a change?" I asked, leaning forward just enough to draw his attention to the V of my dress.

His gaze dropped then traveled back to my face. *This is a new development.* I'd never been the type to overtly flirt like this, though I'd seen Cat do it so often it seemed like second nature to me. I never realized how powerful it'd make me feel.

Jack leaned in closer, the light picking up the sheen of his dark curls. My fingers begged me to reach up and remind them how silky his hair was.

My eyes must have revealed a little too much, because Jack's lips tilted in a knowing smirk. "I don't know," he said, his hand reaching across the table toward me.

My breath quickened in anticipation of his touch, but his hand closed around the beer instead. Slowly, he put it to his lips. Like magnets to steel, my eyes watched as his lips pulled at the bottle, something churning deep inside me. He sat the bottle down and met my eyes. "You're looking a little flustered yourself."

"Pssh, whatever." I sat back and willed my face to cool. "You don't know me."

Jack sat back and slid the bottle over to me. "Not nearly well enough."

I grabbed it and took a sip, my eyes holding his.

What a strange situation I'd found myself in. I had come home filled with dread—not just this weekend, but every single time for years—and yet here I sat, actually enjoying myself. A first in the nine years since I'd left.

And it had a lot to do with the guy sitting across from me. "You know," I started, ready to tell him what just that. "I'm having a—"

"Hey, guys. How's it going?"

Jack and I tore our eyes from each other to find Wes standing at the edge of our table.

Thanks, Universe. I took a huge gulp of my beer. *You're such a dick.*

"Hey, pal. How are ya?" Jack's voice went from silk to steel as he greeted our dinnertime intruder.

"Great." Wes shifted and glanced behind him. "Just, uh, taking Sam to dinner."

"Yeah?" Jack's tone was flat. "Looks like you lost her on the way over." He tilted his head toward the bar.

Sam was perched on a barstool, facing away from us, a drink at her fingertips. Wes looked her way again. "Yeah. We're waiting for our table." He flashed a smile. "So I thought I'd say hi while she got a drink." As he said it, his eyes lingered on me for half a second too long.

It didn't escape Jack. "Well, mission accomplished." He reached across the table and laid a hand over mine, effectively shutting Wes out. "Now, where were we?"

Wes shifted uncomfortably and I caught a flash of satisfaction on Jack's face.

Ugh. No. I would not be a part of this juvenile schlong-measuring. Especially not after Jack and I had already had a talk about this.

Pulling my hand from Jack's, I stood. "I think I'll join Sam for that drink." I held Jack's gaze as I said it, too annoyed to enjoy the instant chastised puppy look on his face. "When you two zip up, let me know."

I marched across the restaurant, leaving the guys behind me.

Sam looked up as I took the seat next to her. "Hey," I said, flagging down the bartender. "How's it going?"

She stabbed a cherry with her swizzle stick, her bottom lip pushed out in a pout that didn't gel with the violence of her gesture. "Oh, wonderful."

I dragged a bowl of pretzels toward me and eyed her. Flushed cheeks, fiery eyes, jerky movements. "Why don't I believe you?"

A laugh, a single, staccato sound, left her. "I don't know." She lifted her glass and drained the drink, then ordered another. "Maybe because I'm alone at the bar, pounding Pina Coladas while my boyfriend wandered off to flirt with his ex?"

Her words smacked me across the face and I reeled back. "I...um..." I stuttered, reaching for the pretzels. "Ah..."

It felt like that bathroom scene at the end of *My Best Friend's Wedding,* only, unlike Julia Roberts, I was innocent.

"You don't have to pretend you don't see it." Sam smiled her thanks at the as the bartender delivered our drinks. "I've heard enough about you to know that you're no fool. And, really, it's no surprise." She stirred her drink more viciously than necessary and spun her stool to face the restaurant. "Those two have always been competitive. Like two puppies fighting over one bone."

"What are you talking about?" I turned my own stool and took a swig of beer. From here, I could see Jack and Wes at our table, tension crackling in the air above them, neither speaking, staring hard at the table in front of them.

I swallowed hard. A memory flashed through my mind. Wes, seventeen and on the verge of graduation. Fuming because Jack had been accepted to the same prestigious college he had, despite his expulsion and slightly less-than-perfect grades.

"I worked my ass off to get into Sutcliffe," he'd said, throwing his arms into the air. "And he just skates through because of his dad. My parents could have bought my acceptance, too, if they had more money than God."

How had I not seen it before? I turned back to Sam in time to see her scooping up her purse. "I'm going to go make that jerk buy me dinner," she said as she hopped off her stool. "Maybe another drink."

She flounced off with more grace than I expected after watching her down those drinks, leaving me alone. Across the restaurant, I caught Jack's eye and my gut twisted.

A realization I didn't want to have settled over me, hot and itchy as a wool sweater in July. Putting my beer and some cash on the bar, I climbed off the stool and headed for the exit.

This was not a game I wanted to play.

11: Coming Clean

I barely made it to the parking lot when I heard Jack's footsteps behind me. "Tierney," he called. "Wait up."

My feet wanted to keep moving, but every other part of me wanted an answer. Needed to know if all of this—the flirting, the fun, the chemistry—was part of a fabricated scenario to rile up my ex.

I whirled around, bringing him to an abrupt stop. "Did you ask me out to screw with Wes?"

Jack shook his head as if he'd misheard me. "What?"

"The birthday party meet-cute, the you-being-a-jerk incident, *this date tonight*." I waved a hand toward the restaurant. "Is it all just to get under Wes's skin?"

A frown nestled between his brows. "Why the hell would I do that?"

Sam's words swirled in my brain. Competitive was one thing. Dating a guy's ex to make him jealous was in an entirely different category. The borderline pathological category.

A category I *really* hoped Jack didn't fall into.

When Jack didn't elaborate, I took a step back. "I'm going to need a *yes* or *no* here, pal." I continued backing up as I spoke. "Otherwise, I'm—"

"No." Jack's hand darted out to grab mine. "I didn't ask you out to screw with Wes." His expression was a blend of frustration and fire and it brought me to a screeching halt. Whatever his reasons were, my body demanded I hear them.

I shook my hair out of my face and lifted my chin. "I'm listening."

Jack pressed his lips together and shoved his hands into his pockets. He looked like he was mulling over the questions of the universe "I asked you out because I think you're funny and smart and beautiful. Always have."

"Always? Since, like, last weekend?"

After a few beats of quiet, he spoke again. "The first time I saw you was on the grand tour of school my first day. You were leaving the library, arms full of books." He stopped, smiled, kept talking. "You were the most beautiful girl I'd ever seen."

My mind shot back to high school. I didn't remember meeting Jack until—

"We didn't actually speak until Spring Thing." His eyes met mine. "I'd been talking Wes's ear off since day one, telling him all about this amazing girl that I just *had* to know."

He paused and started to pace. "So imagine my surprise when Wes moseyed on over that day at Spring Thing—the very day I was finally going to ask you out—and invited you for a walk."

I opened my mouth, but I didn't know what to say. Jack had liked me all along? But Wes asked me out first? Even though he knew that his cousin had a thing for me? What a dick.

"What a dick, right?" Jack echoed my thoughts. "I convinced myself it'd be fine. You'd go on a date, maybe two, then you'd get bored. Because Wes *was* boring. But then one date turned into one year, then two, and then you were engaged. I'd missed my chance." He stopped pacing again and faced me. "So, I knew that when you turned up at your dad's party, I had to talk to you."

He shoved his hands into his pockets and gave me a look—half-smile, half-wince. "So, there you have it. You're not a pawn in some weird family rivalry. You're—"

Without thinking, I stepped forward. Jack watched as I reached up, my fingers gentle in his hair. No words were needed. He'd said enough. Moving another step closer, our bodies just barely touched, but the heat was almost more than I could take.

Jack looked at me, hunger and anticipation darkening his eyes to a deep sapphire. I moved my fingers from his hair to the nape of his neck. My breath quickened as I stood on tiptoe, my eyes fluttering closed. Jack lowered his head, meeting me halfway.

Our lips had just barely brushed when the restaurant door flew open with a bang. Jack and I jolted apart, like two guilty teenagers caught making out under the bleachers.

"I wouldn't care if you bought me every dessert on the menu." Sam stormed passed us, eyes flaring. "You'd *still* be slimy and disgusting and—" She stopped when she saw us. The lot lights caught the bright pink in her cheeks as she shook her bangs away from her face and smiled at me. "I hope you like being the bone."

Before I could say a thing, her heels were click-clacking across the parking lot. We watched as she sifted through her purse and dug out her keys.

Wes pushed passed us, reaching her before she could unlock the car door. "Come on, Sam," he said when he reached her. "Can we not do this again? Give me the keys."

"Screw you!" she shouted, lifting her hand over her head. Wes reached for the keys, but Sam spun away. "If I can't drive, you can't, either." And then she tossed the keys into the wooded area just off the lot.

At Wes's look of shock, Sam laughed. "Gonna be a long walk home," she sang as she teetered away. "Lucky for me, I've got a ride."

Two parking spots away, a bright red Volkswagen sat idling. The driver's side window rolled down and Lola peered out, venom dripping from her glare. Seconds later, their taillights were disappearing in the dark.

Jack and I turned our attention to Wes, who was using his cell phone as a flashlight to locate his keys.

Jack squinted, watching Wes search for a few seconds. "Ahh, dammit." He crossed the parking lot. "Need help, assbutt?"

Wes looked up. "Oh, no. I got it under control." He attempted a smile and went back to his search.

"You look like you've got it under control." Jack pulled out his phone and shone the light on the ground.

I hovered for a few seconds before I dug my phone out of my purse and activated the flashlight. "Here, let me help."

We searched for a good fifteen minutes before Wes admitted defeat. "Well." He shoved his phone into his pocket. "Probably had it coming, huh?"

Jack snorted. "Oh, yeah." His arm snaked around my waist and we headed back to the parking lot together, Wes lagging behind.

"So, I don't want you to take this the wrong way," Jack said just loud enough for me to hear. "But I'm going to offer him a ride home."

I craned my head to see his face. "Why would I take that the wrong way?"

"I mean, I don't know if you noticed, but we were kind of having a moment before all this. A moment I am very much looking forward to finishing." He tilted his head toward Wes. "Driving him home is going to postpone that."

Laughter spilled from my lips. "I see. Well—"

"Hey." Wes caught up, killing my response. "Thanks for your help, guys, but I'm gonna—" he jerked a thumb backward. "Sorry for interrupting your—"

"Get in the truck, man," Jack cut in. "We both know you're not hitchhiker material."

Wes looked like he was about to refuse, but a final glance behind him at the long road home changed his mind. He nodded, contrite. "Thanks.

As we loaded into the cab of Jack's truck, me sandwiched between them, there was no denying it—the moment was officially murdered.

***

"Well, it's been an interesting evening," I said as Jack pulled up outside my parents' house. The drive was only about fifteen minutes, but they were the longest fifteen minutes of my life. Funny how two people could go from Best First Date Ever to this.

I reached for the seatbelt release. "I…uh…had a good time. You know, until—"

"Please tell me you're going to be here tomorrow." Jack turned to me, his eyes hot on mine.

"I hadn't planned to be." I silently begged him for a reason to stick around.

He heard my plea. "You. Me. Tomorrow." In my peripheral, the curtains shuffled. Mom was clearly spying.

"Okay." I glanced toward the house. "I should get inside before my mother comes out and demands you come in for coffee and a midnight snack."

Jack laughed and the sound flowed over me like sun-warmed honey. He reached across the short distance and tucked a piece of wayward hair behind my ear. He looked like he wanted to say something else, but instead he just gave me a grin, leaned across from me, and opened my door.

I climbed out and shut the door behind me.

"Hey," Jack called before I could walk away.

I leaned down to catch his eye.

"Make sure you think all about how bad you want to kiss me." He grinned. "We're gonna pick up where we left off tomorrow." And, with one more smile, he was off, disappearing into the night.

Shaking my head, I laughed to myself as I headed up the walk. He'd done his job with his parting words: I'd be thinking about kissing him all night.

12: Hook, Line, & Smoocher

"Tierney, that boy is here." Dad's voice boomed up the stairs the next morning. "You up?"

"Shit." I bolted upright and shoved my hair out of my face, immediately blinded by the sun assaulting me through the window. It was still *morning*. Who showed up for a date in the *morning*?

"Tierney!" Dad called again, forcing me into action.

"Coming," I called, tossing back the covers. I ran my fingers through my hair and started down the stairs. A silly smile on my face, I raced to the door before Mom could reach it, flinging it open just as Jack raised his fist to knock.

My eyes drank him in. He wore a well-loved pair of blue jeans and black and white Chucks. His t-shirt was plain white but he somehow managed to make it look like a masterpiece. And, as always, his hair had that mussed, just-out-of-bed look. I found myself grinning, not even cranky about the few hours of sleep I'd lost.

While I'd been busy gawking, Jack was taking visual inventory himself. "Def Leppard, huh?" He tilted his head to indicate my t-shirt. "I bet *you* had 'Pour Some Sugar on Me' on your phone."

I ignored him. "What are you doing here so early?"

"I didn't realize we'd agreed on a time," he said, finally dragging his eyes to my face. With a shrug, he added, "I figured last night was kind of a bust, so I wanted to make our second date more memorable. I have things planned. Get your cute ass upstairs and get dressed."

"You're not the boss of me," I said, trying to keep a straight face.

"Fine, keep standing there. But you should know that I can totally see through that shirt."

I looked down, then back to him, crossing my arms over my chest. "Jackass." I slammed the door in his face. I ignored his laughter as I headed upstairs to change.

Once in my room, I tore through my overnight bag. The only other outfit I'd brought with me was the one I'd planned on driving home in—my favorite torn up, worn out jeans and...a white t-shirt. Great. We could be twinsies. With a sigh, I got dressed and ran to the bathroom to wash my face and brush my teeth and hair. Did I have time for makeup? I strained my ear. Mom had invited Jack inside. I could hear them talking in the kitchen.

Thoughts of what she could be saying to him lit a fire under me. I decided to sacrifice the makeup for Jack's sanity. My purse in hand, I started down the stairs.

"Bye, Mom. Bye, Dad," I said, sailing passed the kitchen. "Jack, you ready to go?"

"I, uh, yeah. Thanks for the coffee, Mrs. Chandler. And Mr. Chandler, I'll have to give Hal a call about that muffler. It was good seeing you, I—"

"All right, all right." I grabbed his arm. "Keep it up and they'll have you agreeing to stay for breakfast." I smiled at my parents as I pulled Jack toward the exit. "See you guys later!"

Once we were outside, Jack laughed. "I'm happy to see you, too, sweetheart. But at least let me buy you breakfast before dragging me to the truck to make out."

"Please, pal," I shot back, dropping his arm. "I just rescued you from a world of awkward. Now, about that breakfast…"

Jack rested his hand on my back and led me to the truck. "See, I know they say that imitation is the sincerest form of flattery, but I don't see how it's flattering when you make this outfit look so much better."

"Ha ha," I laughed, wriggling from beneath his arm. "I wouldn't be flattered if I were you. It wasn't intentional. Besides." I pulled open my door and turned to look at him, taking a slow, deliberate journey from his shoes to the top of his mussed mop of hair. "You're wrong."

"Why, Miss Chandler." He braced an arm on the truck, putting me between the door and his body. "Did you just check me out?"

I met his eye, the heat from last night making a roaring reappearance. "You got a problem with that?"

Jack grinned and my breath halted. "No problem at all." He lingered for a second longer before he moved to his side of the truck.

I sagged against the open door and let out a huge breath. If this tension stretched on any longer, it was very possible that I'd burst into flames. Shaking my head, I got into the truck.

Jack looked over. "You ready?"

You have no idea.

***

We drove for about twenty minutes, the air in the cab of the truck heavy. I felt like I'd somehow reverted back to my teenage years, all raging hormones and one-track thoughts. The only thing I could think about was Jack—his hands, his hair, his mouth. It had gotten past mere desire to know what his lips felt like against mine. I *needed* to know.

I shifted in my seat as we whizzed passed the *Now Leaving June Lake* sign. "You're making our date memorable by getting us out of June Lake? Good strategy."

Jack tossed a smirk my way and turned off the main street onto a winding dirt road with trees on either side. We reached a clearing at the end of the drive, a wide, rippling pond in the center. My head whipped over to Jack as recognition took hold.

"Doc McPhee's pond?"

Doc McPhee had been the town doctor for about a hundred years, and he was a cranky old dude. Teenagers were forever sneaking onto his property, having bonfires and parties, skinny dipping...

"We're going fishing," Jack said, tossing me a grin before he got out of the truck.

"Fishing?" I jumped out and followed him to the truck bed. He handed me a tackle box then pulled two fishing rods out. "We're going fishing?"

"Yep." He headed toward the pond.

"So, your big plan is to get me all isolated and alone so you can take advantage of me." I caught up to him and we walked out onto the dock. The breeze coming off the water was cool and glorious. My eyes drifted closed briefly before I looked at Jack.

"Please." He took a seat on the end of the dock, his feet dangling over the edge. "I brought you here so *you* could take advantage of *me*."

I laughed so he wouldn't see how tempting I found that suggestion. "Not likely." Taking the spot next to him. I opened the tackle box.

After a few minutes, we had our lines baited. Jack started to instruct me on how to cast, but I stood and pulled the rod back.

He let out a low whistle as my line sailed smoothly across the water. "Nice."

"I may be a city girl now, but that doesn't mean I forgot how to fish," I said with a grin.

Jack nodded. "Right on. Want to cast mine for me? Because I'm all talk. I have no idea what I'm doing."

I laughed and took his rod. As I flung the line into the water, I said, "So you weren't lying. This really *was* a plan to be alone." I handed him the fishing rod and sat again. "Considering our track record, that's probably a good idea."

He looked over, the wind picking up his hair. "You think so, huh?"

Our eyes held, the air crackling. After a few seconds, Jack finally spoke again. "So. You wanna make out?"

"Shh. You're going to scare the fish off."

He huffed out a sigh and stared out over the water. A few seconds passed before he tried again. "How about now?"

"You're persistent, aren't you?" I tucked my fishing pole into the slats of the dock and turned to look at him. He was leaning forward, his elbows resting on his legs, pole half-heartedly dangling from his fingers. If he got a bite, that thing would be history.

"So, you've got me here, in the middle of nowhere, and you keep insisting we make out. It suddenly occurs to me that I know next to nothing about you." I pulled my leg up to rest my chin on my knee.

Jack groaned and sat his own pole aside. "You're not going to do the 'tell me your life story' thing, are you?"

"Well, no. I don't need to know that you wet the bed till you were thirteen or that you used a Ninja Turtles nightlight all throughout high school. I just want to know a little."

Above us, the sun peeked out from behind a patch of clouds. Jack squinted at me and he looked so cute I almost gave in to his suggestion to make out.

"Tell me about your family." I quelled the urge to lean in. "How'd you end up in little ole June Lake? I mean, aside from the bronze bull incident."

Jack's lips tilted. He turned and sat cross-legged, facing me. "That's a long, tragic story, sweetheart. Are you sure you don't want to start with something lighter? Like the time I pantsed the mall Santa when I was seven?" He smiled as he said it, but I could see a storm behind those eyes.

I crossed my own legs and scooted closer, till our knees were touching. "I can take the tragic story. Unless you don't want to tell me."

His shoulders heaved with a sigh. He looked out over the water and I studied his profile. Finally, he spoke. "My mom died when I was eight. I spent my time split between various boarding schools and summers with Aunt Bonnie after." It was a neat and tidy presentation of his childhood, but I could sense something simmering below the surface.

He still looked toward the water so I reached over and put my hand on his. "What about your dad?" I seemed to remember he was a Big Deal. The Elliott name had been tossed around a lot when Lakeside Gardens was first built. Elliott Enterprises: Real Estate Developers Extraordinaire.

There it was. The first flicker of emotion he'd allowed through. His jaw tensed and he swallowed, dragging his eyes to me. "Busy guy. Lots of business to do, no time for much else. Hence the boarding schools." He picked up a stray stone from the dock and tossed it into the water. "I've got a brother, but we're not really close." Keeping his eye on the pond, he added, "I actually liked coming here. Aunt Bonnie might be a bit much, but she was the closest I could get to my mom after..." He trailed off and looked at my hand on his.

"Ugh. I'm sorry." I squeezed his hand, my heart aching for the little boy he'd been.

Jack flipped his hand over and laced his fingers through mine. "It's all right. I survived. And now I'm here with you, so I'd say things are looking up. Now, if only you'd kiss me. Then, things would be just swell." He looked up and added, "I've been waiting years, you know."

My eyes fell to his mouth. Only inches separated us. I'd just have to lean in...

"Get over here." Jack said, his voice husky, his eyes burning into mine. And who was I to disobey an order like that?

I moved in, closing my eyes as his hands came up to either side of my face. I could feel his breath on my lips as he drew closer and closer.

Suddenly, my eyes flew open. "What if it sucks?"

"What?" Jack dropped his hands, confusion clearing away the heat that had been in his eyes seconds before. "You picked a mighty good time to doubt my kissing ability, darlin'."

I put my hands up in a helpless gesture. "Sorry, it's just...there's been so much build up. There's a lot of pressure for this kiss to be good. What if it isn't? What if—"

Jack cut me off, crushing his lips to mine, his hands pushing through my hair.

And just like that, the world shifted. A whimper left my throat as my hands slid up his arms. Without breaking the kiss, I got to my knees and moved closer. Jack's hands left my hair to trail down my neck and over my shoulders, settling on my waist.

Sparks scattered over every inch of my skin, ending with a full-on lights display behind my eyes. I shoved my hands into Jack's hair and leaned closer until I lost my balance, ending up in his lap. He laughed then, the sound vibrating sweetly through my entire body. Turned out, his laugh felt better than it sounded.

With one hand behind my neck, the other resting on my waist, Jack deepened the kiss, his tongue delving into my mouth, slow, luxurious. The embers burning low in my abdomen roared to life. I brushed my tongue against his and he rewarded me with a delicious groan that broke through whatever semblance of restraint I'd been holding onto. Parting, I straddled him, then smiled before pressing my mouth to his once more.

Jack's hands found the bottom of my shirt and his fingertips played with the naked skin there. My legs began to shake, my lungs ached, my body burned. And yet I didn't want to stop kissing him.

A sound from my left startled us apart. We looked in time to see Jack's fishing pole take a nosedive into the pond. I laughed and shook my head. "You, sir, are a terrible fisherman."

Jack chuckled, reaching up to smooth my hair away from my face. "Doesn't matter. I got what I came here for."

I laughed and moved off his lap. "That makes one of us." Standing, I extended a hand and helped him up. As I straightened my clothes, Jack looked at me, perplexed.

"What did *you* come here for?"

"Food. Which you have yet to provide." I bend to pick up the tackle box and handed it to him. Then I grabbed my fishing pole and reeled in the line. "Also," I said, tossing the pole over my shoulder as I started down the dock. "Can I just point out that I was right?"

"Right about what?" Jack followed me, and once we reached the truck, I turned to him, a smile playing on my lips.

"I told you I wouldn't kiss you again."

"Wait, wait, wait." He stepped in front of me. "All that stuff you said back there about 'what if the kiss sucks?' That was just so that I'd kiss you?" His eyes widened in surprise and I laughed, putting the fishing pole into the truck bed.

"Yep," I said, getting into the truck. "And I'm not even sorry."

13: Desperately Seeking Dobler

Our next stop was a couple towns over, at a diner in Cherry Lake. As we pulled into the parking lot, Jack said, "I figured you'd appreciate a meal without people staring or trying to overhear our conversation."

"You figured right." I looked over at him, a smile taking over my face. He'd very slyly reached across the truck to hold my hand on the way here, and we had talked about how I'd learned to fish. Jack seemed intrigued by the concept of a father taking the time out every weekend to spend with his kids.

Parental quality time shouldn't have been a novelty in his life. It made me mad to know that it was.

The restaurant was a tiny place with butter yellow siding and deep red trim. I leaned forward, reading the sign. "Littlewood's Railway Diner, huh?" I snickered, earning a headshake from Jack. "What? That's funny stuff right there."

Jack gave me a baffled look, but I could see his amusement. "Get out of my truck, Chandler."

"Yessir." I ignored the little thrill that shot through me.

Jack wrapped his arm around my waist. "To be honest," he said as he led us inside. "I laughed the first time I heard the name, too. Only I was meeting the dude this place is named after. Word to the wise, people don't like it when you laugh at their unfortunate last names right in front of them."

"Oh, no!" I stifled a giggle. "How are you still allowed in this place?"

"I've got my ways," he replied, his eyes traveling across the narrow space to a sun-shiny redhead standing at the counter. "Hey, Shannon," he called.

She looked up, a smile on her adorable face. "Hey, Jack," she called. "Be right with you. Sit anywhere."

Something hot stewed in my stomach. I crossed my arms over my chest and followed Jack to a booth. Once we were seated, and nearly blinded by the hellacious shade of yellow vinyl on the seats, Shannon magically appeared at our table. "Did you bring the pie?" she asked, her gray eyes shrewd on Jack's face.

Jack laughed. "Sorry. This isn't a business call. Purely pleasure." He glanced over at me, fire stirring behind his eyes. "Shannon, Tierney. Tierney, Shannon."

I found a smile for her. "Nice to meet you."

A dimple appeared in her cheek. I wanted to hate her for being so adorable, but how could you hate someone that reminded you of a cute little puppy?

"Please tell me she was talking *actual* pie, and it's not a euphemism," I said after she took our orders and disappeared into the kitchen.

Jack wriggled his brows. "You should come over sometime and find out."

"Ha," I said, even as my cheeks filled with heat. "I'm leaving tonight, remember?"

"Dream crusher." He looked utterly devastated. He recovered quickly. "She was talking actual pie." His shrug was going for nonchalance and missed. "A few places in the area sell my stuff. Pies, cookies, whatever."

I leaned forward, my elbows on the table. "That's really cool." I reached for my roll of silverware. "I'd be even more impressed if you'd brought me pie for breakfast." I unwrapped it and pulled a piece of the napkin off. "But since you didn't, I'm afraid you'll have to pay the price." Jack's eyes followed my every movement as I put the paper in my mouth and picked up my straw.

"You won't do it," he said, amusement lighting his eyes. "We're in the middle of a crowded restaurant. People will stare. You hate attention. You—"

I shot the spitball across the table, hitting him right in the chin. The shock on his face was priceless and I couldn't stop the giggles from escaping.

"You think you're funny, huh?" He picked up his own straw and loaded it. Seconds later, I ducked as he fired.

"Ha! Missed." I stuck my tongue out and he started to load his straw again. Before he could shoot, Shannon returned.

"All right, kids," she said, her smile never wavering for a second. This chick was either really, really patient or a spectacular actress. If I were in her shoes, I'd be *thisclose* to cutting a bitch. "Keep it up and I'll make you scrape those things off the walls with a putty knife." She sat our plates on the table, and with a dimpled smile, she was gone.

Feeling thoroughly chastised, I sat my straw down. Meanwhile, Jack kept grinning. He watched as Shannon reached the counter and disappeared into the kitchen. Then he lifted his straw to his mouth.

"Don't you dare!" I looked for our waitress. "She sounded serious. I don't want to spend the rest of my day scraping spitballs off of the walls."

He ignored me and the wad shot from his straw and smacked me on the forehead. "Ha!" Jack raised both arms into the air. "Sparta!"

I tried not to smile. Really, I did. But his jubilance was contagious and within seconds I was laughing right along with him.

"So," Jack said once we sobered. "Def Leppard?"

I blinked at him. "What?"

"Your shirt this morning. You know, the one I could see through..."

"Oh!" I threw a napkin at him. "Yeah. Def Leppard." I stabbed a sausage link and grinned. "The '80's, man. I love everything about that decade." Taking a bite of the sausage, I added, "Is there really a better movie than *Say Anything?*"

"*Say Anything?*" Jack smeared strawberry jam on his toast and looked up. "John Cusack?"

"Oh, yeah." I grinned. "I'm really just a Diane looking for her Lloyd Dobler."

"You want a guy that would creep outside your bedroom, disturbing the neighbors with a boom box blasting cheesy '80's music?" He lifted a brow. "That's borderline stalker behavior."

"Is not." I tossed him a glare. "It's a big, romantic gesture."

"From a creepy stalker guy," Jack added, earning a kick underneath the table.

"I'm just saying." I ignored his laughter. "Had you shown up this morning with a boom box, I may have kissed you a lot sooner."

"I'll keep that in mind." He reached for his water glass. "Though *you* didn't kiss *me*, remember?"

"Well, now you know how to change that."

"Right. By stalking you."

My mouth dropped open. "All right, pal." Picking up my straw, I loaded it with a wad of paper. "You asked for it."

***

By the time we finished our lunch, we had shredded half a napkin between the two of us, shooting many a spitball at each other. Before we left, we cleaned up, because really, what kind of dick leaves a mess like that?

We were still laughing as we walked outside.

"Hey, jackoff," someone said, prompting both of us to turn around. "You don't have food in your own town?"

"Yeah," Jack shot back. "But no one as pretty as you to look at while I eat it."

"Hey!" I said before I really looked at the other guy. Jack was right. He *was* pretty. Tall, with sandy brown hair and a pair of thick-lashed green eyes any girl would kill for. I stared for a few seconds before I realized I was openly ogling the dude. "All right," I said with a shrug. "I get it."

The guy laughed then looked my way. "Hey, I know you. Tierney Chandler, right?" As he said it, he gave Jack an eyebrows-raised look.

"I...uh...yeah." I squinted to get a better look at him. "Sorry, I don't think I know you."

He extended his hand. "Conor Ross. I sat behind you in homeroom for four years."

I took his hand, warmth crawling up my neck to settle on my cheeks. "Oh...okay," I sputtered, trying to picture this gorgeous creature in the halls of Brightwell High. He had Teen Heartthrob written all over him. Surely, I would have remembered if we'd gone to school together.

"You're even more beautiful now than you were then," Conor continued, still holding my hand. His smile crinkled the corners of his eyes and an embarrassingly girlish giggle escaped my lips.

"Th-thank you," I managed just as Jack stepped in between us.

"Okay, okay." He jabbed a finger at Conor. "You. Go be charming somewhere else."

Conor laughed and backed away, his hands up in a 'my bad' gesture. "We still on for Trivia Night at Crowley's next week?" he asked Jack as he eased toward the diner entrance.

"I'll be there," Jack replied. "Beer's on me when you lose."

Conor paused, his hand on the door handle. "Okay, but it's gotta be light."

"Doesn't matter—it's not gonna wash the taste of loser out of your mouth."

A somber expression settled on Conor's face as he pushed open the door. "Nothing does, man. Nothing does."

My eyes followed him until he disappeared through the doors of The Railway. I only blinked when Jack waved a hand in front of my face.

"What? Sorry," I said, an apologetic smile on my lips. "He's just so pretty."

"You know he cries his way through sex, right?" Jack's voice was dry, his arms crossed over his chest as he leveled me with a glare.

"Yeah? How would you know?"

"Everyone experiments in college, Tierney," he said as he crossed the parking lot.

I laughed and followed him. "I don't blame you. If I had the chance, I'd—"

"Ahem." Jack leaned a hand against his truck. "Guy you're on a date with, right here."

I laughed and put my arm around his waist. "I'm sorry. For the rest of the day, I will only objectify *you*."

Jack smiled, turning me so my back was against the truck. "I like the sound of that. Tell me, what does this objectification entail?"

"Ahh, well," I said, putting my arms around his neck. "I could probably start by telling you that I haven't been able to stop thinking of your mouth. Specifically, your mouth on mine. I fear I'm forgetting what it was like to kiss you. I may need a reminder."

"I think I like being objectified," Jack murmured, lowering his head to press his lips to mine.

I melted into him, reveling in the way his lips glided against mine, how his warmth seeped into my body…how we were making out in the wide open for everyone to see.

Pulling my lips from his, I leaned my head against the truck. "You know everyone in that restaurant can probably see us, right?"

He glanced backward and shrugged. "Let 'em watch."

"Oh, no." I laughed and ducked out of his embrace. "There are children in there. And that sweet old couple! I refuse to corrupt them." Crossing my arms over my chest, I raised my brows. "What's next?"

"This here was the part of the date where I would use my considerable charms to convince you to make out with me." Jack sighed. "Now that you've turned me down, I guess I'll just take you home."

I watched as he dragged his feet to the other side of the trick, his hands shoved deep into his pockets, head hung low. Once he got into the truck I looked over, brows raised. "That was pitiful, bordering on pathetic."

"Oh, yeah?" Jack grinned. "Do anything for you?"

Laughing, I gave him a shove. "Shut up and drive."

14: Big Dream Adjacent

Jack drove.

I rolled my window down and reached over, taking his hand. As we entered June Lake, I watched his hair ruffle in the breeze. We were nearing my parents' street. Soon, I'd be getting into my car and driving back to Port Agnes. Back to reality.

It'd been a good day. A day I didn't want to end. Not yet. What did I have to rush back to, anyway? An empty apartment? A pile of work on my desk? A phone call to a sweet old lady, slowly crushing her dreams?

All that could wait.

"Keep driving."

Jack glanced over, looking like he'd just been dealt a Royal Flush. "I knew you couldn't say goodbye just yet."

I dropped his hand to push the hair out of my face. "Don't get too cocky. You have to figure out how to keep me entertained now. And, I feel like you should know, that's no easy task."

We came to a stop sign and Jack looked over. "Oh, I think I'm up for the challenge."

"We'll just see about that." I tried to squelch the heat that bloomed in my cheeks. If the kisses we'd shared earlier were any indication, I had no doubt he could entertain me. But he didn't need to know that.

Jack didn't say anything. Just gave me a smirk and hit the gas.

Twenty minutes later, we pulled into the parking lot of Paul-peroni's, a popular children's arcade in Brightwell. As Jack put the truck into park, I turned. "Really?"

"Really."

I looked at him, then to the glaring neon sign. Did I really want to spend my evening playing silly arcade games in a place filled with shrieking kids? All signs pointed to *No.* "I changed my mind. Take me home."

"Sorry. Too late now. You issued a challenge and I intend to rise to the occasion." He got out of the truck and walked to my side, opening the door. "Out."

I gave in with a dramatic groan, letting him pull me across the parking lot. "This isn't the sort of 'entertainment' I had in mind when said challenge was issued."

Jack paused. "What, exactly, did you have in mind?"

I smiled, seeing a way out of this. "Well, if you come back to the truck, I'll show you."

He tugged my hand, pulling me closer to him. We stood, face-to-face, inches apart. Tucking his index finger under my chin, he lifted my eyes to his and gave me a scorching look. "You know..." he started, moving in a little. "That might have been a good idea earlier." He dropped a light kiss on my lips then moved away, pulling me toward the building again. "But now I'm all excited about kicking your ass at skee ball."

"Ha. You wish." I dropped his hand and ran the last few steps. "I have mad skee ball skills."

"Mad skee ball skills," Jack repeated when he caught up to me. "Is that skillz with a 'z'?"

I yanked open the door. "You don't know about my life."

Jack shook his head and followed me inside. "I don't even know how to respond to that," he said as we approached the hostess.

"Ahh, finally. You're speechless. And it only took all day." I grinned over at him then turned to the brunette.

"Hi!" she said, her voice squeaky. "Are you with the Sanderson party?" She motioned to a group of riled-up five-year-olds and exhausted parents.

"Nope, just the two of us," Jack answered and the girl frowned. "See, this lovely lady is a big fan of your pizza. I told her, 'It might be weird to show up at Paul-peroni's without a kid just for the pizza,' but she insisted. And, really, would you be able to tell this face 'no?'"

I gave the girl a big grin. "I *tried* to talk him into borrowing a kid from our neighbor. They've got about a dozen. They wouldn't even have noticed. But apparently that's kidnapping." I shrugged. "Who knew?"

"Um, okay then. Just...follow me," the girl said, her eyes darting between Jack and I as if she weren't sure she should let us in.

Once we got settled into a table, we ordered a pitcher of beer. Then, armed with pockets full of tokens, we headed to the arcade. First stop: skee ball.

"You're so going down," I said to Jack as we fed the tokens into our machines.

"You wish," he shot back, a suggestive grin on his lips.

Heat flashed low in my abdomen and I looked away. Scooping up my balls, I said, "I'm pretty sure *you* wish."

"Well...yeah. I haven't really made it a secret."

Before I could regain my senses, he turned and tossed a ball up the chute.

"Dammit! You cheater!" I shouted, throwing my own ball. "Dirty, stinking cheater!"

"Hey, it's not my fault you were all distracted thinking filthy, dirty thoughts. And in the presence of *children!* You should be ashamed of yourself." He kept rolling his ball, scoring fifty points with a shout of triumph.

"You started it!" I rolled my ball, growling when it landed in the ten points hole. "I am ashamed of *nothing!*"

"I like a girl with no shame." As he spoke, Jack scored another fifty points. I glanced over and saw his tongue poking out of his mouth as he tried to concentrate.

I rolled another ball, finally hitting fifty. "Uh!" I shouted, aware that maybe I was being a little too exuberant. The little girl next to me widened her eyes like I'd just called her a poopyhead.

The buzzer sounded just as my last ball plopped into the fifty-pointer hole. I looked over at Jack's score and groaned. "No! Twenty points? You beat me by a lousy twenty points?"

Jack threw his arms into the air. "Twenty glorious points!"

"Yeah, well maybe if you hadn't cheated." I crossed my arms over my chest.

"Oh, don't be a sore loser." He put his arm around my shoulder, our prize tickets in his other hand. "I'll buy you something pretty with these babies."

***

Two hours later, loaded down with cheap prizes, we sat in the bed of Jack's truck outside the Shake It Off Drive-In Diner, enjoying drippy, delicious ice cream cones.

"I can't believe you stole that little boy's turn with the Whack-a-Mole," Jack said.

"Hey, that kid had hogged the machine for too long." I licked at the vanilla ice cream. "Better me than the mom with crazy eyes."

"Good point." Jack held out his chocolate and vanilla swirl and I leaned in for a taste.

We sat in silence for a few minutes, eating our ice cream and people watching. Brightwell was a hopping town. People from all the surrounding small towns came here for, well, pretty much everything. As a teenager, I'd made many trips here to escape the June Lake boredom. Bowling, movies, shopping. Brightwell was the metropolis of Greene County.

"I haven't been here in years."

"That tends to happen when you become a social recluse." Jack polished off his cone and wiped his hands on a napkin. "People were wondering if you'd contracted some horrible disease in the big city and that was why you never showed your face."

"Seriously?" I shook my head. "Did they have nothing better to do than speculate about my well-being?"

"People love a mystery. If your plan was to stay out of the gossip mill by keeping your visits short, sweet and invisible, it backfired." He grinned. "I think the latest rumor, before you came back, anyway, had you knocked up with triplets and married to that dude who does the terrible used car commercials. You know, with the naked men in tutus and rodeo clowns?"

I shook my head. "That relationship was doomed from the start. I let him keep the kids—Gunther, Skeeter and Bob—and I kept the tutu."

"Good call," Jack said, nodding solemnly. "I bet you rock that tutu."

"Totally."

I finished my ice cream and brushed my hands on my jeans. The early spring air still had a bite to it and I shivered. Jack lifted his arm and I scooted over, soaking in his warmth. I rested my head on his shoulder and let the silence settle over us like a fuzzy blanket.

"Why did you stay away for so long?"

Jack's voice broke through the stillness and I tilted my head to look at him. If he'd voiced the question in a demanding or accusatory tone, I would have gotten defensive. His voice, though, remained quiet, steady. And so I answered with an honesty that caught me by surprise.

"I was embarrassed."

"Of what?" His hand toyed with the ends of my hair and I snuggled in closer. "What do you have to be embarrassed of?"

I let out a slow, long sigh. "When I broke up with Wes, it was because I envisioned more for myself. More than playing good little housewife to the town hero. I wanted to do something, *be* something. But once I got out there...it's a lot tougher to make it in the real world than I'd anticipated."

I focused my eyes on a tall, skinny guy on roller skates, delivering a tray of food to a car full of rowdy teenagers. They were probably placing bets on how long it'd take him to fall.

"I was going to move to New York," I continued, not sure why I was telling him this. A simple *to avoid seeing my ex-fiancé* would have answered his initial question. Probably would have even been believable. But for some reason, the moment he asked me, I knew I would be honest.

"I *did* move to New York. For six months." I stared at the lines on my palm and swallowed hard. "Did you know that the subway smells like pee?"

"I did not."

Jack laid a hand on my fidgeting ones and I stilled, glanced over, and kept talking. "Well, they do. And it's hot and sticky and people are *mean*." A short laugh escaped me. "I got there, sure I was gonna set the whole place on fire, and...I just didn't." I flipped my hand over and let him lace our fingers together. Squinting against the sting in my eyes, I continued. "I tried, I failed, I settled. So, I came home, took the job with Pencil Pushers, and here I am."

"But you're an editor there, right?" He squeezed my hand. "It may not be The Big Dream, but it's Big Dream Adjacent." His other hand moved from my hair to run down my back, then back up again. He kept going and I closed my eyes, soaking in the absolute comfort of his touch.

"Big Dream Adjacent. Doesn't that sound like a terrible punk rock band or something?"

Jack chuckled and I wanted to move in closer so I could soak in the vibrations. "Big Dream Adjacent, opening for Spunky Boys on Roller Skates."

I smiled, my eyes following the carhop. He'd nearly fallen, waving his arms wildly in the air to regain his balance. The car of teens laughed and booed, hoping for a show. I wanted to applaud him.

"What do you say we get outta here?" I lifted my head from Jack's shoulder. "Maybe hop in the truck and warm up a bit?"

"Are you suggesting I let you objectify me again, Miss Chandler?"

"Well, I might let you objectify me a little, too."

The words were barely out of my mouth when Jack hopped out of the bed of the truck and held out his hand. "My lady."

***

"You, my good sir, are a bad influence," I said as Jack pulled up in front of my parents' house a while later. The clock on the dashboard glowed past midnight. "I have to be to work in, like, eight hours."

Jack leaned an elbow on the steering wheel and rested his head on his hand, looking over at me. "I'd like to apologize, but I wouldn't mean it. And I don't make a habit of saying things I don't mean."

I ran my thumb over the curve of his lips. "I don't want you to apologize. In fact, I want to move over there and pick up where we left off." Him, me, tangled up in the cab of his truck, my fingers frantically toying with the hem of his shirt, his hands scorching up my back.

He scraped his teeth over the sensitive pad of my thumb and my breath caught in my throat. "You don't play fair," I whispered.

"You really have to go?" He flipped my hand over and pressed his lips against my palm, never tearing his eyes from mine.

A tiny sound escaped my throat. "Y-yes?"

"That didn't sound very definite." He began trailing his lips up my arm, pausing at the sensitive skin of my wrist.

"I—yes. I have to go." I yanked my hand away and twisted it in my shirt. With a groan, I threw my head back against the seat. "I don't want to, but yes. Work, or whatever."

Before Jack could say another word—or worse, touch me again—I climbed out of the truck and shut the door. Leaning into the open window, I looked at him. "Today was a lot of fun. Thank you."

Jack tilted his head. "I'm a lot more fun on the third date."

"Is that your way of asking me out again?"

"Eh. I mean, if it's something you're interested in. If not, that's cool." He shrugged and tried to look nonchalant. Tried and failed.

I laughed. "Well, I've got the baby shower next weekend. Maybe after?" That way, I'd have something to look forward to after the torturous afternoon.

"How about before?" His face lit with an idea. "I'm making cupcakes for the shower. You could stop by my place Friday night and give me a hand." He waggled his brows and I shook my head, trying to look stern.

"A hand with the cupcakes, or…other things?"

"Well, I'll leave that up to you, darlin'."

Heat flooded my cheeks as lurid images shot through my mind. Thankful for the darkness, I laughed him off. "I can assure you, you don't want me anywhere near your kitchen."

"Are you telling me you lack…certain skills?"

Meeting his eye, I tossed my hair away from my face. "Oh, I have skills. Just not any that involve a spatula, or whatever you use for the making of the cupcakes."

"No worries. I'm a very good teacher." His lips quirked up. "My place, around six? I'll text you the address."

I stood on the curb, watching as he drove away. I'd just spent over fourteen hours with him, and yet I already couldn't wait to see him again.

I just might be in trouble.

15: Will Edit for Food

"Tierney, can I see you in my office?"

I looked up from a manuscript I'd been editing about the mating habits of army ants to find Ron's head poking out of his office door. "Yeah, sure." Tossing my red pen down, I stood and rounded my desk.

It'd been a long week at Pencil Pushers. A tense week. The usually stuffy office air crackled with an energy I didn't recognize. It had all of us a little on edge. Especially since no one was doing a whole lot of talking. The last time it got weird like this, we'd lost two editors.

I *really* didn't want to join them.

I caught Emily's eye as I passed her desk, and she gave me a smile of encouragement.

Great, I thought. *Emily thinks I'm getting shit canned.*

Wiping my hands on my skirt, I pushed open Ron's office door. "Hey, Ron. What's up?" I took the seat across from him and smiled my *Please Don't Fire Me* smile.

Ron shifted in his seat and straightened his tie. All business. Probably not a good sign.

"You've been with the company a long time," he started, and I swallowed a surge of panic. "Five years now?"

"Six." I knitted my fingers together to keep them from fidgeting. "And a half."

"Right, right." Ron picked up a stack of papers on his desk, straightened them, and sat them back down. "You've done some good work for us over the years. Solid work."

"Thank you." Shifting, I crossed one leg over the other. "I'm glad you think so."

Ron studied my face for a few awkward seconds.

Here it comes.

"Do you like working here, Tierney?" he asked finally, steepling his fingers beneath his chin.

The question caught me off guard. "Oh, uh...of course." I wrung my hands together tighter. "I've learned so much."

My answer was half true, at least. I couldn't afford to lose my job, after all. And if a teensy fib about how much I enjoyed my job kept me in junk food and Netflix, I could manage that.

"All right, then." Ron straightened that damn stack of papers again and cleared his throat. "So, here's the thing."

Oxygen ceased to enter my body. A million little scenarios rushed through my mind. I could crash on Cat's couch for a while, eat *her* junk food for a change. Maybe stand outside the local university with a sign that read *Will Edit For Food*. Students had food, didn't they?

"...and we were considering sending you with her."

I tuned back in as Ron wrapped up. Leaning forward, I rested my chin on my hand. "Uh huh," I said, buying time to figure out what he'd said. "That's interesting."

"Of course, the decision hasn't been made yet. There are a lot of factors to take into consideration. But as soon as we know, you'll know."

"Sounds good, thank you." I stood and smoothed my skirt. "One more question."

He leaned back in his seat. "Sure."

"What, exactly, are we talking about again?"

Ron's eyebrows disappeared into his greased-up hairline and I scrambled to add, "Sorry, it's just...I was pretty sure you were about to fire me, and so I was trying to figure out how I was going to, you know, eat and pay bills and whatnot. So, I..."

A laugh sputtered from Ron's throat. "I'm not firing you. I'm asking if you'd be interested in transferring to our New York office—Myra's flying out today to sort out some last minute details, and we thought it best to send someone from here to join her once things are up and running—it'd be a promotion, of course. Senior editor."

"I...oh." I sank back into my seat, my legs turning to mush. "Wow. That's...wow."

New York. A shiver skittered down my spine. The Big Dream.

"So, you're interested."

Forcing myself to blink, I looked up to find Ron studying me. "I'm...yes." I quelled the butterfly circus in my stomach long enough to feign composure. "Yes. I'm interested."

"Excellent." He readjusted his tie, then the stack of papers, and gave me a nod. "We've narrowed it down to a couple of people. I'll let you know as soon as we've made a decision."

***

For years, the first person I went to with big news was Cat. Happy news, sad news, irritating news—Cat heard it all.

This time, though, there was a different person I wanted to talk to first.

The elevator doors had barely slid shut when Jack answered his phone.

"Why, hello." His voice poured, smooth and warm, through the speaker. I leaned against the wall, my muscles instantly relaxing. "You just couldn't wait till you got here, huh? You had to get yourself a little bit of the Jack sooner."

I laughed. "Damn, you're cocky." His face popped into my head, wide grin and messy hair. I'd be seeing him in a matter of hours, but I had to acknowledge he was right. Silently, of course. He didn't need that oversized ego stroked.

"So you keep saying." He pulled the phone away from his face to lecture Mousse on the lack of manners he'd displayed by putting his paws on the counter. "Sorry about that. You put something delicious in front of that dog and he gets all over-excited. You two have that in common, now that I think of it."

"All right." I left the elevator and pushed open the doors, squinting in the late afternoon sun. "I'm hanging up now."

"Okay, okay. Sorry. I'm done. What's up, doll?"

I glanced up at the building I'd parked in front of, the late afternoon sun glinting off the windows. My stomach flipped as I replayed my conversation with Ron in my head. "The Big Dream, man."

"Is that my new nickname? Because I can get on board with that."

"No," I laughed and jingled my keys in my hand. "The Big Dream. New York." The excitement I'd managed to tamp down all afternoon bubbled to the surface. I hopped up and down in the middle of the street. "*New. Freaking. York.*"

A couple of passersby stared and I took a deep breath, straining for composure.

"Wow." I could hear Jack moving across his house, then a door opening. "That's amazing."

"I mean, it's not official. Ron said they haven't made the decision yet." I moved to the driver's side and unlocked my car. "But..." I trailed off, unable to vocalize the next few words: my dream was finally within reach.

A low whistle filled my ears. "You know what this calls for, don't you?"

Getting into my car, I started the engine. "A few glasses of wine and a shitload of good luck rituals?"

Jack chuckled. "A shitload may be overkill." He paused and I heard the jingle of Mousse's leash. "I don't know any rituals, but I make a mean good luck dinner."

I rested my head against the back of my seat and closed my eyes, a flurry of doubts whirling in my mind.

I'd put in the work, proved myself. I'd been there for six years, steadily getting bumped up on the Pencil Pushers food chain. I'd been Myra's second-in-command for the last couple years, learning everything about her job, soaking in everything she had to teach me.

That job was as good as mine. It had to be.

...right?

No, I couldn't think like that. I had to stay positive. I *would* get the promotion. Ron was a smart guy. He'd see that I was the best choice. He had to...

"How's that sound?" Jack asked, pulling me back to our conversation.

I let out a slow breath and started the car. "Will there be wine?"

"All the wine," Jack confirmed. "Plus, I might even provide dessert."

"Now you're speaking my language." I put the car into drive and pulled onto the road. "Are you thinking cupcakes? Cookies? *Pie?*"

"Me," he replied, deadpan. "I'm the dessert."

"Figures I'd date the only baker in history that refuses to feed me actual dessert." My tone was wry, even as my lips tilted. He didn't need to know I was smiling.

"Fine." He sighed, long and dramatic. "I'll rustle up something else, too. Maybe whipped cream for my—"

"Yep. Hanging up."

Laughter filled my ear and I couldn't help but join in. "I'll see you soon."

16: Magic Potpie

My phone rang about half a dozen times from Port Agnes to June Lake.

"Do you have any allergies?" Jack asked the first time he called.

"Nope."

"Okay, good."

The next time was about ten minutes later: "How do you feel about celery?"

The last one was about twenty minutes ago. He needed to know if I had any objection to peas or carrots. When I told him no, he'd said, "Oh, thank God. I thought I was going to have to start all over."

I smiled, shaking my head. The man couldn't get any cuter if he tried.

Now, I pulled my car into the driveway of a two-story Arts and Crafts style house with olive green siding and stone pillars holding up the front porch. I double-checked the address Jack had sent me the other day. Yep. This was it. Hmm, not what I was expecting.

I walked to the door, taking in the potted plants on the porch and the neatly manicured lawn. I could hear Mousse barking before I raised my hand to knock on the painted-red door.

"Simmer down, big mouth," I heard Jack call from inside. I adjusted my purse strap on my shoulder and ran a hand through my hair, my heart suddenly causing a ruckus inside my chest.

"Yeah, simmer down," I repeated, forcing myself to breathe slowly. "You've been talking to the guy all damn day. No need to act a fool."

"Now, I like my girls a little crazy, but talking to yourself might be crossing a line."

I jumped. Jack stood on the other side of the screen door, a grin on his face, an apron tied around his waist. "I wasn't talking to myself." I held up my phone, which had been in my hand, at my side, the whole time. "Very important phone call."

He raised a brow and opened the screen door. "Get in here."

134

Sliding passed him, I entered the house and knelt to pet Mousse. "Hey, buddy. How are you today?" The dog responded by licking my cheek. I laughed and scratched him behind the ear before standing up.

"I don't know how I feel about my dog getting to kiss you before I do," Jack said and I turned to face him. Tingles all the way to my toes. Huh. Didn't even know that was possible.

"Well, you were too busy being a smartass." I stuck my tongue out at him and turned to walk into the kitchen. "What's for dinner?"

Jack followed behind me. "Food. Sit." He motioned to the small, round table in the corner of his kitchen and I obeyed, pulling out one of the white dining chairs.

He grabbed two wine glasses from the cupboard, then filled them with a luscious red wine. He slid one glass toward me and I picked it up. "Thank you."

His eyes warmed. "So, the job. Who's the competition and how can we sabotage their chances at the promotion?"

Smiling, I took a sip of wine. "I'm pretty sure it's down to me and Emily. She's the boss's son's fiancé." I swallowed the panic that accompanied the thought of Emily getting the job over me. Again, very briefly, I lamented my decision to *not* shack up with Ron, Jr. Then, I looked at the guy sitting across from me. Not a squinty eye or greasy hair in sight. *I win.* "It's very touching that you're willing to cause trouble for someone you've never met just for me."

"Well, eventually, you'll put out and it will all be worthwhile."

"Oh, I see how it is." I sat my glass on the table. "All this—the wine, the dinner, the 'sensitive dude' act—is all just to get me in the sack."

"Uh, yeah." Jack put his own glass on the table and sat back in his chair. "You didn't think I actually *cared*, did you?" His lips twitched with his always-ready smile as he said it and I knew better than to believe his words.

"I understand." I was just as bad at keeping a straight face as he was. "I'm only here for the free meal."

"As long as we're on the same page." He glanced behind him at a kitchen timer sitting on the counter. "We've got about twenty-six more minutes before dinner is ready. Tell me all about the dream job."

A jolt of excitement zapped my every nerve ending. I leaned forward, my elbows on the table. I briefly summarized my meeting with Ron. "It's a huge opportunity," I concluded, sitting back in my seat. "Senior editor. Do you know what that means?"

"It means you're about to grab your dream by the balls." Jack sat back and smiled. He cradled his wine glass between two hands and met my eye. "It means you're going to set that whole damn city on fire."

I warmed. "Senior editor. In New York City." Lifting my glass, I started to take a sip, but another thought stopped me. "It means Needermyer can stop collecting dust!"

"Is…is that code for something?"

I laughed. "No, no. Joy Needermyer. She's an author I've been trying to get published for months. Amazing sci-fi novel. Space ships and battles and...ahh!" I bounced in my seat. "You can read it! When I get her published! Because I'll be senior editor!"

Jack laughed. "I'm looking forward to it," he said as the timer buzzed from the other side of the kitchen. Standing, he crossed the room and opened the oven.

I got up and joined him at the stove. "We're having pie for dinner?" I wrapped my arms around his middle. "It's about time you took a hint."

"Potpie," Jack corrected. "Chicken."

"Oh." I inhaled, the savory scents filling my nose and sending food alert signals to my stomach. "It smells yummy."

"It *is* yummy." He grabbed some plates from the cupboard and motioned for the table. "Now would you sit and let me serve you?"

"Yessir." I dragged my feet across the kitchen floor, even though my insides warmed with the thought that he wanted to take care of me. He filled our plates and brought them over. Then, he took off his apron and sat down.

"Now," he said, picking up his fork. "This here is magic potpie. As soon as you take a bite, you'll forget all about your crappy day." He lifted his eyes to mine and smirked. "Side effects may include wanting to kiss the cook. Hot, passionate kisses. I don't recommend resisting those urges."

"Duly noted," I said as I picked up my fork. "I shall not resist the urges."

***

Jack was right—the potpie was delicious, and I definitely had the urge to kiss the cook. That probably had less to do with the food, more to do with the man, though.

After we finished eating, I got up and helped him clear the plates away. He tried protesting, but silenced when I gave him a dirty look. "You cooked. I'm cleaning up."

He put his hands up in surrender and grabbed a sponge from the sink. Together, we tidied up the kitchen. The comfortable silence, combined with the wine, calmed the frantic *Will I or Won't I Get the Job?* thoughts. Man, this guy was magic.

Magic that I'd be leaving behind if I got the job.

At the sudden thought, I turned to Jack, drinking in his profile as he dried it and put it away. A sharp twinge in my chest, I let my eyes flow over him. New York was so far from little ol' June Lake. So far from Jack…

"It's creepy to stare."

I smiled, shaking the somber thoughts. Another time. I'd think them another time. I hadn't even gotten the job yet. "Sorry. Just feeling that urge you warned me about."

"Oh, well in that case, stare away." He reached for me, a playful spark in his eyes. "Or better yet, come here."

Laughing, I let him pull me against him. I looked up, brushing a lock of hair from his forehead. My heartbeat slowed as he smiled, soft and tender. He lowered his head and brushed his lips against mine, a mere whisper of a touch that sent shockwaves right to the center of my body.

He started to move away but I grabbed his shoulders and leaned in, recapturing his lips with mine. I could feel him smile and little somersaults of happiness rolled through my stomach.

His hands slid up my back and he pulled me closer. Melting into him, I shoved my fingers into his hair and scraped my teeth along his bottom lip. A shiver raced through him. "Careful, darlin'," he murmured against my lips. "You're playing with fire."

I pulled back just enough to see his face. His eyes were heavy-lidded, filled with the same need that coursed through my blood. "I don't mind a little heat," I whispered, not sure he could hear me over the pounding of my heart.

Jack growled before pulling me hard against him. What the kiss lost in gentleness, it gained in intensity. I stood on my tiptoes, trying to get closer, to taste the flames on his tongue. My head spun, my knees shook, every inch of my body sparked with want. I fumbled for the hem of Jack's t-shirt, needing to feel his hot skin against my fingertips. He backed me up against the counter, his own hands lifting my shirt to rove over my belly and up my ribcage.

A whimper left my throat. I tore my mouth from his and yanked his shirt up. He obliged and lifted his arms, letting me pull the shirt over his head. I tossed it to the floor and found his naked shoulder with my mouth. The salt of his skin against my tongue triggered a hunger deep inside me that I needed to satiate.

He thrust his fingers through my hair as I continued to trail kisses over his chest. I listened to his ragged breathing, spurred on by his reaction. My mouth moved lower, nipping and licking over the muscles in his stomach. Almost without thinking, I fell to my knees, enjoying the flash of shock in his eyes.

His chest rose and fell with each breath he took. He looked down at me as my hands reached for the button on his jeans, his hand brushing the hair from my face. I had just pulled the zipper down when a knock on the door froze us in place.

"They'll go away," Jack said, his voice strained. I rested my head against his thigh and willed him to be right.

Whoever was at the door knocked again. "Yoo hoo! Anybody home?"

"Shit! It's my *mom*!" I hissed, moving away from Jack as if he'd suddenly transformed into a pile of rattlesnakes. I scooted against the counter and covered my face with my hands. "Unbelievable."

"I've got the liners for the cupcakes that Julie wants you to use." The doorknob jiggled and I groaned into my hands, knowing it wasn't locked.

Hurriedly, Jack buttoned and zipped his pants. No time to grab his shirt from the floor before my mom came barging in.

"Charla, hey." He walked into the living room, where my mother stood. "Thanks for bringing those by."

"Oh, no problem. It's just so sweet of you to make the cupcakes for the shower. I—you bake with your shirt off?

"Uh. The oven's on. And I got hot."

I snorted then stifled my mouth with my hand.

"Oh, okay..." Mom sounded baffled. After a pause, she continued. "Is that Tierney's car in the driveway? I thought she wasn't due to town till tomorrow morning."

Shit! I thought, sending a prayer to whoever was listening that she didn't come any further into the kitchen.

"Oh. Uh. Yeah. We had dinner together." I could practically hear Jack's brain churning, trying to find a believable reason for why I wasn't in the room. "The...the food didn't go over so well. She's been in the bathroom for, like, twenty minutes."

What? Really, Jack?

"I...I see. Well, I'll let you get back to it, then. You'll bring the cupcakes by eleven, right?"

"Yes ma'am. Thanks again for bringing these over."

I listened as he walked her to the door and closed it behind her. Then, and only then, did I let myself breathe.

Groaning, I struggled to my feet. "Ladies and gentlemen, my mother."

"You know, usually I like your mother, but I sort of want to throttle her right now," Jack said as he entered the kitchen.

His hair was mussed—even more mussed than usual—and his face was flushed. Add to that the fact that he wasn't wearing a shirt, and, well…my mother wasn't stupid. She knew what had been going on.

I met Jack's eye, mortification overtaken briefly by laughter.

"What's so funny?" He crossed the kitchen and backed me into the counter. "I don't see anything funny about this situation."

The giggles increased until I was full-on laughing. "'Uh, the oven's on,'" I said, lowering my voice to imitate Jack. "'I got hot.'"

"You think that's funny, do you?" He wrapped his hands around my waist and tickled.

I tried to wriggle away. "Hey, I believed you! I mean, the oven really heats up the place!" I said through my laughter.

Jack stopped tickling and lifted me up onto the counter, a grin on his face. "How about we give the oven some competition?"

"Ha. Not likely. My mother showing up just when I was about to…" My eyes trailed over his chest and to his jeans. "Well, that was a real mood killer."

A huge sigh escaped Jack's lungs. He shoved both hands through his hair then helped me off the counter. "All right. Let the cupcake-making commence, then."

"I should probably go. I mean, Mom knows I'm here now. I don't need it getting all over town that I stayed the night."

Jack's eyebrows lifted. "Wait. Was that an option?"

I gave a short laugh. "Given what she interrupted, I'd say it was a pretty safe bet."

Jack groaned. "Curse that woman and her terrible timing."

Placing a hand on his chest, I passed him and let my fingertips linger over his still-naked flesh. "Thank you for dinner." I picked up my purse and started for the door.

Jack reached it first and opened it for me. As I headed out, he leaned in and dropped a kiss on my cheek, pausing to say into my ear. "And thank *you* for the blue balls."

17: Cupcakes & Trouser Snakes

Many a suggestive comment and knowing smirk greeted me when I got to my parents' house a while later. I refused to acknowledge my mother's waggling brows and headed straight upstairs for a shower. An ice-cold shower.

Now, it was just after ten a.m. the next morning and the house was filled with clucking hens. I'd been assigned deviled eggs, so I stood in the kitchen, filling the sliced eggs with seasoned yolk from one of those devices with a fancy tip to make the yolk look pretty. *Jack would know what this is called,* I thought, a smile curving my lips.

"That smile wouldn't have anything to do with the visit you paid to June Lake's hottest baker last night, would it?" Betty, my mother's best friend, sang, nudging her shoulder with mine.

My head shot up, my cheeks flaming. "Mom!" I said, catching her eye.

"Oh, no. She didn't say a word. Jerry Hancock saw your car in Jack's driveway. He lives right next door, you know."

Betty put a hand on my arm. "Have you been in the big city for so long that you forgot how quickly word travels back home?"

Across the room, Julie gave me a sympathetic smile. I smiled back, thankful for an ally.

"No, I just underestimated, apparently." I sat the fancy tool down and brushed my hands on my apron. "Eggs are all set."

"Ooh!" One of the other women squealed from the living room. "Speaking of hot bakers—Tierney's boyfriend is here!"

Heat filled my cheeks. "I'm...uh...I have to pee." I didn't want to see Jack in front of all these nosy women. The poor dude already had no idea what he was walking into.

"Oh, no you don't," Julie said, putting her arm around my waist. "Don't let these gossip mongers win." She steered me toward the entryway. "You answer that door and you give them plenty to talk about. Doesn't matter what they say, as long as you're happy, right?"

"Y-yes?" I looked at her. She looked radiant. Big as a house, but absolutely radiant. And she had a point. "Okay. Screw them and their gossip."

"Good girl." She patted me on the shoulder before shuffling away. I sighed and smoothed my hair away from my face, hoping I didn't look as flushed as I felt.

With one final breath, I opened the door. "Hey, you."

"Hey, doll. I'm sure you look absolutely gorgeous behind this mountain of cupcakes, but I can't say for sure until I deliver them to the kitchen. Do you mind leading the way?"

I laughed as I took in the stack of cupcake carriers he held in his arms. All I could see was the top of his hair. "Right this way," I said, putting my hand on his arm. "I see you're a believer of the 'why take two trips when one will do?' philosophy."

"Well, yeah. Who has time for a second trip?" he responded, his voice muffled by trays.

I paused and lifted the top two trays, revealing a pair of sparkling blue eyes. "There you are," I said, my stomach flipping upside down.

"And there *you* are." He grinned, taking me in from the tips of my ballet flats to the top of my French-braided hair. "I was right. You *do* look gorgeous."

I blushed like a schoolgirl. Behind me, I heard a round of snickers.

"We have an audience," Jack whispered, glancing toward the kitchen.

"Yep." I gave him a wry smile. "Isn't it grand?"

As soon as we entered the room, everyone spun around and pretended to be busy. "Too late, ladies," I said as I sat the trays on the counter. "We already saw you spying."

I took the remaining trays from Jack and looked at Mom. Her gray eyes were wide with feigned innocence. "I don't know what you're talking about, sweetie. I've been working on the finger sandwiches the whole time."

"Uh huh." I shook my head at her then looped my arm through Jack's, giving Julie a smile. "We're going to step outside for a moment. Feel free to press your noses against the window to get a better look."

We left the kitchen and went out the front door, pretending not to hear the footsteps following behind us. Once we stood next to Jack's truck, he reached out and straightened the collar of my pink button down. "I'm not going to kiss you because I know that will cause you all kinds of trouble when you head back inside," he said, his eyes alight with a smile. "But just know that it's all I can think about."

I glanced toward the house in time to see the front curtains shuffle. "It's like being under a microscope," I said, looking back to Jack. Crossing my arms over my chest to keep from wrapping them around him, I sighed. "You want to rescue me in a couple hours?"

His lips lifted and I recalled how that smile felt against my mouth last night. My breath caught in my throat and I balled my hands into fists, willing myself to stay put.

"What did you have in mind?" he asked.

I kept my tone blasé. "Oh, you know. Maybe something to eat. A little conversation. Nothing major."

Jack's eyes darkened. "Nothing major?"

I shrugged. "We'll see how the night goes." Then, I stood on my tiptoe and dropped a kiss on his cheek. I started to move away, but Jack's hand found the base of my back, pressing me closer. "What are you doing?" I whispered, glancing back at the house. "People are *watching.*"

"Let 'em watch." Jack's eyes darkened. "I changed my mind. I'm not going to let a couple nosy old ladies keep me from kissing you."

Something in his voice sent skitters of fire through my veins. "Well, if you put it that way..." I pressed my lips to his.

It was a short kiss—the briefest meeting of the lips—but it was enough to make me want more. When we parted, Jack smiled down at me. "See you in a while."

I'd pay for that the moment I went back in the house, but I didn't care. I grinned like a doofus and nodded. With one final wave, he got into his truck and drove off. Once he was out of sight, I took a deep breath and braced myself for certain interrogation.

"All right," I said as I entered the kitchen. "Get it out of your systems."

There was a pause as the half a dozen women looked at each other. My mom—of course—broke the silence. "How's the sex?"

"I...um...well, then." I stammered, stunned. The rest of the room, though, erupted in a whirlwind of giggles and questions.

"Is he a good kisser? He looks like he'd be a good kisser," asked Julie's best friend, Ally.

"Has he cooked for you? He's a great cook!" Betty said. Followed swiftly by Dottie Daniels firing off the winning question: "How big's his trouser snake?"

My mouth dropped open. I closed it, but it fell open again. "I...I'm not...I didn't...ah..." I busied myself with the cupcakes Jack had just delivered, putting them on the carousel display. Should have known better than to open the floor up like that.

Once the task was complete, I wiped my hands on a dishtowel and snuck out of the kitchen, hoping for a few minutes of quiet before—

"Word to the wise, sweetheart."

I stopped short just shy of slamming into Lola. "Sorry, I didn't see you there." I pushed my hair away from my face and started around her.

Before I could get two steps away, she continued. "If you've got your eyes on his bank account, it's nothing to write home about. Daddy cut him off."

I met her eye. "I'm sure if he hadn't, you'd have dug your claws in by now."

Petty wasn't usually my thing, but I'd be lying if I said the look on her face wasn't satisfying.

Pressing her pink-glossed lips together, she blinked. "I don't think I like what you're insinuating."

I laughed and resisted pointing out that she'd insinuated the same thing. "Make sure you try the *deviled* eggs," I said instead, continuing my walk into the living room. "Rumor has it they're your favorite."

18: *Shot Through the Heart*

"Boy, am I glad to see you," I said to Jack a couple hours later. He stood on the front porch, looking like a tall drink of something that could make this entire afternoon disappear. Between the Lola incident and dodging questions about when Jack and I were going to have babies, I was more than ready to be rescued.

Jack laughed and instantly my body relaxed. That laugh, it was voodoo. I was sure of it. "Good, because I'm glad to see you, too," he said. "Now, go change."

I looked down at my floral button-down and skirt. "What's wrong with what I'm wearing?"

"Nothing, if we were having dinner with the Waltons," Jack replied, giving my collar a little tug. "I'm thinking that t-shirt you were wearing last weekend would be perfect."

I swatted his hand away. "Where are we going that requires a Def Leppard t-shirt?"

"Must you be so nosy?" he asked, his eyes playful.
"Hurry up. I don't want to be late."

I huffed out an overly dramatic sigh. "Fine. But I'm going to wear my Bon Jovi t-shirt instead."

Jack's chuckle followed me up the stairs and I shook my head, letting it flow over me. It was like this entire day had been soaked in poison and Jack showed up with the anecdote in the nick of time. My chest lightened as I tossed my overnight bag onto the bed and dug through it.

As I got changed, Lola's words flitted unwelcome through my mind. *Daddy cut him off.*

I knew he had a tense relationship with his father, but she'd hinted at something more. I didn't care about the money, but I *did* care about Jack. What happened that would have—

Giving my head a shake, I decided to push the whole thing right out of my mind and enjoy myself. I had a deliciously adorable guy waiting downstairs for me, and he wanted to take me away from this madhouse. As far as I was concerned, that was all I needed to know.

For now.

A few minutes later, we were walking toward Jack's truck, the sun beaming almost as much as my face. Once we were settled in and on the road, I turned to Jack. "So, I have to say. This whole *Get in my car, but I'm not going to tell you where we're going* game is getting old."

Jack glanced over at me, his brows raised. "What's wrong with a little excitement and mystery?"

"Nothing, as long as you don't turn out to be a serial killer who's going to chop me into pieces and eat me."

"Well," he said as he pointed the truck toward the highway. "I can guarantee at least one of those things won't happen."

It took a second for his meaning to sink in. A shocked laugh escaped my throat, even as fire filled my cheeks. "Do you have to be so vulgar?" I asked, trying for a serious expression and failing.

"Really? Are you trying to tell me you didn't find that funny? Or tempting?" His voice was teasing and it reached into parts of me that I'd nearly forgotten existed.

I forced myself to take a breath before responding. "I do not find the idea of being chopped into bits the least bit tempting."

"And the other?" His eyes flicked my way, taking a brief journey over my body before he looked back to the road. "How do you feel about that?"

Liquid heat melted through my veins, settling deep and low in my belly. I blinked away flashes of the two of us, tangled up together, and straightened my shoulders. "Are you going to tell me where we're going?" I asked, folding my hands primly in my lap.

Jack's laugh filled the truck. "Is that how you're going to play this? You really think I'm going to buy that act after last night?"

"Hey, you started it," I said, closing my eyes against the wave of memory crashing into me. I could still hear the rasp of his zipper...

"Oh," he laughed. "*I* started it? I'm pretty sure you started it the moment you tore my shirt off."

"Yeah, well...you made the magic potpie. Therefore, it was your fault." I stared out the window, putting all my energy into breathing. If I thought any more about last night...well, picking up where we left off wasn't really an option, since Jack was driving.

"In that case," Jack said, his voice tight with restrained laughter and something else that matched my flustered...everything. "I'll take full responsibility."

***

About ninety minutes later, Jack pulled into the parking lot of a tiny, hole-in-the-wall bar in Port Agnes.

"You know," I said, leaning forward to read the sign. "If you wanted me to go home, all you had to do was say so. I could have driven myself."

Jack looked over as he put the truck in park. "I can guarantee the last thing I want is for you to go home."

"Okay, well do I at least need a tetanus shot before I go into this place?" I didn't recognize it. Bars weren't really my scene anyway, and the ones I did go to with Cat were much glitzier than this joint.

"Relax, Princess." He unbuckled his seat belt and got out, coming around to open my door. "You'll like this place." He extended his hand to help me out.

MEIKA USHER

I gave him a dubious look but took his hand anyway. The inside wasn't any better than the outside. Dark and dank. I had to squint to make out anything. A small bar was shoved against the right wall and a smattering of grimy round tables filled the remaining space. Up front, a rickety stage stood. I squeezed Jack's hand.

"Is this where you're going to chop me up?"

"Oh, yeah. In the men's bathroom. Easier to clean up that way." He pulled out a chair for me and I sat, feeling like I needed a bath and a gallon of sanitizer.

I must have looked thoroughly grossed out and uncomfortable because Jack reached over and put his hand over mine. "I'm not compromising your virtue by bringing you here. You're not going catch anything, and the food is actually good. So kick back, have some jalapeno poppers, maybe a beer or two, and relax. You're going to like this. I promise."

I raised an eyebrow, but took the menu he offered. "That's what they all say," I said, softening a tiny bit when I saw fried mushrooms on the menu.

***

Okay, so the food *was* good. By the time I finished my first beer, I barely noticed the way my elbows stuck to the tabletop, or how the grubby ruffian at the bar kept leering my way.

"So, how was the baby shower?" Jack asked over the tinny jukebox music.

155

I leaned in closer, catching a whiff of his shampoo. "Dottie Daniels asked me how big your trouser snake was, if that tells you anything."

A laugh shot out of Jack's throat, his eyes wide with shock. "And what did you tell her?"

I opened my mouth to respond when everything went black. "Great," I muttered. "I'm going to die here after all."

Jack reached through the darkness and took my hand.

"Are you ready to rock?" a voice boomed, and then the stage light up, showcasing four men decked out in their '80's hair band finest.

"What—" I started, looking over at Jack.

"Wait for it." He nodded toward the stage. Seconds later, the opening lines of Bon Jovi's "You Give Love a Bad Name" filled the air. A grin lit up the semi-darkness. I grinned back then turned to watch the performance.

For the next ninety minutes, the band sang cover after cover, hitting all my hair metal favorites. The dirty beer mugs disappeared as they sang "Talk Dirty to Me." The wobbly chair vanished as "Paradise City" filled the room.

By the time the band transitioned into a classic Madonna song, I was thoroughly entranced. The bass guitarist—a wiry little blond chick—took over lead vocals. Jack stood and held out his hand. I glanced at the rest of the bar. No one else was dancing.

"Come on, Chandler. Live a little," Jack said above the music, and that was enough for me to give in.

Taking his hand, I let him lead me to the space in front of the stage. As the melodic strains of "Crazy for You" drifted over us, he pulled me close and wrapped his arms around my waist. With a sigh, I looped my arms around his neck and lay my head on his shoulder.

We swayed to the music, heartbeat against heartbeat, soaking in each other's body heat. The rest of the bar faded away; there was only the two of us. My veins buzzed warm, but I knew that had less to do with the alcohol, more to do with the Jack. Every warm feeling I'd had in the last two weeks had been because of him. How was it possible for one person to ignite so many good things in another person?

Lifting my head, I looked up at him. I wanted to tell him my thoughts, tell him how much I enjoyed every second of his company. But when I opened my mouth to speak, his lips closed over mine. My eyes fluttered closed, my lips immediately responded to his kiss.

Heat simmered below the surface, as it had from the moment we met, but this kiss held more than that. It was soft, searching. Like Jack had been taking a trip down the same path of thoughts I had. Bringing my hand up to the nape of his neck, I gave myself up to his kiss, responding with my own flurry of emotions.

Around us, the song faded and the crowd erupted into applause. We pulled apart and Jack rested his forehead against mine, looking into my eyes. "You want to get out of here?" he asked. "I've got something I want to show you."

19: Starry Night

As we weaved through the streets of Port Agnes, I couldn't keep my eyes off of Jack. Something had shifted between us back there, and it was terrifying and exhilarating all at once. Maybe we were moving too fast, but I could tell we were heading somewhere good. And I didn't want to slow down.

We were driving along the Hope River. This was my favorite part of town. It didn't matter where you were, there was a great view of the river. I was busy watching the way the moonlight glinted off the water when Jack pulled into a parking lot and turned the car off.

We were at the end of Riverview Drive, in front of a darkened building. To the left, a string of businesses, from Downtown Books to that little Sushi place Cat dragged me to sometimes. To the right, the Hope River.

The empty building sat, dark and foreboding, before us. I racked my brain, trying to picture what used to be here, but I drew a blank.

Jack got out and came round to my side. He opened the door and I hopped out. "We're not breaking and entering, are we?"

"Nope." He held up his keys then headed for the building. I stood close behind him, watching for stranger danger, or maybe the cops, while he unlocked the door. Once inside, he flipped on the lights.

A long, narrow, mostly empty space greeted me. I blinked and looked around. Hardwood floors, exposed ceiling beams, ladders and power tools and paints. The far wall was made up of floor-to-ceiling windows, showcasing an expansive view of the Hope River.

"It's not much yet," Jack said, interrupting my inspection.

I turned to him. Excitement and nervousness glimmered in his eyes. "What is it?"

"It's my restaurant." He looked around, seeing it from my eyes. "Well, 'restaurant' might be overstating a bit." Shoving his hands in his pockets, he swung his gaze back to me. "But it will be. Someday."

I took a few steps further into the space. Putting my hands against the exposed brick, I looked back to him. "You're not covering this, are you? Because that would be a tragedy."

Jack joined me. "Wouldn't dream of it."

We turned and I continued talking. "You could line the tables up along the windows, that way people could enjoy that amazing view."

Jack threw his arm over my shoulder and I leaned into him. We stood in silence for about a minute before he finally spoke. "I'm going to call it *Molly's*. After my mom." His voice was soft, and it pulled at my heart like the strains of a cello.

I wrapped my arm around his waist and squeezed. "That's lovely."

"Yeah, well she was a lovely person." I could hear his smile as he spoke.

We stood there in each other's arms, soaking in the silence. After a couple minutes, I spoke again. "When will it be finished?"

Jack released a long, groaning sigh. "Last year. Six months ago. Two weeks ago." He left my side to start pacing. "I've been working on it when I can, between catering jobs, but life gets in the way, you know?"

My conversation with Lola drifted back through my brain and it hit me: Jack wasn't relying on his father's money to make this dream come true. But...why not?

"What..." I started, not sure how to ask it. *If* I should ask it. He looked at me and I swallowed. "I mean, your dad is Lucas Elliott. Surely you've got connections."

He glanced my way, his eyes shuttered. "Connections come with strings attached," was all he said.

The tense line of his shoulders kept me from pushing further. Instead, I reclaimed my position at his side and we watched the way the city lights bounced off the river. It looked like magic, and, gradually, I felt Jack's body relax against mine.

Note to self, I thought. *Don't push the family issue.*

"I bet it's gorgeous in the daytime," I murmured, resting my cheek against Jack's shoulder.

"It's gorgeous now." His voice was quiet. I lifted my head to find his eyes on me, burning like the coals of a campfire in the dead of night.

My breath caught in my throat. I could feel his heartbeat pounding throughout my entire body and it beckoned mine to do the same. Slowly, I pulled my eyes back to his and moved closer, turning into his embrace. I slid a hand up the nape of his neck. He shuddered, his eyes drifting closed.

I threaded my fingers through his hair, fascinated as his breathing quickened. With one last step, I raised my face to his.

I couldn't tell who made the first move. It didn't matter. Our mouths met in a clash of gentle exploration and fierce need. Every breath I'd ever taken had been for this moment. I could feel it right down to my marrow.

Jack's hands came up to bury themselves in my hair as he pushed passed my lips with his tongue. My fingers tightened on his shoulders as desire like thunder rumbled through me. I pressed closer to him and he stumbled until his back was against the window. A groan vibrated from his mouth and my knees nearly gave out from beneath me.

Sliding his hands over my back, he pulled me tighter into him. I stood on my tiptoes, trying to get closer, dying to get closer. Brushing my tongue against his, I gave myself over to the inferno burning inside me.

With another groan, Jack moved his hands to my shoulders and broke the kiss. "I don't know if you noticed," he said, his voice husky, his breath ragged. "But there are a lot of windows here. And while I want you so badly I can't think straight, I'd rather continue this somewhere more private."

I leaned my forehead against his chest and fought to breathe. He was right. We couldn't stay here and put on a show for all of Port Agnes.

His hands continued to trail up and down my back, his heart pounded loud in my ears. It was clear that he wanted me as much as I wanted him. So, why stop? Why end our night going separate ways? I searched my mind for answers and came up empty. With my heart slamming hard, I raised my head and looked into his eyes. "My place is only ten minutes away."

***

The cab of Jack's truck sparked with the heat radiating from our bodies. I breathlessly gave him directions to my apartment and willed him to drive faster. For some reason, the damn man insisted on driving the speed limit.

Once we reach my building, it was a quick trip upstairs. As I fumbled with my keys, I glanced over at Jack. He gave me a smile that sent tingles all over my body. The knob turned in my hand and I pushed open the door, trying to calm the sudden nerves in my stomach.

Jack followed me inside, momentarily distracted by the new surroundings. I glanced around, seeing my apartment through his eyes. White walls, yellow floral curtains, sea foam green couch with multi-colored throw pillows. It was neat and clean, as always. Not a thing out of place.

I hung back as Jack walked through the room, pausing at the framed print of Van Gogh's *Sunflowers*. "Most people go with *Starry Night*," he said, his eyes finding mine.

With a shrug, I moved across the room. "Yeah, well. I do what I want."

A lopsided grin spread across his face. "I like the sound of that."

I laughed and patted his cheek. "It's cute how you think that includes you."

"Doesn't it?" Two small words. Three syllables. That was all it took to bring the heat roaring back. My eyes dropped to his mouth, then back to his eyes.

"Do you need anything?" I asked, a voice somewhere in the back of my mind reminding me to be a good hostess.

Jack shook his head, holding my gaze with his molten one. The air left my lungs at warp speed. "Good," I said and then we crashed into each other. What was it about this man that beckoned me to let go? To lose control? This wasn't me.

Oh, but it was someone I very badly wanted to be. Someone I used to be. Someone I wanted to be again.

Especially if being that person meant that Jack would keep kissing me like this.

Sparks flew behind my eyelids as he tore his lips from mine and found my neck. Feeling the world around me swirl, I held tight to his shoulders. "What are you doing to me?" I whispered, as he nipped at the sensitive spot between my shoulder and neck.

"Whatever you want me to," he murmured back, his voice low and sexy in my ear.

An involuntary sigh left my lips. I tilted my head to give him better access to my neck and held on for dear life. Jack began trailing his lips back up my neck and along my jawline. "What do you want?" he whispered once he reached my ear.

I opened my eyes then to find Jack gazing down at me. He dragged his knuckles over the same path his lips had taken. My eyelids fluttered, but I held his stare. "You."

That was all it took for Jack to reclaim my lips with his. In two short steps, he landed on the couch, pulling me down with him. I found myself straddling him. I could feel him straining against his jeans and liquid fire pooled low inside me. "What do you want?" he asked again and my whole body quivered.

His fingers dug into my waist and I struggled to breathe. Forcing my eyes open, I gripped his shoulders tight and whispered, "I want you to touch me."

He held my eyes as his thumbs slipped under the bottom of my shirt to my naked skin. "Here?" he asked.

Just at that small contact, my skin caught fire. It only served to fuel the greed inside me. I shook my head. "N-no."

In a smooth movement, he gripped the bottom of my shirt and pulled it over my head. The cool air kissed my skin and I gasped. My chest rose and fell at a rapid pace. Jack's eyes hungrily drank me in, lingering on the black lace that held my breasts in place. Leaning forward, he trailed the tip of his tongue along the edges of the lace, his hot breath sending a shower of shivers over my entire body. "Here?" he asked again, his lips lingering over the sensitive flesh of one breast.

"Good place to start," I answered, pushing my fingers through his hair. He growled and tugged my bra straps down, pulling a nipple into his hot mouth while his hand covered the other. I gasped, my fingers tightening in his hair, as his tongue flicked over the sensitive peak. As if of their own accord, my hips began rocking against him. The friction of his jeans between my thighs sent fissures straight to my center like a flaming arrow to a bulls-eye.

I closed my eyes and threw my head back, giving myself over to this moment, those hands, that mouth. Tightening my thighs around his hips, I ground myself into him, wanton need overtaking any semblance of shyness I may have felt.

Jack pulled his mouth from my breast and I whimpered my protest. He chuckled, the sound vibrating through me. I opened my eyes to find him looking up at me, his eyes burning bright. "Do you have any idea how sexy you are?" he asked, his voice low and gravelly.

My cheeks burned even hotter, but I held his gaze as I reached behind me and unclasped my bra, the hunger in his eyes making me brave. His gaze darkened and fell to my chest. "And you really do have a great rack."

I laughed just as Jack's hands encircled my waist. Before I could register what was happening, he had me onto my back and was dropping hot kisses over my naked shoulder and across my chest. My hands roved over his back until I found the hem of his shirt. I pulled until he obliged and sat up long enough to remove the barrier of clothing. When he returned to me, his mouth found its way right back to my breasts.

"Mmm," I moaned, arching my hips to get closer to him. He reached between us and parted my knees, situating himself snugly between them, his mouth never leaving my breast.

My breath came quick and harsh. I dug my heels into the couch and watched the sparks shooting behind my eyelids as Jack pressed closer, his hardness grinding into my aching heat. "There," I rasped, my lungs aching for air, body lamenting the barrier our clothes provided. His teeth scraped one nipple while his thumb grazed over the other.

"Yes," I whispered, the word coming out broken and ragged as a wave of bliss washed over me. My abdomen tightened as my hands moved over his back. I wrapped my legs around his waist and held tight as he moved against me.

"Jack." His name left my lips as I felt myself losing control. "God, Jack."

"Mmm," he murmured against my breast, and the strain in his voice only spurred me on. Closer and closer, I approached the edge, feeling more frenzied with each passing second. My skin burned, my lungs ached, everything inside me screamed for release. Jack's mouth switched breasts, and his tongue began flicking rapidly over my sensitive nipple. The muscles in my belly squeezed hard and tight.

"Please, please, please," I whispered, desperate for release.

"Come for me," Jack murmured, and the growl in his voice pulled at something deep and primal within me. My fingernails dug hard into his shoulders and I threw my head into the couch.

"Don't stop," I managed, nearly crying with need.

With one final motion, Jack thrust himself hard against me and I pushed myself into him. Everything exploded then. A strangled sound escaped my throat and I held on tight as wave after wave of fire crashed over me. Jack groaned, the sound muffled by my breast, and I shoved my fingers into his hair, dragging his mouth up to mine. I kissed him as the waves eased into a gentle ebb and flow.

"Holy shit," I said once we parted. Jack laughed, his blue eyes shining down at me.

"You going to make it?" he asked, brushing the hair away from my face. A self-satisfied smirk curved his lips. I thought about lecturing him for being cocky, but considering the little aftershocks still pulsing through me, I decided he'd earned a little cockiness.

Nodding in response to his question, I said, "I think I'll make it."

"Good." His eyes darkened and before I could register what was happening, he was sliding down my body, his fingers working at the button on my pants. "Because I'm not done with you."

20: Killer Umbrella

Sleep pulled at my eyelids as Jack and I lay in my bed the next morning, a tangle of arms and legs. I rested my head on his bare chest, my fingertips tracing over the smattering of hair on his chest. A smile touched my lips. Lifting my head, I looked at him.

"Hey you," he murmured, his hair thoroughly mussed.

"Hey." I pressed my lips to his chest. "How's it going?"

He grinned and I tingled. "It's going real good, darlin'. How about you?"

I moved up until we were face-to-face and kissed his smiling mouth. "Eh."

"*Eh*?" Jack repeated, raising his brows. "Really?"

Hiding my smile against his chest, I shrugged. "Yep. Eh."

"Oh, you think you're funny." His hands slid beneath the tangled sheets, his eyes glittering.

"Oh, no," I said, realizing what he was up to. "Don't you dare." Too little, too late. His fingertips found my sides. I squealed, trying to wriggle away. "Stop!"

He chuckled, one arm holding me in place while the other tickled relentlessly. "Take it back."

Giggling, I squirmed and kicked. "Okay, okay, okay!" I reached between us and grabbed his hand, trying to stop the assault. "You're a magnificent sex god and I am more than just 'eh.'"

"Magnificent?" he repeated, his hand stilling at my waist. "I like the sound of that."

Still smiling, I reached up and made a poor attempt at smoothing his hair. My heart swelled against my ribcage and I blinked as a wave of tenderness washed over me. "G-good," I managed, shoving my emotions aside for further examination later. "Now, don't tickle me again or I might have to use my sweet ninja moves on you."

"I'll keep that in mind." His eyes left mine to travel over the naked flesh that had been exposed in my struggle to get away. "I'd really like to use some sweet moves on you right now. Magnificent, even." As he said it, he ran his hand up my naked leg and over my belly.

Moments earlier, I'd been completely satiated. Now, the always-burning embers roared to life. "You're trying to kill me," I groaned, moving just enough to give him better access. He leaned on one elbow, watching my face with intense eyes as his hand moved lower and lower, grazing the place aching for his touch.

"Sweetheart, trust me. I like you much better when you're living and breathing." Watching my face closely, he slid his fingers into my slick heat, finding my pulsing center. Never breaking eye contact, he began to move, slow and soft. My breath caught in my throat and my eyelids fluttered closed.

"Keep breathing," he whispered as his fingers picked up the pace. And then his lips were on my skin, nipping and licking a burning trail over my chest. I gasped as his tongue flicked over a nipple. "There you go."

With a whimper, I reached up and grabbed his head, pushing his mouth back to my breast. He chuckled but obliged, pulling my nipple into his mouth. My entire body rocked with pleasure, my fingers tightened in his hair. I lifted my hips off the bed, silently begging him to keep touching me. He obeyed, moving his fingers faster and faster. "Ohgodohgod," I chanted, pushing my heels hard into the bed, arching closer to his hand.

Jack pulled his mouth from my breast and I could feel his eyes on me. "You feel so good." His voice, deep and raspy, flowed over me.

"*Holy shit*, don't stop," I managed, my hands moving to grip the sheets, my entire body arching toward him.

"Wouldn't dream of it," he murmured before reclaiming my nipple with his mouth.

Pressure built inside me with each passing second and, desperate for release, I ground myself into his hand.

Gripping tight to Jack, I pressed my head deep into my pillow and groaned. His fingers slipped lower and he entered me with one quick thrust. I tightened around him as he curved his finger, finding a spot deep inside me that tore another long, loud groan from my throat. And then I slipped. Right over the edge.

"Oh, God. Jackjackjackjack." My nails dug hard into his back. I moaned a string of nonsensical words as white-hot sparks radiated through me.

Jack lifted his head from my breast, his fingers still deep inside me as I pulsated around them. "Deep breaths," he murmured, his husky voice tinged with amusement. "Don't die on me now."

I laughed and turned my head into the pillow as the waves began to subside. "I think it's too late. I'm dead."

Gently slipping his fingers out of me, Jack slid up the bed and turned so that we were face-to-face. His blue eyes were dark, an underlying heat simmering beneath the surface. "I don't know," he said, his lips quirking. "If this is what it's like to be dead, I might just take it."

I wriggled closer and ran my hand over the side of his hair, stopping at the nape of his neck. As my heart rate slowed to a normal pace, the thudding desperation was replaced with a tenderness so unfamiliar to me I didn't know if I should be scared of it. Making the decision to face it instead of hiding, I lifted my face and pressed my lips to Jack's.

The kiss was soft, warm. He moved his mouth over mine and I kissed him back with every ounce of that unfamiliar feeling coursing through my veins. I could feel his hardness pressing against my leg, and I was suddenly filled with the desire to make him feel as good as he'd just made me feel. Moving onto my elbow, I pushed closer to him until he lay on his back. Pulling my lips from his, I smiled up at him. "Don't forget to breathe."

"Wh-what?" He blinked, understanding dawning on his face as my mouth moved against his naked chest. Lower and lower I went, leaving a trail of kisses behind, until I sank my teeth into the deliciousness of his hipbone. He hissed and I smiled, anticipating the moment I pulled him into my mouth.

Settling myself between his legs, I ran my hands over his thighs and caught his eye. The liquid fire in them ignited a heat in me that I hadn't felt before. That I could put that look in his eyes...

Holding his gaze, I ran my tongue along the hard length of him, relishing in the gasp that escaped him. I was just about to pull him into my mouth when a loud bang startled us apart.

"...the hell?" I muttered, tilting my head to listen. "What *was* that?"

"I think it was the door." Jack's voice was tight. "They'll go away."

I nodded, turning back to him. Taking him into my hand, I leaned down, only to be interrupted again. This time, the sound was closer. "Seriously," I muttered. "No one even knows I'm in town."

"Well, then they'll give up." He grinned. "Where were we?"

Laughing, I replied, "About...here." His breath caught as I gripped him and brushed my lips over him.

"All right, I know you're in there!" A voice broke through the moment, coming from right outside my bedroom door. "And you should know that I'm armed!"

"You gotta be shitting me," I muttered, getting off the bed. Grabbing the sheet, I wrapped it around myself and gave Jack an apologetic smile. "This should only take a minute." Giving him one last, longing look, I opened the door and slipped out.

"What are you *doing?*" I hissed as I found Cat standing at my door, an umbrella held up like a baseball bat.

"Oh, thank God. It's just you!" Her arms drooped and she smiled with relief. "I heard noise and I thought someone broke into your apartment."

"And...you were going to kill them with an umbrella?" I tightened the sheet around my breasts. "How'd you even get in here?"

"Keys. Duh." She held up a key ring and I recalled giving her a spare a while back when the cable guy had to come for a repair and I had to work all day. "You've got a guy in there. As your best friend, it's my duty to scope him out. Make sure he's worthy. Especially since you don't usually bring guys ho—"

"Shh!" I grabbed her arm and steered her away from the bedroom. "Could you keep it down? I'd rather not advertise to my neighbors that there's a guy in my bed."

"Sweetie, I hate to break it to you, but the entire building knows you've got a guy in your bed. You weren't exactly discreet." She grinned, her dark eyes sparkling. "He must really know what he's doing."

I didn't know it was possible, but my cheeks grew hotter. I opened my mouth, but a sound from behind us cut me off.

Jack walked out of the bedroom, in jeans and nothing else. He cleared his throat and ran a hand through his hair. The grin on his face made it clear he'd heard Cat's comment.

So damn cocky, I thought, even as my eyes drank in the trail of hair disappearing into the waistband of his jeans.

177

Cat glanced at me and crossed the room. "You must be *Ohgodohgod.* I've heard a lot about you."

"Cat!"

He grinned. "Good to know word gets around. I'm Jack."

"Cat," she replied, assessing him with her eyes. She turned back to me and mouthed *Nice.* "So, Jack. What are your intentions?"

"Oh, god," I muttered, putting a hand over my face.

Cat turned to me and waved me into silence. "Yes, I know his name. Now let him talk."

Jack laughed. "Well," he replied, not an ounce of awkwardness in his voice. He was so easygoing, so laid back. I really dug that about him. "My intentions are to provide as many earth-shattering orgasms as possible, for as long as possible, until Tierney gets sick of having me around."

My mouth dropped open. Cat laughed. I peeked out between my fingers in time to see her high fiving him. "My man." She nodded her approval. "Well, I should let you get back to it, then." Brushing passed me toward the door, she added, "At least turn on a TV or something. Because, really. Mrs. Wallace on the top floor can't take such scandalous behavior."

Once she closed the door behind her, I looked at Jack. He was still grinning, looking all sorts of smug. "So...uh...that's Cat," I said, motioning toward the door.

"I like her." He crossed the room to wrap his arms around me. With a deft motion, he loosened the sheet and let it drop to the floor. "Now, what do you say we give Mrs. Wallace something to be scandalized about?"

21: *Like Magic*

A few hours later, grinning like idiots, we headed outside to Jack's truck. "You know," he said as he opened the passenger door. "I'm thinking that maybe we should go back inside. Hole up in your bed all day. Maybe all week."

I smiled and leaned up to kiss him. "Alas, real life will eventually come banging at our door."

"Holding an umbrella?"

I snorted. "Sorry about that."

He lifted a shoulder, his lips curving wickedly. "No worries. If she hadn't shown up, we wouldn't have had super hot sex on the living room floor."

A flush crept over my cheeks. Lurid images flashed through my mind. My sheet hitting the floor. Jack's hands roving over my skin. Me, shoving him against the wall and dropping to my knees, picking up where we'd left off minutes before...

"Yeah, well," I said, looking at the ground. Jack put a finger under my chin, bringing my eyes to his.

"I don't want this date to be over." His eyes simmered with warmth and called to the place inside me that had been trying to escape all night. I reached up and pushed his hair off his forehead, smiling when it moved right back into place.

"I don't either."

We stood there for countless seconds, holding tight to the last strains of magic, neither of us willing to move, to break the spell. Finally, I reached into Jack's jeans pocket and grabbed his keys, an idea taking hold. "Get in. We're going for a drive."

***

A little while later, I pulled into an empty parking lot back in June Lake. Jack glanced over at me. "You know Spring Thing isn't until *next* weekend, right?"

I grabbed his arm. "Spring Thing is next weekend?"

Spring Thing was an annual fair that brought together June Lake and a few of the towns around it. It was a place for local businesses to sell their wares, all the while loading up on fair food and riding carnival rides to their hearts' content. It'd always been one of my favorite things when I lived here.

Jack laughed and got out of the truck. I unbuckled and opened my door in time for him to meet me with his hand extended. I took it and got out. "Yeah," he said, closing the door behind me. "Which is why I'm a little confused as to why you brought me to the fairgrounds."

"It's one of my favorite places in June Lake." Linking my fingers through his, I pulled him forward, my eyes taking in the wide expanse of empty space before us. "I love how it can look like this," I waved my free hand toward the field, "but then like magic, there are lights and people and rides."

We walked toward the edge of the field, toward a copse of trees. I dropped his hand and sat in the grass. "I don't know. It's silly."

Jack plopped down beside me, leaning his back against the trunk of a tree. Lifting his arm, he issued the silent invitation and I took it, nestling into him. "It's not silly," he said, kissing my temple. "You should come next weekend. We can have elephant ears and shop and ride the bumper cars. In between running things at my booth, of course."

I tilted my head to look at him. "You're going to have a booth?"

"Yep." He smiled, pride warming his face. "Cookies, cupcakes, pies. The usual lineup. Should be fun."

I smiled back. "Very cool." A warm breeze drifted over us and I closed my eyes. "The Ferris wheel was always my favorite," I said suddenly. Opening my eyes, I looked up, watching the fluffy clouds drift across the bright blue sky. "Something about feeling like I'm on top of the world. It's like..." I trailed off, suddenly feeling self-conscious. "It's...great."

"Great?" Jack repeated, catching the shift in my voice.

"Yep. Just great." I crossed my arms over my chest and rested my head against his shoulder. "Anyway," I said by way of changing the subject.

After a few seconds, Jack spoke again. "Why do you do that?"

I glanced over, the mid-afternoon sun catching a glint of sapphire in his eyes. "Do what?"

"You have these moments of absolute freedom, you're so passionate. And then, you become so...restrained." His voice remained level, his hand didn't stop stroking my bare arm. Even still, I paused, looking over at him.

"I don't know what you're talking about."

His lips tilted slightly. "Really? The Ferris wheel is 'just great?' 'Great' is a lukewarm word. I've known you long enough to know that you are anything but lukewarm."

Slowly, I turned my body toward him until we sat facing each other. I took my bottom lip into my mouth as his words sank in. I'd done it my entire life. There had always been a part of me that stayed hidden, worried about what others would say. Slowly, though, from the moment he'd offered me a drink at that party, Jack had been chipping away at that reserve. I didn't even feel like the same person with him. I became more myself than I ever was with Wes. With anyone.

And I loved it.

"What do you like about the Ferris wheel?" Jack's quiet voice pulled me back to this moment.

Before the ever-present censor could kick in, I answered. "Since I left June Lake, I've spent so much time on the ground. So much time struggling, trying to reach my goals. Something about being up there, seeing the world so small below, it's always made me believe I can be more than what I am." I exhaled, long and slow, and finished. "I...I haven't felt like that in a long time."

The silence following my words made me tense. Staring at my hands, I added, "I don't know. It's stupid."

"I don't think it's stupid." Jack reached across the distance and moved my hair from my face. "I think it's vulnerable and human and brave."

I scoffed, still not looking at him. "I'm probably the least brave person you'll ever meet."

"I don't know." His fingertips tilted my chin up so I had to look at him. "It took a lot of courage to know that life here in June Lake wasn't something that you wanted. It was brave to walk away from it when everyone was telling you it was the best thing for you."

"Yeah, but at what cost?" I splayed my hands in front of me, meeting his eye. "I've been stuck in the same job for the last six years, a job I took because I couldn't make it in New York. In the meantime, Wes has taken over the clinic, just like he always talked about. I just...feel like I'm running behind."

Jack winced imperceptibly at the mention of Wes, but he brushed it off so fast I nearly missed it. "You can't spend your life comparing yourself to others, Tierney. It'll drive you crazy."

I watched his face, his words swirling in my mind. While I absorbed them, he continued. "You'll get where you're going. You're just taking your time getting there. Grinning, he added, "Which will make that promotion you're about to get so much sweeter."

I returned his smile and took his hand in mine. Something in his words resonated deep within me. Something in his words hit home deep inside his own soul. I watched his eyes, wanting to know more. When I spoke, my voice was quiet, gentle. "Who are you comparing yourself to?"

Jack looked at me and I could see the wheels turning in his mind. Maybe wondering how much to say. Maybe wishing he'd just kept his mouth shut. Whatever the thoughts going through his head, he began to speak anyway.

"When your father is Lucas Elliott that comes with a lot of expectations." He shifted, stretching his legs out in front of him.

Lucas Elliott. A name synonymous with wealth and power. I knew from earlier conversations that Jack hadn't spoken to his father in years. Now, I wondered why.

"I can't imagine the pressure that must put on you." I stretched my legs out and rested them against his, leaning back on my elbows. "My dad ran the car repair place and I felt like I couldn't measure up sometimes. I mean, I couldn't even tell you where the carburetor is in my car."

"Yeah, you should really know that. Your dad's a mechanic. There's no excuse." He bumped his leg into mine and smiled, but the twinkle didn't reach his eye. "Anyway, it's not dear old dad."

I tilted my head, turning his words over in my mind. "Your brother."

Jack gave a curt nod and focused his eyes on something in the distance. I'd only ever met Lucas Elliott II once, at a family get-together, maybe Wes's parents' anniversary, the first year Wes and I were together. I had a vague vision of an icy blue stare and a head of neat dark hair. He'd stayed all of an hour before ducking out.

"Luke was a good little soldier from the start," Jack said now, bringing my attention back to him. "Went to the fancy schools, didn't get in any trouble, got straight A's. Graduated from Sutcliffe with honors. He'd been groomed since practically birth to be Dad's right-hand man." He lifted a shoulder and tried his best to look indifferent. He didn't fool me, though. I saw beneath the carefully still mask.

"That's what he's doing now. Running Elliott Enterprises while Dad does whatever a cold-hearted bastard with too much time and money does. Plays golf? Skins puppies to turn them into fur coats? I don't know." He plucked a blade of grass and studied it. "Meanwhile, here I am. Broke, with indefinite plans to open a restaurant." He laughed, a short, bitter sound. "To say I'm not the favorite son would be a massive understatement."

And there it was: the unspoken reason why *Molly's* hadn't opened its doors. In comparing himself to his brother, Jack had paralyzed his own success.

Anger bubbled up inside me, at his father, and his brother, for making him feel anything less than the wonderful man he was.

"Fuck 'em."

Jack's eyes flew to my face, wide with surprise. I shrugged. "You heard me. They're both epic assholes and they don't deserve to claim you as anything, much less family."

He smiled—a real one that actually reached his eyes—and said, "You've got a filthy mouth, Chandler. I like it."

I got to my knees and moved up the length of his legs until I sat on his lap. "You know, that's not the first time today you've told me how much you like my mouth."

A chuckle, low and sexy, reverberated through him. "And I meant it both times." He leaned in and pressed his lips to mine. Despite the flirtation, the kiss was soft and sweet. I put my hands on his shoulders and kissed him back, my heart thumping unevenly in my chest. Melting into him, I gave myself up to the wash of emotions flowing over me.

When we parted, I rested my head against his forehead. "You know what else?"

"What?"

"You're gonna open that restaurant, and it's going to be amazing. That, my dear, is the ultimate Fuck You."

Jack's lips tilted in the most adorable half-smile I'd ever seen. "Thanks, doll." Then, he kissed me again—long and sweet.

"So, what do you say?" he asked moments later. "You, me, next weekend? We get on that Ferris wheel and picture ourselves conquering the world together?"

"It's a date. Now, I'm absolutely starving, so I think we need to locate some food before I waste away."

"Aww, and here I thought we were going to make out some more." Jack watched as I got to my feet, then took the hand I offered. "There's no one around for miles. Could have been fun."

"Good God, man," I muttered, giving him a yank. "You are insatiable."

"Your fault." He threw his arm over my shoulder and we started toward the truck together. "You walk around looking all sexy and expect me to resist?"

"I'll try to remember that for our next date. I think I have a mu-mu in my closet…"

"Mmm, now *that* sounds sexy. Make it happen." We reached his truck and he opened the passenger door, pulling the keys from my pocket. "In fact, maybe you should wear it tonight. To the thing I'm about to ask you to." He paused, giving me his most endearing smile.

"What thing?" I leaned a shoulder against the truck and tried not to smile in return.

"You know the brother I just ranted on and on about? He's going to be in Port Agnes tonight, and wants to meet for dinner. I could really use a friendly face." His eyes flickered and he added, "Plus, if you wear something low-cut, I'll spend the entire night thinking about your rack, and I won't even notice my brother's there."

"So, let me get this straight." I met his eye and cocked my brows. "You want to take the chick you just started sleeping with to meet the brother you detest?"

"Well, yeah. Is that…is that not something that people do?" He did his best to look earnest and my lips twitched. Then, he pushed out his bottom lip and channeled his best labradoodle impression. "Please?"

"Dude, you don't fight fair," I groaned, resting my head against the truck.

"So, is that a yes? You'll rescue me from a night of awkward silence with your pretty, pretty face?" He batted his lashes and I sighed, giving him my most put-upon look.

"It's a yes. But you owe me, pal."

Jack grinned then, and pulled me against him, trailing his lips down my neck. "I'm okay with that."

22: Meet the Elliott's

"Dinner is canceled," Jack said later, putting his arm around my waist and nuzzling my neck. We ended up back at Jack's place, where I let him show me his appreciation. For two hours. Stretching, I turned my head toward him. I felt *very* appreciated.

"Let's just stay here. All night. All the nights in existence," he continued, his voice muffled as he buried his nose in my hair.

"Mmm." I brushed the hair off his forehead to press my lips to it. "If you figure out a way for that to happen, let me know. In the meantime, I'm sad to say that we have to get up. Familial obligations await."

His shoulders tensed and he looked up at me. "I don't wanna."

I continued brushing my hand over his hair, letting him hold tight to me. "The company might suck, but there will be food. And food makes everything better. Them's facts." I rested my hand against his cheek, loving the way he leaned into it. "Up we go."

Jack released a huge sigh and rolled over onto his back. "You're lucky you're cute," he said, watching me closely as I stood and crossed the room. "Otherwise, I'd tell you just what you could do with that bossiness of yours."

I raised my brows. "You like it."

"You're right. I can't help it. It's hot when you get all authoritative on me." He leaned up on his elbows and grinned. "Go on, tell me what to do again."

I tossed his shirt at him, smiling smugly when it hit him in the face. "Get up. Jackass."

Jack obeyed, getting up from the bed. "Fine, but just know that now I'm unhappy *and* turned on."

"Ahh, just the way I like my men." I started out of the room. "I'm getting in the shower. If you can manage to keep your hands to yourself, you're welcome to join me."

"I make no guarantees." He followed behind me, his hand cupping my ass. "But I'll do my best."

Twenty minutes and countless foiled attempts at getting handsy later, we emerged from the shower and finished getting ready. I glanced at the bedside clock. "We're going to be late."

Jack straightened the collar on his pinstriped button-down and shrugged. "You sure you don't want to cancel? My brother's a dick, anyway. Probably would do him some good to be stood up."

Leaning my shoulder against the doorframe, I studied Jack's face. "You can't just promise a girl a free meal and then back out." I gave him a playful smile, but he couldn't muster one of his own. Very un-Jack-like. Pushing away from the door, I looped my arm through his and moved to the bed. We sat on the edge and I reached up, turning his head to face me. "What's up, pudding pop?"

Seconds ticked by, the quiet only interrupted by Mousse wandering into the room, then back out. Finally, Jack cleared his throat. "I apologize in advance if I turn into a first-class asshole in that restaurant." He scrubbed a hand over his face. "My brother tends to bring that out in me."

"Hey, man. I get it." I bumped my shoulder with his. "Sometimes, Stephen and I—"

"It's not like that." His lips twisted wryly. "There's no reliving childhood memories or lighthearted bickering." The smile turned to a laugh, one void of amusement. "Nothing lighthearted about *our* fights."

His hands twisted in his lap, tension running laps through his body. I reached over to still him. "Tell me about it."

Jack swallowed, his gaze falling to our hands. "I always wanted to study cooking. Then, I got accepted to *Pâtisserie Paris*. In France." His fingers intertwined with mine, then untangled. "My father flipped. I either go to Sutcliffe or I'm disinherited." He rejoined our hands. "I was seventeen. A kid who just wanted his dad's approval. So, I caved."

I squeezed his hand. I knew how that pressure felt. The pressure to be something you weren't sure you wanted to be.

"After college, I had Dad on one side, threatening to disown me if I didn't take the position he'd created just for me. And Luke on the other, guilting me with the whole *Just be a good son* spiel."

He stood, pacing. "*Dad's not getting younger,* he said. *He just wants to spend time with you.*" Swinging to look at me, he gave a sardonic smile. "But I wasn't interested in sacrificing my happiness for my father again. So I turned him down."

"And that's when your dad made good on his threat." I filled in the ending. Anger simmered hot in my veins on Jack's behalf. "Fucker."

Jack laughed—a real one this time. "Yeah." He plopped down next to me. "It all turned out, though. I worked my way through culinary school. Not the fancy French one, but hey, I came out all right. And soon, I'll have my own restaurant." A crooked smile stumbled over his lips as he looked my way. "Well, soon-*ish*."

"Screw your brother." My arms encircled his waist and I squeezed tight. "Let's stand his sorry ass up."

Jack's laugh vibrated through me. "Nah. Let's just get it over with." He stood and held his hand out to me, a gentle smile on his lips. "Besides, you're right. Food does make everything better."

***

The air in *Venezia's* smelled like heaven and homemade Italian bread. Jack and I walked in, arm-in-arm, and the host immediately showed us to our table.

Luke stood as we reached him. "Jack." His voice was cool, his eyes even cooler.

I hung back, absorbing the striking similarities in these two men. Luke was a couple inches taller than Jack, but they shared the same dark hair and piercing blue eyes. Only, Luke's were missing the ever-present light. He was handsome, yes, but his jawline was too sharp, his lips too serious. Like if I dared to make a joke in his presence, he'd merely pat me on the head and tell me I was being silly.

"Luke," Jack responded, his own voice taking on an icy tone I'd never heard from him. "How've you been?"

"Good. Busy." Luke's eyes flickered over to me then back to Jack, surprise on his face. "You brought a date."

I smiled and held out my hand. "Hi," I said, forcing brightness into my voice. "I'm Tierney."

Luke took my hand and smiled. *Ahh, there's the resemblance,* I thought. Still not as nice as Jack's smile, though. "It's a pleasure to meet you, Tierney."

"I assume you ordered wine," Jack cut in, forcing Luke to drop my hand.

"Of course." He moved to pull out my chair just as Jack did the same. Jack shot a glare at him and he put his hands up and moved to his own seat. "I hope Chianti meets your approval."

Tension spark between them like a downed power line in a rainstorm. I, for one, didn't feel like getting electrocuted. "Chianti, huh?" I took my seat and shook open my napkin. "Who's liver are we eating?"

Half a laugh left Jack before he covered it with a cough. Across from me, Luke's lips tilted maybe a centimeter upward. Ahh, progress. "So, Luke," I continued, anxious to crack the weirdness like a walnut. "I've heard a lot about you."

He glanced up sharply as he filled our wine glasses. "Yeah?" He looked at Jack, then back to me. "So? Do I *look* like Satan?"

I opened my mouth to tell him I'd always pictured Satan in a bowtie when the host approached our table. "Here you are, Mr. Elliott," he said with a hefty dose of butt-kissery. "Anything else I can do for you, sir?"

It took me a full five seconds longer than everyone else to realize that the *Mr. Elliott* our host was referring to was neither of the men currently seated.

Lucas Elliott the first tilted his head, dismissing the host, as he took the seat next to his eldest son. "I would imagine," he said, his arctic eyes flickering my way. "That I'm Satan in this story. Am I right?"

"You—you're not wearing a bowtie," I stammered, reaching for my wine glass. Lifting it to my lips, I took a hearty sip. "Pretty sure Satan wears bowties."

"Bow...tie?" Jack repeated, looking to Luke as if he had the answers.

Luke shrugged. "She's your date, man."

"You are correct, dear," Mr. Elliott ignored his sons, focusing on me. "I'm afraid I don't own a single bowtie." He extended his hand across the table and, with a glance toward Jack, I took it. "Since both my sons have forgotten their manners, I'm afraid I don't know your name."

"Tierney." He gave my hand a quick squeeze and I yanked it back. "Tierney Chandler."

A smile flashed over his face, illuminating those Disney prince genes he'd passed on to his offspring. Only, he looked more like a villain. *No one charms like Jack's dad, no one cheats like Jack's dad, no one disowns their son for baking things like Jack's dad...*

I gave myself a mental shake and refocused before I launched into a full-on reenactment of *Beauty and the Beast*. Not the time or place, dammit.

"Good to meet you, Ms. Chandler," the elder Elliott said as he picked up his wine glass. He rotated it in a slow circle and watched the rich liquid swirl. He didn't look up as he spoke again. "Jack. How have you been?"

"How about I save you some time?" Jack said instead of answering. "I'm not interested in the 'new position' that just opened up with Elliott Enterprises." His father looked up, a spark of surprise flaring then dying on his face. "I haven't been for the last three years you've tried to rope me in," Jack went on, "and I won't be for the next three years—or ever."

Around us, the clink and buzz of the restaurant continued, but at our table, silence was the guest of honor. Jack kept his eyes trained on his father, not an ounce of warmth to be found. Beneath the table, he reached for my hand. I took it and squeezed.

Finally, Luke cleared his throat. "Well. Now that that's out of the way."

"We can get back to pretending we give a shit about each other's lives?" Jack leaned back in his seat, his free hand reaching for his wine. "All right. If that's the game you want to play. How's everything?"

I winced at the coldness in Jack's voice. He'd warned me, but I was still caught off guard. Not a trace of the Jack I'd come to know—my Jack—to be found.

Mr. Elliott sat back and picked up his wine again. He seemed to measure his words carefully. Finally, he looked up and held Jack's gaze, his eyes flint, Jack's steel. I watched the sparks shoot across the table and held my breath.

"I've missed you."

The words ricocheted like bullets across the atmosphere. Jack reared back and blinked. "You know how to find me."

"Yes. And I've called," Mr. Elliott said. His fingers rested on the stem of his glass, his eyes on Jack's face. "And emailed."

Jack pulled his glare away. I looked from him to his father to Luke. Three sets of blue eyes, varying degrees of torment rumbling below the surface. Three equally stubborn faces, holding the storms at bay.

Communication was not strong with these guys.

Jack broke the silence first. "Anyway." He tossed his napkin onto the table and pushed his chair back. I followed his lead. "It's been swell, but I really think we should be going."

"Jack." His father's voice was soft enough to stop him. "Stay. Have dinner. I'd like to hear about how you've been."

He seemed to genuinely mean it. Jack must've caught that, too. He paused, and I could see the thoughts tumbling around in his brain. I waited for his cue, ready to sit back down.

Looking from his father to Luke, Jack shook his head. "Nah." He put his arm around my waist and we backed up. "I'm good."

23: A Heart Thing

"You sure you don't want to go back in there?" I asked as we stepped out onto the sidewalk. I looped my arm through Jack's and cast a surreptitious look at his profile. The muscles in his jaw worked overtime as he thumbed through his wallet for the valet ticket.

"I'm sure," he said with a glance my way. Short and to the point. He hadn't shaken his *dealing-with-my-family* vibe yet.

"Okay." I watched as he handed the ticket to the valet and barely managed a polite smile. I tried again. "But the food smelled really yummy, and your dad seemed sincere, and—"

"My father is only sincere when he wants something." He kept his eyes fixed on something across the street. "Luke has failed for years to convince me to come work for Dad. I assume this was his way of getting the job done."

"You assume wrong."

We turned to find Luke standing behind us. Jack's gaze barely met his brother's before he turned back around. "You're wasting your time, Luke."

Not to be deterred by the ice in his brother's tone, Luke forged ahead. "Look, I know we haven't exactly had the best relationship—"

"Relationship?" Jack took a step toward Luke. "We see each other once, maybe twice, a year. You don't know a thing about me."

Luke's lips thinned. He nodded. "Fair enough. But that man in there, he's our father." He gestured toward the restaurant. "And he's been trying to contact you for months."

I hung back, taking in every gesture, every expression exchanged between them. Jack shrugged, deceptively casual, while a plethora of emotions simmered beneath the surface.

"Why would I pick up the phone?" he asked. "Why would I read the emails? So he can tell me what a disappointment I am? How hard he's worked to provide for me, and he *just wishes I would appreciate it?*" A bark of laughter punctuated his sentence. He shook his head. "I don't need him to tell me something I already know."

"He's sick, Jack." Luke's words fell soft, but their effect was anything but.

The tension left Jack's body, puddling at his feet. "What do you mean?"

"He had a scare last month." Luke pushed his hair away from his forehead and exhaled. "A heart thing."

"What happened?" A new energy emanated from Jack as he faced his brother. Fear. Worry. "Is he okay?"

I eased closer, rested my hand on Jack's arm, waited alongside him for Luke to answer.

"He's fine," Luke finally said. "Or, he will be. Doc's got him on new meds, he's changing his diet, getting more exercise in than walking a golf course, and..." he paused, warily meeting Jack's eye. "Cutting back on work."

"And there it is." Jack turned away, walked a few paces up the sidewalk, then back toward us. "Pops can't work, so he's calling in reinforcements."

"That's not it at all." Luke's eyes sparked with sincerity. "A man has a heart attack, he reevaluates his life." He paused and glanced behind him as if he were checking on their father. "It's not about business."

The air between them thickened. Every fiber of me wanted to wrap my arms around Jack, squeeze him tight, take him far away from this conversation.

The valet shuffled over, keys in hand, snapping the tension like a rubber band.

Jack took the keys and cleared his throat. "Forgive me," he said to Luke, "if I have a hard time believing you." He jingled his keys and put an arm over my shoulder

Luke pressed his lips together and nodded. "I hope you reconsider." With a wave, he opened the door to *Venezia's* and disappeared inside.

"Are...are you sure you don't want to..." I started, choosing my words carefully. "I mean, I don't want to overstep, but—"

"Thank you for coming tonight." He dropped a kiss on the top of my head, cutting off any persuasive words I might have had. "Now, let's get out of here."

***

The ride back to my place was dense with silence. Words and sentence fragments rolled around in my brain as I tried to come up with the perfect thing to say that would turn Jack around.

I had nothing.

We came to a stop outside my building. Jack left the truck running. I fiddled with the seatbelt clasp and searched my brain one more time. I'd seen torment on his face back there. Indecision. I knew part of him wanted to go back, to talk to his father. The bigger part, the part that had been burned one too many times by those sparks of hope, kept him from giving in.

"I'm gonna head home." Jack's voice cut through the quiet and my eyes found his silhouette. His fingers did a nervous dance on the steering wheel as he glanced my way.

"Okay." I reached for the door handle, but stopped before I touched it. I had to try. "Look, they're probably still at the rest—"

"Let it go, Tierney." He met my eye, his filled with storm clouds, though his voice remained level. "Please."

I wanted to respect his words—really, I did. But my mouth had other plans. "You don't want to at least hear him out? I think—"

"Look, not to be a jerk." His fingers stilled and wrapped around the wheel. "But this isn't really your business."

"I know." I turned in my seat to face him. "And I get it. I—"

"You don't get it." His stare stayed focused ahead of him. "Your family is straight out of a sitcom from the '90's—complete with quirky toddler."

"Hey, now." I lifted a hand, bringing his words to a stop. "Her quirkiness is damn adorable."

"Oh, I agree." He glanced my way long enough to pass me a quick smile. "The point is, my family isn't like yours. We're screwed up." His shoulders lifted. He refocused his stare out the windshield. The nervous tapping of his fingers against the steering wheel started again. "A health scare isn't going to change that."

There was finality in his tone. *Case closed*, it said. *Moving on.*

But every molecule of energy emanating from him contradicted that. I knew that if I got out of the car without doing everything I could to sway him, I'd regret it. *He'd* regret it.

"But what if it will?"

A long sigh left him. He dropped his head to the steering wheel and I could see his struggle to find his next words. I took his silence as my chance to build my case. "People change, Jack. Especially when they're forced to reassess their lives. If he's sick, I'm sure he's scared. He just wants to—"

"Get out." He didn't look up when he said it. For a moment, I wondered if I misheard him.

"Jack, I—"

"I'm not doing this with you, Tierney." He lifted his head and scrubbed a hand over his face. When he turned toward me, the look in his eyes was so far removed from my Jack that, for a moment, I didn't recognize him.

His voice was flat as he continued. "Look, this has been a lot of fun, but that's all it is. You don't know me. You don't get to tell me how to handle my family."

"Oh." I shook my hair away from my face and blinked. Hard. "Okay." I reached for the door handle and told the shudder in my chest to fuck off.

As I pushed the door open, Jack laid a hand on my arm. "Wait. I'm sorry. I just—"

"No, no. You're right. I'm sorry. I shouldn't have pushed." I shook off his touch. "It's not my place." I climbed out of the truck and tried for a smile. Didn't happen. Instead, I tossed him a wave and slammed the truck door.

I didn't look back. Didn't wait around to see if he got out of the truck. Didn't listen for the engine revving as he drove away.

Nope. I simply marched into my apartment building and to the elevator. Pushed the button, got inside, waited as it lifted me to my floor.

And tried not to think about the wrenching inside me.

This has been a lot of fun, but that's all it is...

Silly me. I thought we were more than that.

24: Sugar Helps the Sorry's Go Down

The next morning, I got to the office about five minutes late—not bad, considering how long I spent staring at my phone, willing it to ring.

The regret of letting Jack leave last night was more intense than watching a slasher film before bed, even though you know it'll give you nightmares.

Because, hey, at least the nightmares ended when you woke up.

I wanted to call him. In fact, I almost did. About thirty-three times. But each time, I tossed my phone aside before I could make the connection.

Space. He needed space.

Maybe a lot of space.

Maybe permanent space.

The thought kept me up all night, and with the rise of the sun, I realized something: he had a point.

It really wasn't my place to advise him on his family. I'd been seeing the dude a few weeks. And, while it hurt to hear him say it, he wasn't wrong—I didn't know him. Not as much as I wanted to.

I hoped it wasn't too late to fix that.

I entered the office, phone in hand as I considered calling Jack, for real this time. Staring at his contact info, I nearly collided with someone. "Oh! I'm sorry!"

"It's all right. No harm done."

I shoved my phone in my purse and forced my focus back to the here and now. Myra stood in front of me, her blue eyes bright behind her thick-framed bifocals. "You're back from your trip?"

"Oh, no. Haven't left yet." She smiled, her eyes crinkling. "I just met with Ron—gave him my recommendation for the senior editor position." Her brows wriggled. "I'm looking forward to taking on New York with you."

My hands and feet went cold. "You mean—"

"Well, nothing's official, of course." She continued to smile. "But I did give Ron a shining recommendation for you. I told him if he didn't give you that job, his head was full of pumpkin guts."

I returned her smile, trying to tamp down the excitement boiling up inside of me. *Nothing's official,* I told myself. *Don't get your hopes up yet.* "Thank you so much, Myra. That was very sweet of you."

"Sweet, hell. It's true." She slapped my arm with her free hand, her face stern.

I thanked her again for the recommendation and then she was on her way. I tried not to dance my way to my desk, smiling good morning to Emily on the way.

At least I can keep hope alive for a few more days.

***

Excitement, plus lack of sleep, plus boy problems, equaled a total lack of concentration.

By lunchtime, I had reorganized my pens—first by color, then by size—assembled an impressive chain of paper clips, and created a fashionable collection of Post-It hats the framed picture of my parents on my desk.

Yet my to-do list remained untouched.

I was a shoo-in for the promotion. Which meant I'd be moving. Which meant I'd be leaving Jack behind.

Maybe our fight was a good thing—he wouldn't even miss me when I left.

The hollow feeling in my chest told me I was wrong.

Rocking my chair from side to side, I blew out a deep breath. How had it taken me this long to realize the implications of The Big Dream?

My parents grinned at me from their spot on my desk, Mom sporting a bright fuchsia Post-it fedora, and another pang hit me. From Port Agnes, I was only ninety minutes away from everyone. New York City was much further…

I shoved away from my desk and grabbed my phone. I needed food. "Going to lunch," I called to Emily, who had been on the phone all morning. Unless her client was named Mr. Schnookums, it wasn't a business call.

Without missing a beat in conversation, Emily waved me off.

A few minutes later, I'd shoved myself into a corner booth at a crowded restaurant down the street. The waitress didn't bat an eye when I told her I'd be dining on apologies and coffee for lunch. She delivered the latter with a smile and a cinnamon roll.

"Sugar helps the sorry's go down," she said when I looked up.

"Oh. Ha." I picked up my fork and stabbed the pastry. "Thank you."

She waved off my thanks, her dark eyes warm. "Good luck."

Once she was gone, I released the fork, watching as it slowly drooped to the side, peeling away layers of delicious cinnamon roll with it. My phone sat next to the plate, silent and waiting. Judging.

Leaving things like this was not an option. Even if— by some miracle—I got the promotion, I didn't want to chase this dream without Jack's support.

"Ahh, dammit." Blowing out a quick breath, I picked it up and swiped to unlock it. Within seconds, I had his contact information pulled up. "Just do it. Call him."

"Well, hello, stranger."

Cat slid into the booth across from me, a whirlwind of red hair and sass. "And *hello*, beautiful." Without skipping a beat, she picked up my abandoned fork and dug into the roll.

"Were you *following* me?" I asked, flipping my phone over. "Also, sure. Help yourself."

"Don't mind if I do," she replied around a mouthful of food. "And, yes. Totally following you. How else am I supposed to know where we're meeting for lunch, since you didn't bother to tell me?" She shook her hair away from her face and ripped off another piece of roll. "I'm really starting to feel like yesterday's pizza here. You know, still awesome—some might even say better—but you kinda forget it's there because you're so distracted by the new meal in front of you."

I rolled my eyes and took the fork from her. "When have you *ever* forgotten about pizza?"

"Never." She raised a hand to get the waitress' attention. "But you have."

"Only because you finish it before I remember it's there."

"Yeah, yeah. That's not the point." The waitress returned, and Cat rambled off an order that sounded like enough to feed three people. "And another one of these," she added, waving at my cinnamon roll.

"I don't know how you do it," I said once the waitress was gone.

Cat slid the plate toward her and yanked the fork from my hand. "Easy," she said, popping another bite into her mouth. "Like this."

I shook my head and cradled my coffee cup in two hands. My phone seemed to glow from its place on the table, and I tapped my fingers against my mug to keep from reaching for it.

What would I even say when he picked up? *If* he picked up? *Hey, so about last night. Sorry I—*

"Hello?" Cat waved a hand in front of my face. "Are you daydreaming about the Giver of the Orgasms over there?"

"What?" I blinked. "No. What are you—"

"I mean, I *saw* him," she continued as if I hadn't spoken at all. "He's definitely drool-worthy. And, well, everyone within a three-block radius knows he's good in the sack."

I flushed as she said it, and she kept talking. "I just need to know where this is going. You're spending an awful lot of time together, and you haven't stopped grinning like an idiot for days. Now, I admittedly know next to nothing about relationships and all the crap that comes with them, but you've got *smitten* written all over you. I feel like I have a right to know if this guy is planning to steal my best friend from me."

"Chill out, *Mom*." I rolled my eyes and reached for the last piece of cinnamon roll. My stomach revolted at the thought of food as the realization that I'd also be leaving Cat behind hit me. "Not likely to happen," I said after I swallowed. I'd tell her about the job offer later. "We, uh, actually had a fight last night."

"Uh oh." She rested her chin in her hand. "Is that why you've been staring at your phone this whole time? Waiting for the *I'm sorry* call?"

I started to deny it, but she cut me off. "Screw that. Call him and demand your apology." Before I could stop her, she grabbed my phone from the table and unlocked it. "No one keeps my best friend waiting. No matter *how* nice his penis is."

The waitress arrived with Cat's food as she said it, and I didn't know where to focus first. Apologize to the waitress for Cat's lack of filter, move my coffee cup out of the way so she could put the food down, or attempt to get my phone out of Cat's hand.

As I was clearing the table for the waitress, Cat was putting my phone to her ear.

I made the wrong choice.

"Cat, no." I shot to my feet and reached for the phone. My elbow whacked the waitress' tray. Issuing a string of sorry's, I steadied it. Once disaster was averted, I turned back to Cat. "You are fired from best friend duty unless you give me that phone *right now*."

She blinked, took the phone from her ear, and shrugged. "Here you go."

"Thank you," I sighed, sinking into my seat. The waitress finished unloading Cat's feast, and left us alone. Looking at Cat, I continued. "Where are your boundaries, woman? I don't need you to call up some dude I'm shagging to demand apologies. For all you know, *I'm* the one who screwed up."

As Cat buttered her toast, she tilted her chin toward my phone. "If that's the case, now's a good time to apologize, don't you think?"

"I didn't say I *did* screw up. Just that I might have. And anyway, I'm not sure I like him enough to apologize. I just—"

Cat cut me off with the most obnoxious throat clearing of all time.

"Holy hell, woman. That's why you *chew* the food first." I tossed my phone on the table and reached for her second piece of toast. "Besides, his penis isn't *that* nice. It's only okay, really. I've—"

She cleared her throat again and I looked up. "*What* is your deal?"

With wide eyes, she looked from me to the phone. "*Ahem-HEM.*"

I glanced down to find Jack's face grinning up at me. It took about ten seconds and three muffled *hellos* to realize what Cat's deal was. She'd called Jack.

And he'd heard everything.

215

25: *Only Okay*

"You're a bad best friend." I glared at Cat and picked up my phone, making sure to put my hand over the speaker. "Bad, bad best friend."

She barely glanced up from the plate of scrambled eggs she was salting. "Yeah, yeah. Thank me later."

"You're paying for my breakfast," I said before I headed for the door.

Once outside, I took a deep breath and put the phone to my ear. "*Heeeey.*"

Silence.

Had he hung up? I had to admit, I half-hoped he had. At least then, I'd have time to scrounge up excuses for what he'd overheard. I could make up one hell of a story to explain away the comment I made about his—

"So, it's *only okay*, huh?" Jack's voice came through the phone, heavy with amusement. "A less secure man would be really hurt by that."

My face burned and I was thankful he couldn't see me. "Well, it's a good thing you're not one of those men."

"Exactly."

He paused, and I searched the air for my next words. The apology I knew I owed him. The assurance that I'd keep my nose out of his business, the—

"So, listen," Jack said before I had my thoughts together. "I'm sorry about last night. I was a jerk and you didn't deserve it. I—"

"Wait, *you're* sorry?" I leaned against the building, bafflement fuzzing up my brain. "I'm the one who should be apologizing. You were right—your relationship with your family isn't any of my business. I don't know you, and—"

"You know me better than most people in my life." His voice was warm with sincerity. "That was a shit thing to say. And I'm sorry."

"Apology accepted." I leaned my head against the cool brick behind me and let the warmth seep through the phone. "I'm sorry, too."

"For saying my penis was only okay?" The teasing was back in his tone. I had *missed* this Jack. "Thank you, I really appreciate you saying that. For a minute there, I was questioning everything I knew about myself. I mean, does that mean I'm a bad kisser, too? And that my magic potpie isn't so magical? My entire life was turning into a question mark."

"Shut up," I laughed. "Jackass."

His laugh flowed through the phone. As it eased to an end, he continued talking. "I didn't mean it, you know."

"Mean what?"

"The thing about this being fun."

"Oh, so it's not fun?" I made light to hide the jab that was still aching from his words last night. "I think you're pretty boring, too."

"You know what I mean." His voice went from light and teasing to stretched-thin and nervous. "You and me. It's more than just fun."

"Yeah?" I couldn't stop the smile from taking over. *More than just fun.*

Which would make it that much harder to leave…

I watched a herd of businessmen cross the street and shoved that thought aside.

"So, it occurred to me," Jack continued as the last of the businessmen reached the curb. "That you never got your dinner last night."

"Yeah, well." I glanced through the restaurant window at Cat happily attacking a stack of pancakes. I swallowed the mounting sad and focused on Jack. On this moment. I hadn't even gotten the job yet. Possibly wouldn't get it at all. No point in steeping myself in guilt and remorse just yet. "A PB&J ain't Italian, but it got the job done."

Jack groaned. "A PB&J? I sentenced you to a dinner of PB&J? I'm a monster."

"I mean, I wasn't going to say anything, but now that you mention it…"

"Let me make it up to you."

Cat caught my eye and waved. I took visual inventory of the food in front of her. Yep. I'd be leaving this place still hungry. "Tonight?"

"Tonight," Jack confirmed. "I'll pick you up at seven. We can go back to *Venezia's* and get you some damn spaghetti."

"I was really hoping for lasagna..."

"Or lasagna. Or linguini. Or whatever else you want on that menu."

I watched as Cat flagged down the waitress and paid the bill. My stomach rumbled at the loss of all that delicious breakfast food. "Will there be dessert?"

***

"Oh, would you stop pacing? You're making me nauseous." Cat leaned her elbows against my kitchen counter and shook her head. "You're acting like this is your first date with the guy."

"Well," I replied, smoothing imaginary wrinkles in my borrowed blue dress. Jack would be there any second and I had used up the last six hours to obsess over our date. "It's our first date after our first fight, so—"

"So, you're worried about the makeup sex." Cat nodded and swung to open the freezer. "That's understandable. I mean, if it's too good, you're setting a high standard for the rest of your relationship. If it's bad, he's gonna wonder why he bothered making up with you in the first place." She pulled out a box of pizza rolls. "I would *not* want to be you right now."

"Please. Drain my fridge *and* my self-esteem." I glared at her and gestured toward the kitchen. "Help yourself."

"Kidding, kidding." She sailed to the microwave and popped the pizza rolls in. "I'm sure it's going to be a very lovely date, with makeup sex that is just the right amount of smokin'."

"Why do those things sound so patronizing when you say them?"

Cat shrugged. "Because I think relationships are society's way of forcing us to shackle ourselves to another human being and give birth to the next generation of poor saps that think all they need is love?" She smiled brightly and whirled to glare at the microwave. "But, hey. That's just me."

Before I could formulate a response, there was a knock at the door. "Try to keep your cynicism to yourself for five minutes, okay?" I said as I crossed the room.

She gave me a thumbs up with her free hand, the other holding a plate of pizza rolls.

Taking a giant breath, I pulled open the door. Jack stood in the hall, looking like every hero in every romantic comedy ever. Fancy suit, nervous smile, and a damn dozen roses.

"Hey." He held out the flowers.

I smiled and breathed in the scent of roses. "I feel like Julia Roberts in *Pretty Woman*."

"You feel like a prostitute?" Cat called from the kitchen. "Hi, Jack."

Burying my face in the bouquet, I stepped aside to let Jack in. "Hey, Cat." He crossed to the counter. "How are you this lovely evening?"

"Clearly not as good as you." She came to a stop across from him and bit into a pizza roll. "You've got I'm-Gonna-Get-Laid Face."

"Oh, my God." I dropped the roses into a pitcher and sat it on the counter between them. "What are you even doing here?"

Cat shrugged, undeterred. "I have no food in my place." Taking her plate, she sailed around the counter and into the living room. "And I can't remember my Netflix password."

I grabbed my purse from the counter and threw it over my shoulder. "You're never out of food."

"What are you trying to say?" she asked around a mouthful of pizza roll.

Behind me, Jack snorted. "Don't encourage her," I grumbled, looping my arm through his. "Lock up when you leave," I called to Cat as Jack opened the door.

"Don't worry," she called back. "I'll be gone in time for your Bone-a-thon!"

I pulled the door shut before she could add anything else. "I swear," I said, refocusing my attention on Jack. "It's like having a teenage boy around all the time. The food, the TV, the—"

Jack shut me up with a kiss.

If I felt like Julia Roberts in *Pretty Woman* earlier, I felt like I was in *Notting Hill* now.

Only, Jack was probably a better kisser than Hugh Grant.

His hand rested against my cheek as he kissed me. His lips were soft, his touch gentle. Like I was something to be cherished.

My heart thumped unevenly as I pushed my fingers into his hair and I kissed him back, cherished him back, until the walls spun around us and the floor dropped from beneath our feet.

Pulling his lips away, Jack rested his forehead against mine and stroked my cheekbone with his thumb. "I missed you."

I blinked, forcing my eyes to focus on his. Inside, my heart kicked it up a few more notches. "You, too."

He smiled and my heart stuttered. Tucking a piece of hair behind my ear, he dropped a tiny kiss on my nose and backed away. "Good. I would hate to take a girl to a fancy dinner if she didn't even *miss* me. I mean, I suppose the dinner would go a long way toward making her miss me, but do I really want someone who only misses me for the foo—"

I gripped the front of his shirt and pressed my lips to his. A surprised noise vibrated through me, but melted into a groan as I stood on my tiptoes and deepened the kiss.

His tongue slid hot over mine and any control I'd had evaporated. Stepping forward, he pushed me against the closed door. As he buried one hand in my hair, the other landed on my back, urging me closer, tighter against him, until I could feel his heartbeat through my entire body, until his body heat melted my bones, until—

Until the door shook behind me.

My eyes flew open, Jack's lips left mine, and we both stared, confused, at the source of our interruption.

"Dinner first, dessert later, kiddos," Cat called from the other side of the door. "Have fun!"

With a labored sigh, Jack pushed away from the door and extended his hand to me. "At least she didn't threaten me with an umbrella this time."

I laughed, my fingers tangling with his. "Small victories, man. Now, about that food…"

He pulled me away from the door and draped his arm over my shoulders. "Food's the last thing I want in my mouth right now," he murmured as we headed toward the elevator.

I stopped. Looked at him. Then back to the door. Heat flooded through me, from the roots of my hair to the tips of my toes. "Cat!" I called, turning on my heels. "Cat, you gotta go!"

26: Dessert is Off the Table

Cat didn't go. We went instead.

Jack enforced her *dinner first, then dessert* rule. He made conversation over appetizers, charmed me over wine, and force-fed me lasagna till I couldn't move.

Okay, that last part wasn't true—I ate the lasagna willingly.

By the time we arrived back to my apartment, making with the sexytimes was the last thing on my mind.

"All right. Bye, now," I said to Jack as I unlocked the door. "Thanks for the food."

"But...what about dessert?" Jack put on his puppy dog eyes. "I was promised dessert."

"You should have thought about that before you fed me." I pushed open the door and let him follow me inside. "Full Tierney is sleepy Tierney."

He shut the door behind us and took my purse from my shoulder. As he hung it on the hook, he said, "I can get on board with sleepy Tierney."

I awkwardly kicked off my shoes and looked at him. "What?"

He toed off his own shoes and loosened his tie. "Couch or bed?" Tossing his tie on the counter, he started unbuttoning his shirt. "The couch forces us to be closer, but the bed is probably more comfy."

My brain processed his words one at a time, then strung them together to form sentences. I shook my head. "I'm sorry. What?"

Jack laughed. "What's the matter, darlin'?" His shirt joined his tie. "Didn't expect me to stick around once dessert was off the table?"

I looked at the guy standing in front of me, from his socks to his plain white t-shirt, and something inside me went all mushy. Could've been my heart. Maybe just my pancreas. Either way, I closed the distance between us and wrapped my arms around his neck. Leaning up, I pressed my lips to his. A soft kiss, not seeking anything more than the sweetness of this moment.

When we parted, I smiled. "Couch." Threading my fingers through his, I turned and pulled him toward the living room. "I could stand to be a little close to you right now."

***

I woke up in a tangle of limbs and blankets. Snuggling deeper into the warmth, I opened an eye.

"Hey." Jack grinned down at me. "Morning."

"Is it?" I stretched my arms over my head and groaned. "Morning, I mean."

"Sort of." He dropped a kiss on my jaw and pushed a piece of hair from my forehead. "I've got to get home. Pies to bake and whatnot."

"Mmm, pie." I wriggled in closer. "Don't you think it's too early for the dirty talk, pal?"

A chuckle vibrated through him, sending tingles over me. "It's never too early for dirty talk."

"Especially when it involves pie." I sighed. "Do you really have to go?"

"'Fraid so." He lingered long enough to run his fingertips over my exposed belly. I shivered. He groaned. "You're not making it easy, though."

I smiled, keeping my eyes closed. "Good."

He went quiet, his fingers still trailing across my skin. After a few seconds, he said, "If it weren't for my morning breath, I'd kiss the snark right out of you."

I arched my back, leaning into his touch. "If it weren't for *my* morning breath, I'd let you try."

"Try?" His fingers hovered

"Well, yeah." Tossing the blanket aside, I sat up and put my feet on the floor. "The snark never leaves. It's just...there."

"Ahh." Jack sat up next to me. A hand smoothed my hair away from my face. "I wouldn't want you any other way." Leaning in, he pressed his lips to my neck, sending a thousand tiny shivers over my skin.

I lifted a hand and pushed my fingers through his hair, holding him close, urging him to keep kissing me.

He obliged, his lips moving up my neck to nip at my earlobe. A whimper left my lips. I turned my head just in time to catch his lips with mine.

The kiss was softer than I expected. Jack's hand was gentle on my cheek as his lips moved against mine. The room didn't spin. The ground didn't drop from beneath my feet. My clothes didn't demand to be ripped from my body, and my blood didn't turn to fire.

What *did* happen was much bigger.

My heart—that lump inside me that had kept me alive thus far—shuddered, stalled, then slammed hard against my chest. As if it were saying, "Hey! Hey, you! Pay attention to this! This is important!"

Jack must've felt it, too. His lips stilled against mine and, slowly, he moved away. His eyes were hazy as he looked into mine. "Hey," he said, his lips curving with a smile.

"Hey, back." My fingers were still in his hair, so I extracted them to rest my hand on his cheek. He leaned into my touch and my heart did that weird skipping thing again.

"Tierney, I—"

The rattling of my doorknob interrupted him. Seconds later, Cat sailed through the door. "Oh, you're up," she said as she caught sight of us. "Don't mind me. I'll be gone so fast you won't even know I was here." She marched into the kitchen and swung open the fridge. "It's just that I woke up craving carbs like a beast, so I was about to have a bagel when I noticed that my cream cheese has green crud growing on it. And you can't have a bagel without cream cheese, right?"

Jack rubbed a hand over his face and leaned back. "Way to ruin the moment," he called toward the kitchen.

"Sorry, dude," Cat called back. "It was an emergency."

"A cream cheese emergency?" I stood and ruffled Jack's hair. Then, I joined Cat in the kitchen. Reaching passed her, I grabbed the tub of cream cheese. "You're abusing your key-holding privileges," I said, holding the tub just out of her reach.

She reached for it and missed. Grimacing, she crossed her arms over her chest. "Fine. Won't happen again."

"Thank you." I handed her the cream cheese and she whirled away.

"Nice to see you again, Jack," she said with a wink, pulling the door closed behind her.

I shut the fridge and headed back to the couch. "Sorry..." I trailed off as Jack grabbed my hand and pulled me down next to him. He laced his fingers with mine, and instantly, I forgot what I was saying.

"I have a proposal for you," he began, watching our fingers twist together.

"Don't you think it's a little too soon to propose?" My eyes found our hands, too. "I mean, I've got t-shirts older than this relationship."

"Ha." He stopped fidgeting and held my hand in his. Looking up, he went on. "I didn't make the greatest impression the other night with my family. I was hostile, impatient, rude—"

"All true," I interjected. "But I get it. There's stuff there that I don't understand. You don't have to—"

"I want a second chance." His fingers tightened slightly on mine. "To show you that I'm not a jerk."

"You...you want to have another dinner with your father and Luke?" I raised my eyebrows, part of me hopeful for reconciliation, part of me dreading the explosion.

A laugh left Jack. "No. God, no." He cleared his throat and dropped his gaze. "Uh, dinner with the rest of my family."

I blinked. Narrowed my eyes. Shook my head. "You want me to have dinner with the Nolan's?" I laughed—a short sound, void of amusement. "You know your beloved aunt hates me, right? Like, she wants very bad things to happen to me."

"Eh, she's harmless." He grinned. "Besides, I like you, and I want them to know that."

That brought me to a stop. "It...it's kind of a big deal, then. Like, bringing a girl home to meet the family, big."

"I mean...yes and no. You already know them. They know you. We're just...establishing a new dynamic. I'm telling you. Once you go from Wes's evil ex to my beautiful and charming girlfriend, they're going to love you."

Something tilted inside me. "Girlfriend, huh?"

"Yeah, you got a problem with that?" His voice was teasing. "I mean, I could call you 'That chick I sleep with sometimes,' or 'She Who Has the Great Rack,' if you prefer."

"No, no." I laughed. "Girlfriend's good. Kind of has a nice ring to it."

"I thought so. Anyway, what do you say? Want to meet the family?"

A long groan left my lips. "You know what's going to happen, right? I'll go from Wes's evil ex to the woman who's corrupting another of her precious boys. The end result? An elaborate scheme to end my life. It was nice knowing you, pal."

"Well, in that case, I feel as though we should spend as much time together as possible before your untimely end." He leaned in as he said it, emanating with charm. "What do you say?" His lips trailed over my jaw, nearing my mouth. "I promise I won't let my aunt murder you."

I turned my head, all kinds of mushy feelings flowing through me. Pushing my fingers into his hair, I sighed. "Fine. Okay. But if I die, it's on your hands."

27: Pot Roast Predicament

The day arrived, dark and gloomy, like Mother Nature knew this was my last day of existence. Bitch could have at least given me some sunshine.

I stopped by Cat's apartment before I headed to June Lake. "You know the drill." Leaning against her doorframe, I leveled a tragic look on her. "Wipe my hard drive, toss the Beanie Babies, maybe run a vacuum."

"I really don't think Jack's aunt is going to murder you." Cat rolled her eyes. "Just in case, though, can I have your Netflix password?"

Shooting her a glare, I pushed away from the doorframe and started down the hall. "It's biteme123. It was really nice knowing you."

The drive was too short. Before I'd managed to adequately prepare myself for the evening, I was pulling into Jack's driveway.

He met me at the door, looking yummy and comfy. I pushed out my bottom lip and gave him my best puppy eyes. "I don't wanna."

"Get in here," he said, opening his arms. I stepped forward and let his warmth envelop me. He kissed my hair and I breathed him in.

"You smell like pie," I murmured against his chest, the turmoil inside me calming.

He laughed and I loved the way it vibrated through me. "Thanks." With one hand, he reached behind me and closed the door, the other arm still firm around me. "You smell like fear."

I pulled back. "I feel like that wasn't a compliment." Sniffing myself, I glanced at him. "Do I really smell?"

"Relax," Jack said, pulling me back to him. "I was only kidding. You smell delicious." As if to prove his point, he buried his nose in the space behind my ear.

I shivered. "You're not a nice guy."

"Let's be honest." His hands moved down my back and I arched into him. "You don't like me because I'm a nice guy."

"I beg to differ. I happen to think you're a very nice gu—"

My last word got caught in a sigh as Jack nipped the sensitive skin at my neck. I felt him smile and I pushed my fingers through his hair and brought his face to mine. Our lips clashed in a hot, hungry kiss. We stumbled backward with Mousse dancing at our feet.

"We're going to be late," I murmured, even as I reached for the buttons on his shirt.

Jack pulled my skirt up, his fingertips skimming my thighs. My knees shook and I clung to his shoulders. "Well, then we should stop," he whispered as his hands moved higher up my legs.

"Or we could just not go." His fingers traced the outline of my underwear and my breath caught. "I...I like that idea."

He chuckled, husky and sensuous. "We won't be that late." His eyes narrowed on my face, and I fought to keep mine open. "Just a few minutes."

"That doesn't sound promising," I managed, digging my nails into his shoulders as his thumb hooked into the elastic at my inner thigh.

His eyes shimmered like the midnight sky. "No, darlin'," he murmured, backing me into the living room. My legs hit the couch as he finished. "I only need a few minutes for you."

I sank to the couch, my legs no longer willing to hold me up. Seconds later, Jack joined me, shoving my skirt up to my waist. And then...well, I didn't care how late we were.

***

We were the last to arrive.

As we hit the front porch, it began to sink in. Once upon a time, I'd practically been family. Now, I was as unwelcome as an infestation of termites. Now, I was on the arm of someone else.

Should be a good time.

"Too late to change my mind?" I whispered, my hands fidgeting in front of me as we stood at the front door. "We could hit the highway and—"

Jack cut me off with a kiss, hot and quick.

"What was *that* for?" I asked when he pulled away.

He shrugged. "Just wanted to kiss my girlfriend."

My insides went all gooey. What was it about that word that—

"You know, before my aunt murders her," he added, rapping his knuckles on the door.

I let out an indignant squeak as the door swung open. Bonnie Nolan, blond hair and fake smile, greeted us. "Jack, there you are, sweetie!"

Well, greeted *Jack.*

"Dinner smells wonderful." Jack hugged Bonnie, who barely seemed to notice I was there. "You remember Tierney." He pressed his fingertips into the small of my back, urging me forward.

Her eyes dragged across me like tiger claws, but her smile held. "Of course I do. *So* good to see you, Tierney."

I gave her a smile that I was sure looked more like a grimace. "It's good to see you, too, Mrs. Nolan."

She nodded, unable to muster another fake-ass nicety, then headed into the house.

As she walked away, I leaned closer to Jack. "She's going to poison my pot roast, isn't she?"

"And ruin the meal she's been slaving over all day by having to dispose of a dead body? She wouldn't dream of it." He put his arm around my waist and we followed her inside.

"You're trading me plates. Just in case."

"Oh, I see how it is. It's okay for *me* to keel over dead, just as long as you're okay." Jack placed a kiss on the top of my head.

"Hey, man. It's a dog eat dog world out there."

"Just make sure to wear something low-cut to my funeral, and we'll call it even."

I laughed. "Deal."

We entered the dining room just as Bonnie walked out of the kitchen, holding a basket of rolls.

"Jack is here," she called toward the living room as she set the basket in the center of the table. Once it was perfectly arranged, she straightened and ran her hands over her apron.

The rest of the Nolan clan streamed through the doorway, starting with George—the Nolan patriarch.

"Why, hello, Tierney," he said as he passed me. His smile held echoes of his son's, and I warmed. He'd never been anything but kind to me. Almost made up for Bonnie's malice. "It's good to see you again." As he spoke, he gave my shoulder a squeeze.

I smiled back—a real one this time—and patted his hand. "You, too."

A cloud of blond curls hovered behind him. George stepped away and I screwed my smile on tighter, ready to play nice with Wes's bubble-gum-sweet girlfriend.

"Hey, Sa—"

"Try again," the blond said, her hazel eyes sparking with amusement. "Subtract the frizzy hair and glitter lip gloss..."

My mouth fell open. "Darcy?"

Wes's little sister—who wasn't so little anymore—grinned and pulled me in for a hug, officially giving me the warmest welcome of the evening. "I've gotta tell you," she said as we parted. "Mom is *not* pleased with this whole Jack thing." She glanced her mother's way and continued in spite of the glare Bonnie sent her way. "She thought she got rid of you for good."

"Darcy, that's enough!" Bonnie snapped. "Why don't you come help me in the kitchen?"

"Mmm, nah. I'm good." She put her hand on my back and gave me a push. "Tierney would *love* to help, though!"

Bonnie's eyes scraped over me, then to Darcy. Sighing, she turned on her heel. "Fine."

With a glance toward Jack, I followed her into the kitchen. "Smells goo—" I started, cut off when she thrust a ceramic bowl in my hands.

"Here. You can scoop the mashed potatoes into this." Spinning around, she grabbed a knife from a drawer. The tip glinted in the light.

This is it. This is where I die.

A tiny smirk played across her lips as she plunged the knife into the hunk of meat on the counter. "You like pot roast, don't you, dear?"

Pot roast? *You gotta be kidding me.*

Shaking off my feeling of inevitable demise, I nodded. "Yeah. Pot roast is good."

Dramatic. I was being dramatic.

"Good." She gave a single nod. "Start scooping."

We worked for a couple minutes, with only the sound of Bonnie's knife scraping against the plate and the disgusting *plop* of potatoes filling the silence.

"So, Tierney."

I jumped, the spoon clattering to the counter. "Yes. Hi. Yes?"

Bonnie's pale brows lifted, judgment lighting her eyes. "Potatoes in the bowl, not on the counter," she said, handing me a towel.

"Sorry." As I cleaned up the mess, I sent *help me* vibes to Jack, willing him to come to my rescue.

No luck.

"I remembered you don't like mashed potatoes, so there are tater tots in the oven."

"Oh." I looked at her, then back down to the bowl of potatoes I'd been scooping. One nice gesture, neutralized by a vindictive one. "That's very thoughtful. Thank you."

She nodded and spun, a platter piled with pot roast in her hands. "All right, then," she said, forging ahead as if she hadn't just showed kindness to the enemy. Well, sort of.

The moment I entered the dining room, it was like I'd stepped back in time. Same rose-covered wallpaper, mahogany dining set, and forest green carpet. Same place settings and china set.

Same boy sitting in the same chair.

The last time I'd had dinner here had been to celebrate my engagement to that boy.

While Bonnie had barely cracked a smile all night—not dissimilar to tonight, actually—the rest of us were floating.

Especially me.

I'd just said *yes* to the perfect guy. Our perfect life glowed on the horizon.

But somewhere along the way, shadows of doubt eclipsed the glow. Somewhere along the way, I decided it wasn't the life I wanted.

And so I ended it.

"I hope everyone brought their appetites," Bonnie sang as she rejoined us. "Tierney, your tots."

I shook the tendrils of memory away and took the bowl from Bonnie's outstretched hand.

After I gave Wes the ring back, I wondered if I'd made the right decision, if I'd end up regretting it. And, every once in a while, maybe I had.

Now?

Wes glanced at me from across the table, a golden reminder of my past. One chair over, all sparkling eyes and sweetness, Jack winked at me and patted the empty chair beside him. I took the seat and felt the warmth of his hand on the back of my neck. Tension melted from my body. With a smile his way, I reached for the tater tots.

Bring on the poison, Bonnie. I didn't regret a damn thing.

28: Inappropriate Ex/Current Girlfriends

My "bring it on" bravado did not last long.

Over poison-free pot roast, Bonnie regaled us with tales of Wes's latest victories at the vet clinic. While we slathered butter on our rolls, she went on about her darling son's contributions to the community. Once the red velvet cake was served, she'd moved on to another person entirely: Sam.

"It's just a shame that darling girl of yours couldn't be here tonight," she said to Wes, her fork catching glints of light as she spoke. "I would have *loved* to hear about how school's going." Pausing, she glanced my way. One of her brows lifted. "Sam is a teacher at June Lake Elementary. Second grade."

I nodded and choked down the mouthful of sawdust I'd been eating. "How nice."

"Yeah," Wes cut in. "She had a thing with her co-workers." His eyes remained on his plate, fork gripped tight in his hands. The tips of his ears were tinged with scarlet and his shoulders were all scrunched up. He'd never liked being the center of attention. Of course, that never stopped Bonnie from putting him there.

"That's too bad," Bonnie continued, oblivious to her son's discomfort. "I would've *loved* to hear her thoughts on my new red velvet recipe!"

"It's a little dry."

All eyes swung to Jack. He shrugged. "Probably not the recipe, though. Maybe you just baked it too long."

If I could freeze-frame the look on Bonnie's face and whip it out anytime I needed a pick-me-up, you bet your sweet ass I would. Hiding my smile behind my water glass, I looked away before I lost it to the laughter threatening to take over.

"Jack Christopher Elliott." She set her fork down with the utmost restraint. "I have never over-baked a cake in my entire life."

"Ooh." Darcy leaned forward. "She middle-named you."

Jack grinned, seemingly unaffected by the dreaded middle-naming. "There's first time for everything, right?"

"Careful," Darcy murmured, eyeing her mother warily. "She's gonna blow."

Sure enough, Bonnie's face had transitioned from its usual pallor to a deep red. She blinked and blew a slow breath out of her pursed lips. "No, no. It's fine." Picking her fork back up, she dug into her cake. "Your honesty is always appreciated, dear."

Jack's grin held. "And, hey. If you ever need advice—"

"Anyway," Bonnie cut him off before he could insult her any further. "Wesley, you'll take leftovers to Sam, won't you?"

At the sound of his name, Wes's head shot up. He glanced at his mother, then to each of us. "Sure, yeah," he managed, holding my eye. "Why not?"

Now, it'd been nine years since I'd seen the dude, sure. But we'd been together for a long time. Which meant I spoke fluent Wes. Or at least I used to. And that look on his face was classic *Help me.*

Clearing my throat—partly because the cake really *was* dry, but partly to divert Bonnie's attention—I said, "I don't know what Jack is talking about. This cake is *divine.*"

It was Jack's turn to bite back the laughter. I ignored him and took a gulp from my water glass. "Not dry in the *least.*"

Bonnie narrowed her eyes on me, and I shriveled in my seat. Man, that woman was scary. "I'd appreciate it if you kept your sarcasm to yourself, young lady." A pause, then she redirected her attention to Jack. "You know, Jack. It's a good thing you waited until now to start dating Tierney. Just think: you could've gotten kicked out of a *second* high school back then."

Ouch.

I knew where she was going with this. And I couldn't believe she hadn't let it go. "No one got kicked—" I started, but Bonnie wasn't having it.

"Only because George and I begged the principal to go easy." Her eyes flashed. "You could've jeopardized Wes's entire future. All because you just *had to* ride your father's motorcycle through the halls of the high school."

"It was a harmless prank." I splayed my hands in front of me. I couldn't believe I was defending something Wes and I did as teenagers. "We didn't think we would get—"

"That's the problem with you. You don't think. You're impulsive and indecisive and selfi—"

"That's enough." Wes sat his fork down and straightened his shoulders. "There's a fine line between being concerned and being cruel, Mom. And you're crossing it."

Bonnie blinked. "I just—"

"Thank you for dinner," he continued, gliding over her protest like it didn't exist. "I think I'm gonna head home." Pausing, he added, "Without leftovers for Sam."

I didn't miss the smirk that came with the last part. As if standing up to his mother weren't enough, he had deprived her of bonding with her would-be daughter-in-law.

It really *was* all about the little victories, wasn't it?

Bonnie sputtered and stalled, struggling to regain her composure. "All right," she finally said, pushing away from the table. "Let me walk you out."

Wes stood. "I can see myself out," he said. "Enjoy your dessert."

All eyes were on Wes as he rounded the table and disappeared through the doorway. Silence followed.

With a glance at Jack, I scooted my chair back. "I'll be right back."

I reached the front porch just as Wes was descending the stairs. "Hey."

He turned, the porch light catching his surprise. "Hey."

"I, uh, just wanted to say thanks." I jabbed my thumb behind me. "For what you did in there."

"Oh, pssh." Wes waved a hand. "You kidding? That was fun." He grinned and, for a second, I caught a glimpse of the old Wes. The one the old Tierney adored so much.

The one old Tierney smashed into the ground.

The thought came out of nowhere. I blinked. Shifted and fidgeted. And then: "Listen, I'm sorry."

Wes's brows furrowed. "For?"

I walked down the steps and stopped in front of him. "You know, the whole dumping you and running off thing." Glancing toward the house, I added, "And for showing up here tonight. With Jack."

He winced—just barely. "Yeah. *That's* a little awkward." Rubbing the back of his neck, he squinted up at the house. "You serious about him?"

I followed his line of vision, catching a glimpse of Jack helping Darcy clear off the table. His easy smile as he joked with her, the warmth that I could feel even from here. The patience and ease and Teflon...ness that he displayed— even with dear Aunt Bonnie. Especially with her.

Yep. I wanted him in my world.

Looking back at Wes, I smiled. "Yeah. I think so."

Wes nodded. "I figured," he said. "He doesn't usually bring girls home."

I brushed off the tingle of pleasure that came with that revelation and volleyed Wes's question back at him. "What about you?"

He gave a short laugh. "With Sam? No. We broke up."

"Oh, really?" I crossed my arms over my chest. "Your mom seemed to think she was the marrying kind."

Wes sighed and sat on the bottom step. "That's because my mother just wants to see me settled down with a nice girl so that I can give her grand babies and the perfect little life she's always wanted for me."

I joined him on the step. "You don't want that?"

Wes's shoulders lifted. "I don't know what I want." He looked at me, conflict clear on his face. "Can I be honest here?"

My stomach tensed. *Please don't be that scene in every romance where the heroine's ex proclaims his undying love for her when she's all ready to move on.*

"S-sure," I stammered, willing myself to teleport out of here. Or rewind time. Something, anything, to end this conversation.

"I envy you."

"Wes, I—" I stopped mid-rejection, his words sinking in. "You envy me?" I frowned. "Why?"

"You got out." He said it as if it were the most obvious thing in the world. "You went after your dreams, didn't let anyone tell you what you wanted." As he spoke, he studied his intertwined hands. "Not even me."

I opened my mouth, apology at the ready, but he stopped me. "No, I get it." He raised his head, meeting my eye. "It sucked, but I always got it. It's just..." Trailing off, he found something behind me to study.

"Just...what?" I prompted, the feeling of dread not quite dissipated.

Something bad is afoot, my mind sang. *Head back inside. Make nice with Bonnie and go home with the boy you came with. This will not end well.*

When Wes continued, it was with a bemused smile. "Dating you was the most rebellious thing I'd ever done."

"What?" A laugh spilled from my lips before I could stop it. "What do you mean?"

"Even in high school, you knew who you were. Wouldn't let anyone convince you otherwise" He looked away. "Wouldn't let *me* convince you otherwise."

"Um...thanks?" I sputtered, my brain trying to process what he was saying.

But he wasn't finished.

"I'd dated cheerleaders and student council members and athletes. Girls deemed 'appropriate' by my family—by everyone in this damn town. Then there was you."

"I...was inappropriate?" I frowned. "I don't know how to take that."

He looked at me, eyebrows raised. "Do I need to bring up Bessie?"

A laugh shot from me. "I forgot about Bessie!" The gigantic cement cow that had sat outside Udder Delights Ice Cream. Wes and I hitched it to my dad's pickup one summer night and drove off.

Doc McPhee did *not* appreciate finding the old gal on his farm the next morning.

Nor did he appreciate the—

"And the skinny-dipping?" Wes held up his hand, two fingers extended. With a third, he added, "Or the water tower." Four. "Oh, how about the time we made out in the—"

"Okay, okay." I grabbed his hand and stopped the counting of my many teenage indiscretions. "You're right. Inappropriate sums me up."

Wes laughed. "But it was a good thing. You didn't give a shit what anyone thought of you. I admired you for that." He smiled. "Still do."

A hurricane of reactions battled inside me. Nostalgia cast a warm glow over his words, but beneath it, I knew the cold shock of reality was waiting. Wes and I didn't work for a reason. Multiple reasons. A super long list of reasons.

So, why did this feel like...

"When we broke up," he continued, "I reverted back to my old self. Following the rules, checking the boxes." A long sigh left his lungs. His hand found the back of his neck again. "I'm *tired* of checking boxes." He looked at me. Something on my face must've indicated my inner freak-out. "Don't worry," he said with a wave of his hand. "I'm not professing my undying love here."

"Oh, thank God." I sagged against the porch railing, relief heavy.

His lips twitched. "Thanks."

I laughed. "Oh, no. No offense, man. It's just..." I searched my brain for the perfect analogy. "You've only gotta watch a movie once to know how it ends, ya know?"

Our eyes met and he nodded. "Yeah. I know." He pushed to his feet and held his hand out to me. I took it and he pulled me up. "Here's hoping for a happy ending next time around, huh?"

29: And the Poison Spreads

As I watched Wes disappear into the darkness, the smile still lingering on my face faded. The girl he'd described—the one who didn't care what people thought—what happened to her?

I'd always just assumed I grew up. And got boring along with it. When was the last time I'd done anything spontaneous or dangerous or any of the other -ouses?

Man, I missed that girl.

As I turned toward the house, I wondered if I could talk Jack into a midnight swim…

I stumbled to a stop on the last step, surprised to find Bonnie standing at the top.

"Oh, hey." Grabbing the railing, I straightened my spine. "Didn't see you there."

"It's not going to work, you know," she said. The porch light behind her obscured her face, giving the whole moment a *now would be a good time to run,* feel.

"What?" I pushed my hair away from my face. "What are you talking about?"

"Wes has moved on. He's happy." Her lips spread in an almost gleeful smile. "It's too late."

Eyeing the closed door behind her, I tried to plan my escape. "I don't know what you're trying to say, but—"

"You're using Jack to get closer to Wes." Bonnie took a step to the side, blocking my view. "It's obvious."

"*What?*" Cold showered my flesh, followed by a rush of heat. "You can't be serious."

"Why else would you start seeing Jack?" Her arms crisscrossed over her chest and her chin lifted, defying me to deny it. "You could've found someone else—anyone else."

"That's not—"

"Frankly, it's despicable. Jack is a good man. A nice man. He doesn't deserve to be used by some—"

"I know." I hiked up the last step and stood level with her. "I *know*. That's why I'm with him." I met her eye. Outrage blended with fury, causing an earthquake inside me. "Not because of some sick scheme to get Wes back." Glancing behind her, I saw Jack move passed the window, and my heart clenched tight. "For you to even *think* that I'd use Jack like that..." I shook my head. "He's too sweet and kind and—"

"Too good for you."

"What?"

"He's too good for you." Bonnie's eyes slid over me, her lip curling. "Both my boys are."

My mouth dropped open but no sound came out. Didn't matter. She wasn't done.

"You weren't good enough for Wes then. You're not good enough for Jack now. They deserve better than an underachieving troublemaker who's only going to bring them down. You're—"

"Done," I cut in, meeting her cool gray eyes. "I'm done letting you treat me like this. I understand why you don't like me. Maybe I've earned it. But here's the thing: it was *nine* years ago." I threw my hands in the air, years' worth of pent-up frustration reaching its limit. "We were kids! Get the hell over it."

The screen door slammed shut, punctuating my words. We turned to find Jack standing in the doorway. "What's going on out here?" he asked, looking from me to Bonnie.

"Oh, hello, dear." Bonnie blinked half a dozen times and gave him a wobbly smile. "Tierney and I were just…" She trailed off and looked my way. The light pouring from the window caught a glimmer of moisture in her eyes. *Oh, you gotta be kidding me.* "Catching up," she finished, putting a hand on Jack's arm.

Jack covered her hand with his, narrowing his eyes. "Are you okay?"

"Fine." Sniffle. "I'm so glad you could make it tonight." Another sniff, followed by a series of blinks, and one single, lonely tear. Straightening her shoulders, she gave his hand a squeeze. "I'd better get started on those dishes." Before she turned away, she caught my eye, her lips tilting in the slightest of smiles.

Oh, she was good.

As Bonnie vanished into the house, Jack turned to me. He'd bought her act—I could see it on his face. Before I could utter a syllable, he said, "I'm going to go inside and make sure she's all right." His eyes flickered over me, anger like bee stings on my skin. Without waiting for my response, he opened the door. "I think you should wait out here."

***

The drive back to Jack's house was heavy with unspoken tension. I rehearsed a million different things to say—from defending myself to apologizing—but I couldn't bring myself to say any of them out loud.

This was a different level of mad than last week's father incident. A level of mad aimed specifically my way.

Which was bullshit. He hadn't even *asked* me what prompted the argument with Bonnie. He'd simply taken her word—and who knew *what* she'd told him.

That girl is evil, Jack, I could hear her saying. *You should have heard the way she yelled at me!*

At the thought, a silent, unamused laugh left my lips.

Jack glanced my way. "Something funny?"

"Not in the least." I shifted in my seat and let my eyes trace his profile. An ache radiated inside my chest as I pictured him leaving me alone on that porch. "I could've used your support back there."

"You mean when you were attacking my aunt after she welcomed you into her home?"

"You're kidding, right?" Disbelief had my head spinning. "She spent the entire night treating me like a parasite."

"She's just looking out for me." He pulled the truck into his driveway and put it into park, keeping his eyes straight ahead. "She doesn't want me to get hurt."

"And she decided from the moment I stepped foot on that porch tonight that I was going to do that." I unbuckled and faced him. "No, before that. She spent the entire evening punishing me for something that happened almost a decade ago. And you let her."

Jack tightened his hands around the steering wheel and bowed his head. "The woman is practically my mother, Tierney. What was I supposed to do?"

"Wes didn't have a problem stepping in."

The words were out before I could stop them. Jack's entire body tensed. Lifting his head, he met my eye. "And there it is."

Apology hovered on the tip of my tongue, but I pushed my next words passed it. "I showed up with you. As your *girlfriend*. And you sat there, silent, while your aunt ripped me apart. So, yes. I appreciate that he spoke up. Someone had to."

"Maybe you showed up with the wrong guy, then." He didn't break eye contact as he said it, and challenge flashed across the distance.

"Oh, don't try that shit with me." I shook my head. "I'm with you because I want to be with you. Not him. All I'm saying is that—"

"I should take a cue from good ol' Wes?" His eyes clashed with mine. "Is that it?"

"I didn't say that."

"You didn't have to. You've never had to." Yanking the keys from the ignition, he shoved open his door and got out.

I followed. "What's that supposed to mean?"

"We both know I'm the runner-up here." He stopped abruptly and faced me. "Why are we even pretending otherwise?"

"Did Bonnie tell you that?"

"It doesn't matter," Jack said instead of answering my question. "You're leaving, anyway." Moving around me, he continued up the walk. "I was just a small town distraction on your way to the big city."

The words were like a direct hit to my heart. I stepped back, eyes wide on his face. "That's how you see me?"

"Maybe." He let his keys dangle from his fingers, a sneer twisting his lips. "What's that saying about history repeating itself?"

Fury bubbled in my bloodstream. I balled my hands into fists to keep from punching the smirk right off his face. Inside the house, Mousse barked in anticipation of his daddy opening the door. Well, he was going to have to wait a damn minute. "You really want to compare yourself to Wes?" I took a step closer. My heartbeat slammed loud in my head, my limbs buzzed. "*Wes* is the one I left, the one I hurt." Another step. "And he *still* thinks I'm a decent human being."

We were inches away from the door now, and Mousse was going insane. I had to raise my voice to be heard over him. "He doesn't buy the story Bonnie's selling." Lifting my chin, I let my eyes clash with his as I nailed my next words home. "He *never* has." I jabbed a finger in Jack's direction. "Compare yourself to *that*."

I brushed passed him, our shoulders bumping. Fishing my keys out of my purse, I pulled open my car door. Bonnie should've just poisoned the damn pot roast.

30: Some Old Lady

I walked into work the next morning heavy with relief. Work would distract me, keep me from obsessing about last night's fight, stop me from returning one of Jack's calls from last night, from driving back to June Lake.

Of course, work would also eat my soul, but sometimes you had to take the good with the bad.

Emily met me at the office door. "You have a visitor." Her baby doll eyes blinkity-blinked at me. "Waiting at your desk."

My breath caught in my throat. I grabbed Emily's arm. "Who is it?" I couldn't see Jack now. My willpower only applied if I didn't have to look him in the eye when I stood my ground.

"I don't know." Emily extracted herself from my grip, her brows dropping. "Some old lady."

Relief like a waterfall flowed over me. An old lady, I could deal with. A Jack, not so much.

"Thank you." I pressed my cold hands to my burning face. "And I'm sorry." Giving her a smile, I marched ahead.

My steps slowed as I reached my desk. A tiny woman with fire engine red hair leaned against my desk, eyeing me over her cat's eye glasses. I recognized her right away.

"Mrs. Needermyer, hi." I smiled and extended my hand. "I wasn't expecting you."

She twisted her peacock-hued beads and waved me off. "Call me Joy. Mrs. Needermyer is my mother-in-law."

"Okay, Joy." I motioned for the empty chair beside her. "Have a seat. Do you need anything? Coffee? Tea? Wat—"

"I didn't come to chit-chat." She pushed her glasses up her nose and leveled me with her stare. "I got your latest email."

I winced. Another revise and resubmit. "Yes. I'm sorry about that. I—"

"I'm not getting any younger, you know." She patted her scarlet hair. "I just turned sixty-nine last week."

"Happy birthd—"

"Thank you." She smiled to take the sting out of her interruption. "The point is, I don't want to reach seventy, seventy-five, eighty, still trying to get this dream off the ground."

From the corner of my eye, I saw Emily sneaking glances our way. Over her shoulder, Ron sat in his office, pretending not to listen. Cowards. I stifled a growl and focused on Mrs. Needermyer. "I understand your frustration, Mrs. Needer—"

"Joy."

"Joy." I straightened my shoulders and smiled. "I'm sorry this whole process has taken so long. I can assure you that I'm doing my best to—"

"I know you are." She reached over and patted my arm. "But I'm impatient."

"Well, if you could just wait a little longer..." I trailed off, unsure of how much to say. Should I tell her about my potential promotion? Did I really want to make promises I wasn't sure I could keep?

"It's already done." She waved a hand toward Ron's office. "We've terminated my contract. If I didn't know any better, I'd swear that fellow was glad to be rid of me."

"Oh, no. That's not—"

"No need to sugarcoat it." She gave me a self-deprecating smile. "Nothing personal. Sometimes, the thing you think you want just isn't what you need." She gave my shoulder a squeeze and whirled away. "It's been a pleasure, Ms. Chandler."

I watched her disappear and sank into my seat, deflating like a balloon. Was...was I just fired? I'd put so much into that manuscript. Time, energy, passion...and *poof*. Gone.

My eyes swept over my desk, cluttered with folders and sticky notes and paperwork. Mrs. Needermyer's book was the first thing I'd been excited about in a while. A long while. Now, it was back to—

"Tierney, good morning."

I looked up to find Ron hovering over my desk. I nodded my greeting and began piling the folders into a neat stack.

"So, listen." Ron adjusted his tie and shifted his weight. "Now that the Needermyer manuscript is off your plate, I'd like you to take over the Amish cookbook. Myra was working on it before she left, and she recommended that you finish it up."

I paused in my task and looked up. Two different thoughts flashed through my mind. One: *Holy shit. Amish cookbook. Can you say boring?* And, two: *Myra recommended me. That must mean Ron thinks I'm ready for the promotion.*

Smiling, I stood and reached for the folder he was holding. "Glad to do it, Ron. Thanks!"

Ron nodded and backed up a couple steps. "Excellent. Thank you, Tierney."

Once he was gone, office door shut behind him, I sat again. Opening the folder, I skimmed over the first page. Amish Friendship Bread.

Well, *that* was certainly less exciting than an epic spaceship fantasy…

***

I spent the rest of my day dreaming about the tube of chocolate chip cookie dough in my fridge and the unwatched episodes of *My Boyfriend the Vampire*. Nothing like a long night of self-indulgence to slap a Band-Aid on what was ailing you, right?

I had just peeled back the wrapper on my cookie dough, ready to eat it like a banana, when my phone rang. Mom's face flashed up at me, and relief buzzed through my veins. Well, relief with a dash of annoyance. Had the town gossip mill done its duty already?

My finger hovered over the Decline button before I realized that Mom would just call again. And again. Until I picked up.

"Hey, sweetheart," she said when I answered. "How are you?"

"Oh, you know." I bit into the dough. "Living the dream. What's up?"

"That's actually why I'm calling you. Is everything okay?"

I sat up straighter and swallowed. She couldn't have already heard about the drama with Bonnie, right? Or the break—

Cutting that thought off before it could finish, I sat my cookie dough aside. "What do you mean?"

"Jerry Hancock told Dottie Daniels who told me that Jack left his place in the middle of the night last night. And he's still not home." Mom paused. "I figured you'd know something."

"So, you're calling me to verify some silly gossip you heard over your morning coffee?" I tamped down the annoyance—both at my mother and at my inability to contribute. "Sorry, can't help you."

"Sweetie, I'm just concerned is all." Mom's tone shifted to something resembling genuine. "Dottie called Bonnie this morning, and Bonnie just went on and on about her new recipe book—and how rude you were last night, but that's a conversation for a different time, sweetheart. Anyway, she didn't say a word about Jack. Which is just odd, don't you think?"

She waited for me to pipe in, but I stayed quiet. Picking at my nail polish, I tried to come up with a logical reason for Jack to take off in the wee hours. I left him a mess last night, but I'd left him at home. It would've made sense, maybe, if he had left right after me—if he had decided to go for a drive, to clear his head, or to come after me. But he wasn't here, and my phone had only rang once or twice after I left.

My stomach burned. *What if something happened to him?*

"So, you don't know anything." Mom's voice dragged me back to the moment. "If *my* boyfriend disappeared in the middle of the night, I would want to know why."

"Mom, don't you have anything better to do than participate in juvenile gossip?" I snapped. "I've got to go."

I hung up and winced. Shit. I'd have to apologize for that. Later. Now, I had to find out what was going on with Jack.

I picked up my phone and stared. I hadn't heard from him all day.

My stomach twisted tighter. But what if he wasn't calling because something was wrong? Immediately, I thought of his dad. Luke seemed worried about the old dude. What if something happened again?

What if Jack needed me and I wasn't there?

Shit.

Pulling up his information, I hit Call before I could change my mind. It didn't even ring on his end. Just went straight to voicemail. I hung up and stared at my phone. Had he changed his number? Blocked me? Or maybe he didn't get cell service where he was. I tried one more time, with the same result. Sitting up straighter, I searched my mind.

Aside from his place in June Lake, and the restaurant-in-progress here in Port Agnes, I had no idea where he would be.

I glared at my phone. One person would know. Unfortunately, this person was the last person who'd ever tell me anything. Thinking about Jack and whatever he was facing right now, I knew I didn't have a choice.

Minutes later, after a phone call with Wes to get the necessary phone number, I dialed.

"Hello?" Bonnie said, her voice as sweet as frosted sugar cookies. Ha. Frosted sugar cookies sprinkled with death, maybe.

"Hi, Bo—Mrs. Nolan. It's Tierney. How are you this lovely evening?" I put as much warmth and sunshine as I could into my voice with the vain hope that she wouldn't immediately hang up.

"Tierney," she repeated, all the sweetness gone. "How can I help you?"

"I...I just got off the phone with my mom. She expressed some concern for Jack. I was just...calling to see if everything is okay?" I bit my thumbnail and frowned, hating the uncertainty in my voice. Hating that I had to come to her when I should've been with Jack already.

"I'm sure if Jack wanted you to know, he'd have called you." There was a bit of pleasure in her voice, and I had to bite the inside of my cheek to keep from saying something snarky. "Now, if you don't mind," she continued. "I've got a casserole in the oven."

And then silence. I pulled the phone away from my ear and glared. Well, that was pointless. With a sigh, I dropped my hand to my lap and let my eyes drift over the room. I settled on the Van Gogh print. My memory flitted to a night a few weeks ago. Jack, moving through my space for the first time. The way he'd grinned at me when he saw the print. Then...everything that followed.

That'd been the beginning of something unexpected. Something life-changing. Something that made me feel alive.

The things Jack had given me in our short time together far outweighed the pride that kept me from reaching for that phone again.

Biting back a groan of dread, I dialed Bonnie's number.

"Hello?" she said again, the same sweetness in her voice. It was like she didn't even have caller ID.

"Look." I cut her off before she could hang up. My voice came out clipped, direct. "I know you hate me, but I care about Jack. And if he needs me, I'd like to be there for him. Now, if you don't mind, could you tell me where to find him?" I paused for breath before adding, "Please."

Silence emanated from my phone. I started to pull it away, thinking Bonnie had hung up again, but then a long, labored sigh filled my ear. "Fine. He's staying at his father's house, in Port Agnes. Do you have a pen?"

31: Enter the Dollhouse

I pulled into a long, tree-lined driveway and turned the car off. Leaning forward, I peered through the windshield. I didn't know what I'd been expecting. A full on, Beverly Hills-style mansion, complete with marble walkways and a sprawling lawn? An intimidating, angular modern masterpiece with a fountain smack in the middle of the drive?

What greeted me met none of my expectations. My eyes roved over the tall, ornate Victorian house before me, and I found myself immediately charmed. With its pale blue, shingled siding and white gingerbread woodwork, the house was every little girl's dream come true. Lucas Elliott, mogul of business, family tyrant, lived in a dollhouse.

The thought distracted me just enough to get me out of the car. Gripping my purse tight, I stood frozen to the cobblestone walk. Somewhere in that big, pretty house, was Jack. What would I say to him when he opened that door?

I had no flipping clue.

With one final breath, I straightened my shoulders and marched up the stairs. My knuckles connected with the lead glass door before I noticed the doorbell. I gave it a push, listening to the chime echo inside the house. Twisting my purse strap, I waited. After about thirty seconds with no answer, and no commotion inside, I tried again.

Nothing.

Wiping my hands on my jeans, I looked around. I could go home and try again later. I knew me, though. It had taken thirty minutes and several pep talks to get me out the door. I wouldn't come back. So…now, what?

I plopped down in one of the wicker chairs on the wrap-around porch and crossed my arms over my chest. *Now, I wait.*

***

20% Battery Remaining.

I dismissed the alert on my phone and dropped it to my lap. I'd just spent forty-five minutes playing one of those stupid candy-matching games. My brain cells were leaping from my ear like my head was the Titanic. Taking a deep breath, I crossed and uncrossed my legs. The sun had set, the temperature dropped. I hadn't brought a jacket.

I wrapped my arms around myself and rubbed my exposed skin. Did I have the right house? Had Bonnie given me the wrong address?

Picking up my phone again, I unlocked the screen and started to pull up Jack's number. Maybe I could try one more time, and if he didn't answer, I'd take the hint and—

The crunch of tire on gravel jolted me out of my thoughts. I looked up to find a sleek black Jaguar pulling into the driveway. It parked next to my considerably less fancy Ford and the driver killed the already-quiet engine. I stood, my phone clattering to the porch.

"Shit." I scrambled to pick it up just as two sets of footsteps started up the walk. Straightening, I shoved my phone in my pocket and wiped my hands on my jeans. I looked up in time to see Luke coming up the stairs. The porch light caught the surprise in his blue eyes when he saw me.

"Hello." He nodded his head toward me. His lips tilted in a sort of friendly, mostly confused smile and, again, I noticed how pretty he was. Damn, this family had good genes.

I raised my hand in an awkward wave as Jack reached the top step. He looked less surprised. Probably because he'd recognized my car. I drank him in, taking note of the dark shadows beneath his eyes and the stubble on his face. His hair was messier than usual, his shirt rumpled.

I stepped forward, ready to pull him into my arms, before I caught myself. I settled on a smile. "Hey."

Jack attempted a smile in return, but his lips barely lifted.

My eyes flicked between the two men, taking inventory. No dad. Which meant…

"I'm going to head inside," Luke said, and I blinked. I'd forgotten he was there. "You're welcome to join us for dinner, Tierney." He held up a takeout bag for reference before unlocking the door.

Once he disappeared, I turned back to Jack. "I—I won't stay long. I just…I mean, I just wanted to see—" I stopped and exhaled. "I called you."

His eyes met mine, exhaustion not completely masking the fear that swirled in them. "I know."

"I…" I glanced down at my phone, then back to him. "Is everything okay?"

His eyes flickered over me, impatience blending with uncertainty. He wanted to tell me to leave. I could see it. Something stopped him, though. And that something was all I needed to stay.

"Your dad?"

"Your dad?"

Jack gave a slight nod. "He's in the ICU."

I felt his words like a punch to the gut. Without waiting for an invite, I stepped forward and wrapped my arms around Jack's middle. He hesitated for a moment, his body tense against mine, before giving in. He pulled me tight to his chest and buried his nose in my hair. I closed my eyes and let him hold me, giving him all the warmth and comfort I could muster.

We stood there for a while. Jack's heart beat hard against my chest and I hugged him as tight as I could. Finally, he spoke.

"You're cold."

"Been here a while." I let my hand move in slow circles across his back.

He soaked it in, releasing a sigh into my hair. "Why'd you come?" he asked a few seconds later.

I pulled back slightly so I could see his face. I wanted more than anything to run my fingertips over his cheek, to smooth away the worry and fear that was settled into the creases around his eyes and mouth. But I resisted. "My mom called. Mentioned something had happened. I…I needed to know you were okay. I needed to be here for you."

His brows furrowed, but he didn't say anything, so I rested my head on his shoulder. A few seconds later, he spoke again. "You hungry? Luke got a ton of food from a place he insists has the best Chinese in Port Agnes. And, honestly, I'd love someone else to talk to for a while."

"Is it from Stu's?" I asked, my stomach suddenly rumbling.

Jack moved away, giving me one of his eyes-narrowed looks. "How'd you guess?"

I lifted a shoulder. "It really *is* the best Chinese in Port Agnes."

"Well, then you're definitely coming in." He linked his arm through mine and opened the door. We entered the house together, and I braced myself against the little fissures of heat that crackled between us. Too easy. It'd be too easy to fall back into Us. I had to remember why that was a bad idea.

No matter how good he'd felt in my arms back there.

***

The first half of the meal was quiet, tense. No one spoke much. No one really ate much, either. I wanted to ask what about their father, but I was afraid to make things worse. So, instead, I sat next to Jack and shoved Lo Mein into my mouth for about fifteen minutes straight, letting my eyes taking in my surroundings.

We were seated at the butcher-block island, in the center of a bright kitchen, lined with white, glass-front cupboards. It was such a warm, homey space. I had a hard time imagining either Luke or their father actually using it. Jack, though. Jack, I could see here.

As the thought flitted through my mind, I looked over. Jack's eyes were glued to his plate, which was still mostly full. His shoulders were slumped, but there was a distinct tension radiating from him. I hated this. I hated not being able to *do* anything.

Casting a glance over at Luke, who had been shooting furrowed-brow looks in Jack's direction all night, I willed him to speak up. Something warm and sharp flickered in his bright blue eyes. Looked an awful lot like concern, if you asked me. And yet he kept staring at his plate, pretending no one else was there. What *was* that?

I reached under the table and took Jack's hand in mine. He jumped slightly, like he'd forgotten I was there, but then squeezed my fingers.

"So," I said finally, dropping my fork. This silence had to end. "That's a mighty fancy car you got there, Luke. Get you anywhere with the ladies?"

Luke's head jerked up, his eyebrows raised nearly to his hairline. "Uh," he started and I sat back, intrigued. I had yet to see the elder Elliott unruffled. For that matter, it was rare to see Jack unruffled. Another shared trait. I'd bet these two had no idea they had so much in common.

"Well." He tapped his chopsticks against the rim of his plate. "Can't say that I've really tried."

Beside me, I saw Jack's lips quirk. Obviously, he was enjoying his brother's discomfort as well.

"Huh." I reclaimed my fork. "That's a shame. Maybe you should let me borrow it sometime. I could probably pick up *tons* of chicks."

Jack snorted and Luke let out a surprised laugh. "I would be lying if I said that I wouldn't like to see you try. I'm not sure my brother would be all right with that, though."

"You kidding?" Jack shot back, a smile—the first real smile I'd seen tonight—on his lips. "People pay good money to watch movies that start like that."

My mouth dropped open, but only silence came out. Both men laughed and I looked from Jack to his brother, enjoying the matching grins on their faces. I was having dinner with the most gorgeous men in all of Greene County. Cat would be so jealous.

Feeling like I'd accomplished something, I took a bite of my Spring Roll.

"So, Luke." Jack stood and headed for the kitchen. "You got any beer?"

32: Soap Suds & Sadness

Two hours and a six-pack of beer later, Luke had retired to bed, leaving Jack and I alone in the kitchen. While Jack cleaned up the remnants of dinner, I carried a stack of dishes to the sink and started to fill it.

"There's a dishwasher," he said as he dropped empty Chinese containers into the trash. "You don't have to do that."

I shrugged. "It's relaxing."

He came to stand next to me as I dropped the plates into the sudsy water. I watched from the corner of my eye as he rolled up his sleeves, my mouth suddenly going dry. Was I really objectifying the poor man while his father was laid up in the hospital? What was *wrong* with me?

"Your ass looks fantastic in those jeans, by the way." Jack's voice was low, gruff.

My eyes shot to his, heat flaming my face, even as I felt vindicated in my own thoughts. "I thought you were a boob man."

His lips quirked and he lifted one shoulder. "That doesn't mean I can't appreciate a great ass, too. I'm an equal opportunity ogler."

I smiled and shook my head, diverting my attention back to the dishes. So easy, I thought for the second time that night. It'd be so easy to...

"Thank you," Jack said suddenly, and my hands stilled mid-scrub.

I turned my head. "For what?"

"For being here. You didn't have to, and I can't imagine Aunt Bonnie was pleasant to deal with when you called to find out where I was." His eyebrows lifted as if he expected me to deny it. I didn't, so he continued. "Anyway, I know we're not...anymore, and I appreciate that you came."

I shrugged, tearing my eyes from his to stare at the soapy water. "Just because we're not...anymore, doesn't mean I don't care."

"I know." His words were soft and I felt my gaze drawn back to his. His eyes had melted to warm puddles of blue, a soft smile curved his lips. My heart lurched and I released the plate I'd been washing to turn my entire body toward him.

Jack handed me the dishtowel he'd had draped over his shoulder and shifted to face me, too. Slowly, as if he were afraid I'd run like a startled deer, he reached out, pushing a tendril of hair off my forehead. My breath stilled. I watched his face as his fingertips brushed my cheek. Helpless, I leaned into his touch.

His eyes flickered and he greedily pushed his fingertips through my hair. A tiny sound escaped the back of my throat and I stepped forward, letting him pull me into his arms. No one said a word. We just held each other's stares as we inched closer and closer, until Jack ducked his head, pressing his lips to mine, soft, hesitant. He started to pull away, but something in me, something I'd been ignoring all night, roared to life. I reached up and pressed my fingertips into the nape of his neck, bringing his mouth back to mine.

It was a tender kiss, a cautious kiss. As if neither of us were sure what the other wanted. Jack's palm pressed into the small of my back and I moved closer, until I could feel the heat of his skin, the pound of his heart against me. His touch remained gentle as his hands came to rest on my hips. My pulse echoed loud in my ears, asking me—begging me—to take this further, to deepen the kiss. To undo the last twenty-four hours and—

As soon as the thought formed, I froze. Squeezing my eyes shut, I put my hand on Jack's chest and broke the kiss. "I...I'm sorry," I murmured, staring at the buttons on his shirt.

Jack cleared his throat and dropped his hands from my hips. "Me, too." His tone made it clear that his sorry wasn't for the same reasons as mine.

He rubbed a hand over his face and an enormous breath left his lips. After a few seconds, he gave me a half-smile before taking a step back. "Those dishes aren't going to wash themselves."

I blinked, then jumped for the out he was giving me. "Right." I turned back to the sink.

We stood side-by-side, me washing and Jack drying, for a long stretch of quiet. Once I submerged the last couple dishes, I glanced over at him and spoke. "How's your dad?"

It was why I'd come, why he looked so stressed and exhausted. We needed to talk about it.

Jack's shoulders immediately tensed. "Stable," he answered, drying the inside of a water glass. "For now."

"What happened?"

Setting the dish aside, he pushed away from the counter and shoved his fingers through his hair. "From what I've gathered, one moment he was fine, playing a round of golf with some business partners. The next, paramedics were wheeling him off Hole 9. Massive heart attack." He sat and rested his elbows on the table.

I crossed the kitchen and took the seat across from him, resting my hands in the middle of the table, an open invitation. He took it, lacing his fingers through mine.

"The entire drive to the hospital, I just kept thinking…what if he dies? What if he dies thinking that I hate him?" His eyes were wide on my face, the fear in them shaking me straight to my marrow. I gripped his hand tight, feeling tears prick my own eyes.

"I already lost my mom." His voice was gruff as he continued. "Luke and Dad…they're all I have left. What if he dies before I can fix it?"

He looked like a terrified little boy. My heart cracked for him. Standing, I rounded the table and pulled him to me. His head rested against my belly and I brushed my hand over his hair. I didn't know what to say. I couldn't tell him everything would be all right, because how did *I* know that? I couldn't tell him his dad would be okay, that he'd have time to mend bridges, that his dad had to know he loved him…there were no certainties. I didn't want to lie to him.

So I just held him tight. I held him for as long as he needed me to. And when he finally moved away, I rested my hand against his cheek and kissed his forehead.

"I don't know what's going to happen with your dad." I looked into his bright and terrified eyes. "No one can really know what life will bring. I think all we can do in times like these is…is hold onto the ones we love." As I said it, I was thinking of Luke, and the worried looks he'd been passing to his little brother all night. When Jack met my eyes, though, my words took on another meaning. "I…I think that's something," I finished, ignoring the sudden tremor inside my chest.

Jack nodded, his stubble rough against my palm. "It's something," he repeated, standing. He pushed my hair away from my face and smiled. "Thanks again. For being here."

I gave him a shaky smile. I wanted to say, *Of course I'm here. I will always be here. Because I sort of really care about you. Possibly even love you.* Instead, I ruffled his hair. Now wasn't the time to lay *those* particular things bare.

A little while later, we stood side-by-side in the driveway, saying our goodbyes. I didn't want to go. I didn't want to leave him alone.

It must've shown on my face, because Jack bumped his shoulder into mine. "I'll be all right, darlin'. Get out of here. You look exhausted."

I opened my mouth to deny it but yawned instead. I rested my head on his shoulder and watched the light glow from inside the house. After a few seconds of quiet, I glanced up at Jack's profile. "Come with me to Spring Thing this weekend." Stephen had guilted me into coming to watch Rory dance on Saturday. Maybe Jack could use the time away.

He glanced over, eyebrows lifted. "Because cotton candy makes everything better?"

I scoffed. "No. But bumper cars do."

Something twinkled in Jack's eyes, and I spoke again before he could. "Make one joke about rear-ending and I'll rescind my invite."

"Fine." He sighed and leaned his back against Luke's fancy pants car. "I could use a break for a little while. The hospital is trying to steal my soul."

"Okay. All right. I'll, um, pick you up around eleven on Saturday? Maybe?"

His expression darkened briefly. "Can I let you know later?"

Just in case things take a turn. He didn't have to say it. I heard it, anyway.

And I said a silent prayer that, for Jack's sake, that didn't happen.

33: *Concrete Ribbon*

Jack was sitting on the front porch Saturday morning as I pulled into the driveway, looking like an excited kid. An excited kid with a naughty secret.

We'd been talking since I left him on Thursday. His dad was on the upswing, so he felt comfortable leaving the hospital for the day.

As soon as I got out of the car, his grin went from *I'm super excited* to *I didn't mean to do it, I swear.*

"What's that look for?" I asked, leaning against the porch rail. "What did you do?"

"Ah, well what had happened was..."

He was interrupted by Luke poking his head out the door. "Morning, Tierney. Thank you for inviting me. Would you like a cup of coffee for the road?"

"I...uh, sure!" I said, giving him my best smile. Once he was back inside, I turned to Jack. "Luke's coming?"

Jack pushed to his feet. "Well, I told him this morning what my plans were, and he looked sort of...bummed. And, then I thought, he's stressed, too. Maybe more than me, because he's closer to the old man. I figured he could use some time away, too. Otherwise—"

"Otherwise, he'd sit up at that hospital all alone." My heart twisted as I pictured it. Luke, sitting by his father's bedside, rumpled suit and distress lines around his eyes. "Yeah, good idea. He should definitely come." I reached up and gave his hair a ruffle. "This should be a very interesting day," I started, gesturing toward the car.

"Hey, buddy!" Cat leaned out from the passenger seat to wave like a maniac. "I call shotgun!"

Jack's eyes moved to my face and I gave him a shrug. "She met me at my car this morning, declaring she needed some 'best friend time.' How could I say no?"

Cat caught sight of Luke, coming out the door with a cup of coffee in each hand. "Scratch that," she called, pulling herself out of the car window, all Dukes of Hazzard style. "I'll sit in the back. With the hot new guy."

Luke glanced from me to Jack, his eyes narrowing in confusion—maybe even fear. Which was generally the reaction Cat got. "Cat, Luke. Luke, Cat." I gestured between the two. Taking the coffee Luke held out to me, I added, "Luke is Jack's brother."

Cat sidled over to Luke, putting on her most suggestive smile. "Hey, there Jack's brother. Tell me, has anyone ever called you God?"

"*Aaaaand,* we're leaving." I stepped forward and steered Luke to the front seat. "I think you should sit up front. With me. Jack, you don't mind, do you?"

Jack was too busy laughing to answer. While Luke got settled into the front seat, I shot Cat a look. She shrugged and mouthed *What? He's hot,* then got into the car.

As Jack moved passed me, he murmured, "This day just got a whole lot more interesting."

He wasn't lying. The drive to June Lake alone was a barrel full of monkeys. Insane, poo-flinging monkeys. The craziest of which sported red hair and a mouth without a censor. Jack didn't make matters better, though. He simply encouraged Cat's loud mouth and inappropriate conversation topics.

By the time we pulled into the fairground parking lot, Luke looked like he wanted to disappear into the upholstery, and I wanted to jump out of the moving vehicle. Jack, though. Jack looked like he was having the time of his life.

"Seriously," Cat was saying as I parked the car. She'd leaned forward and was talking to Luke, her hand resting on his shoulder. "You've got really gorgeous hands. I bet you really know how to use them."

Luke, poor Luke, cleared his throat. A flush had begun creeping up his neck about twenty miles ago, around the time Cat asked him if he had ever had sex in a public place. Now, his entire face was tinged with red.

I put the car in park and glared at Cat. "Could you keep it in your pants? You're making us all uncomfortable."

"I'm not uncomfortable," Jack said and I craned my neck to give him the evil eye. *Not helping*, I mouthed. He just grinned. Much like at dinner the other night, seeing his buttoned-up, serious brother flustered gave him satisfaction and amusement.

Cat sat back in her seat with a dramatic sigh, mumbling something about being "cockblocked. I ignored her and gave Luke a smile. "Sorry about this."

Luke shrugged. "Pssh. I'm fine." He brushed my apology off. "I'm a serious, straight talking business man. Nothing gets to me. I'm unflappable." He returned my smile, looking just like his brother.

I laughed and started to reply when Jack leaned up, planting his face between Luke and me. "So, are we going to get out of here, or what?" he asked, sounding cranky. "I don't know about you guys, but I'd kill for some cotton candy right now."

Luke cleared his throat and undid his seatbelt, all business again. "Cotton candy for breakfast?" he asked, his eyes darting to his brother. "Don't you think you should start with something a little...healthier? Like a corndog?"

"Hey, man," Jack shot back, getting out of the car. "Both those options are better than that health-nut crap you made me eat yesterday."

"You mean the bagel?" Luke's tone was wry, his brows raised. I leaned back in my seat and listened to the banter, which was the easiest I'd heard it so far. Maybe all this time together was doing them some good.

"Yeah. The bagel. The *plain* bagel. With no cream cheese. Who does that?"

"I'm with Jack on this one," Cat piped in. "It is simply criminal to eat a bagel without cream cheese." She leaned forward and gave Luke a look. "It's like I don't know you at all."

I put my hand on her forehead and pushed, and she took the hint, returning to her seat. "So, corn dogs first." Pulling the key out of the ignition, I unbuckled. "Let's get to it, then."

***

A couple hours later, Cat was high on cotton candy and the presence of hot dudes, while Luke finally seemed to let loose a little. They were currently laughing as they attempted to toss Ping-Pong balls into fishbowls.

"I bet you twenty bucks Cat makes her shot before Luke." Jack's voice was right next to my ear and I started.

"Deal." I shook his hand. "You should know, though, that I've seen Cat play many a game of beer pong. Always ends with her blitzed out of her mind."

"Yeah, but you've never seen Luke play basketball. Or attempt to play. He's like a baby giraffe learning to walk."

I snorted, then covered my mouth as I glanced over at him. "You're an ass."

"Yes, but an honest ass. Look. Did you see that? The ball just bounced off that carnie."

He was right. Luke's ball arched high in the air and landed with a soft thud against the bearded, sweaty man's chest. My snort turned to a laugh and I turned, burying my face against Jack's shirt. "I can't look."

"Maybe we should get out of here before they realize we're together." As he spoke, he put his arm around my waist, and I let him. It felt too good to resist. "That way, if the carnie snaps, he'll only murder the two of them."

"Might be a good idea," I replied, not sure if I agreed because I didn't want to be seen with such terrible sportsmen or if I just wanted to be alone with Jack.

Who was I kidding? It was the last one.

"What do you say we hit up that Ferris wheel?" Jack's arm tightened around my waist and he steered me away from the slow-motion car crash just as Luke's second Ping-Pong ball smacked the dude right in his beard.

"I think that is a fabulous idea." I ignored Cat's cackle of laughter. She certainly wasn't helping Luke's case much.

The line at the Ferris wheel was short. Apparently, most people shunned the tame ride in favor of the Tornado Twister or the Pirate Ship. Poor bastards. They had no idea what they were missing.

We reached the front of the line quickly and loaded into a cart. Once the lap bar was secure, we moved upward and stopped while the next passengers climbed on. After a couple minutes, the ride was loaded and ready to go.

The Ferris wheel jerked to life, lifting us high above the ground. With wide eyes, I took in everything around me. The expanse of blue sky, the vivid green trees waving in the warm breeze. In the distance, I could make out Old Man McPhee's pond, and beyond that, the highway, a concrete ribbon leading out of town.

I looked over at Jack, his eyes almost bluer than the sky. "I used to dream about the day I'd hit that highway and never come back."

Jack stilled, glancing over with question in his eyes. I wasn't sure why I'd said it, but once the words were out, the rest of the story began to tumble after.

"That's how I knew it was over with Wes." My eyes found that road again as we made our upward climb. Jack's arm came to rest over the back of the cart and I resisted the urge to nestle against him.

"That spring," I continued, "we came back home for break. For the first couple years after we started dating, I'd stopped thinking about my escape. I looked forward to heading off to college, sure, but I knew I'd be back. I loved Wes, and I wanted the life we talked about. The fairy tale bullshit, complete with white picket fences and babies and homemade apple pies."

"I prefer cherry pie myself," Jack cut in, lightening the mood. His fingertips stroked my shoulder, left bare by my sundress.

"You know? Me, too." I forced myself to ignore the little shocks that accompanied each touch of skin on skin, forced my head to remain upright, not rested on his shoulder where it so wanted to be.

"I make a mean cherry pie. You should try it sometime." He grinned. "Anyway." His voice was soft, interested. "You were on the Ferris wheel alone..."

"Right. For the fourth year straight. He'd never even *try* it. Which was whatever, really. It was my thing, and it had never bothered me before. But for some reason, this particular time...it got to me. I asked him to join me, and he got this weird look on his face, like I'd just asked him to murder and eat his kid sister or something."

"That's a weird comparison."

"Yeah, well." I shrugged and looked over. The wind caught Jack's hair just right and it looked like a dark cloud around his head. Like a habit I couldn't break, I reached up and tried to smooth it down. It wasn't until I caught the flicker in his eyes that I realized what I was doing. "Sorry."

"Don't be," he murmured, his words almost carried away on the wind. "You were saying?"

I cleared my throat and twisted my hands together in my lap. "Did you know I got into NYU?"

"Wow." Jack let out a low whistle. "I did not know that."

"I didn't tell many people." I shrugged. "I chose Central Michigan because it was closer to Sutcliffe." The wind whipped my hair into my face, and I brushed it away. "Anyway. Earlier that day, I'd overheard my parents talking. About how they wished I'd gone to NYU instead. How my mom didn't want me to end up like her—happy homemaker in a small town. *She had big dreams,* she said. *And she's giving them up.*"

I shook my head, reliving those moments. "I hadn't seen it until then—I spent my whole life staring at that highway, dreaming of the day I'd be on it. And then...I stopped." Taking a breath, I looked at Jack. "I knew then that I didn't want to marry Wes."

I blinked, my eyes suddenly burning. I'd never told anyone this story. Not even Cat, who knew pretty much everything about me. Why was I telling Jack? Now was probably not the time to share bits of my soul with this man. Not when we were somewhere in a weird, murky middle ground. Were we friends? Acquaintances? Was I just sticking around long enough to help him through this stuff with his dad? Then what? Then I'd go back to my life, he back to his? We'd move on with our lives as if the other had never existed?

Even the thought hurt like a jagged glass bottle stuck right in my gut. No. That wasn't what I wanted. Not at all.

So...what, then?

Squinting at the horizon, I cleared my throat. "So...um. There's that."

Jack pulled me closer to him, and I finally gave in to the urge I'd fought earlier, snuggling tight against him. "So, how about now?" he asked and I tilted my head to look up at him. "Do you feel like hitting that highway and never coming back?"

My heart lurched and I forced myself to breathe. I knew my answer. Knew it to the very marrow of my bones. But once I said it, I couldn't take it back. Did I want that?

Looking into his eyes, I knew that I did. "I want to drive away because I know it's the right thing to do. But..."

"But?"

I held his gaze, the blaze burning in his eyes matching the one in my heart. "Wherever you are is where I want to be."

I'd barely finished speaking when Jack's lips crashed into mine. I gripped the front of his shirt and held on tight as he kissed me, need and desperation clashing to create a hurricane of fire that I was helpless to resist.

And, if I was honest with myself, I didn't want to resist it. Not now. Not ever.

Maybe, just maybe, we could make this thing work. Maybe—

"Ahem." The sound of a man clearing his throat brought our moment to an end. We parted to find the Ferris wheel operator glaring at us. "Time's up."

34: Something in the Fair

We wandered the fair for a while after that, hand-in-hand. Initially, we'd been looking for Luke and Cat, but they'd vanished. Somewhere in the back of my mind, I worried that the bearded man had actually murdered them. When I voiced my worry, though, Jack assured me that they were fine.

"Probably," he added. "Most likely. At the very least, they're tied up somewhere, and will be freed as soon as Luke offers to pay off Carnie Carl."

I took his word for it and allowed myself to enjoy this moment, enjoy the weightlessness of Jack's shoulders. In a while, he'd get back to real life. In a while, he'd have to deal with his sick father and what might happen.

In a while, I'd have to face real life—and make some big decisions.

For now, though...for now, we were happy.

I wanted to cling to that for a while longer.

"You got the time?" I asked him as we paid for frozen lemonades and elephant ears.

Jack pulled his phone from his pocket. "Quarter to four."

"Shit!" I tucked my lemonade in the crook of my elbow and shifted my elephant ear to my now empty hand. Taking Jack's hand in mine, I rushed forward. "Rory's got a show in fifteen minutes. Stephen'll kill me if I miss it."

Jack laughed and let me drag him through the crowd. "You know, you could've mentioned this earlier."

"Yeah, well maybe if someone hadn't pulled me behind the funhouse to make out, I would have remembered," I shot back. Maybe a little too loudly, as Dottie Daniels gave me a scandalized look. I grinned at her and kept moving.

"No, no, no," Jack said. "I mean, earlier than that. I refuse to take the blame for your tardiness, when you didn't even mention darling little Rory's recital until *right this minute.*"

I looked back at him long enough to stick my tongue out. He merely grinned and my heart sputtered.

A few seconds later, we reached the stage, which was located at the far end of the grounds. We found Stephen and Julie at the base of the stage, Stephen crouched down in front of Rory. The little girl looked adorable in her black leotard and red tutu, polka-dotted wings strapped to her back.

Julie caught sight of us first. She smiled and waved, then said something to Stephen, who looked up as we reached them.

"Aunt Tee-Tee!" Rory said, jumping up and down. "Do you like my costume? I'm a ladybug!"

"You're the cutest ladybug in all the universe," I said as she barreled toward me. I scooped her up and smacked a kiss on her soft cheek. "Did mommy do your hair for you?"

Rory reached up and squeezed her poufy ponytail. "Yep. My ribbon matches." She grinned and I melted. Gah. How did my brother make such a cute kid?

"So, Jack." Julie brought my attention back to the grown-ups. "Tierney didn't mention you'd be here." She passed me a look, her dark eyes twinkling.

Jack lifted a shoulder. "She didn't tell me, either. So we're both surprised."

I opened my mouth to say something snarky just as Cat and Luke wandered over, looking rumpled and flushed. My already-open mouth dropped even further. Cat, catching my look, merely shrugged unapologetically. Luke, though. Luke looked pretty damn pleased with himself.

Giving my head a shake, I ignored them and put Rory down. "All right, shortcake. Get out there and shake your stuff like there's no tomorrow."

Rory giggled then skipped off to the rest of her troupe.

"Luke, my man," Stephen said, grasping the other man's hand. "Good to see you."

Luke smiled, managing to remember his usual persona in the nick of time. I crossed my arms over my chest and bumped my shoulder against Jack's. "Can you believe this?" I whispered.

Jack grinned. "Yeah. Awesome, right?"

"Damn right," Cat butt in, coming to stand next to me. "Let me tell you. The Jackster isn't the only Elliott who can make you see God."

"Cat! Really?" I glared at her, even as Jack's shoulders shook with laughter.

"You know what? I'm done with all of you." I shook the hair out of my face and went to find a seat.

Cat and Luke? Unbelievable. I didn't even want to *think* about where they—

"Behind the funhouse," Cat said, catching up to me. "Right after you and Jack—"

"Jack and I did not!" I sputtered, heat filling my face.

"Oh, I know. You're way too uptight for that." She found a row of empty seats and sat down. "Anyway, don't go getting your panties in a bunch. It was a one-time thing. He needed to decompress, and I...well, have you *seen* him?"

Luckily, the rest of the gang joined us, bringing an end to the conversation. Not so luckily, I knew I'd hear all about it later. Jack took the seat next to me, resting his hand, palm-side up, on my knee. I laced my fingers through his and then all else was forgotten.

How did he *do* that?

It didn't matter. All that mattered was, I didn't want him to stop.

***

After Rory's performance—without incident—Jack took my hand and steered me through the crowd. We stopped at the Strong Man game long enough for Jack to prove his manliness. It took three swings of the hammer, but he managed to ring the bell. He grinned as he handed me a giant stuffed alligator. "For the lady" He bowed with a flourish.

I accepted the butt-ugly thing with a laugh, and we continued on.

"Have you heard anything about your promotion?" Jack asked as he threaded his fingers through mine. His tone was light, but the question was like a cannonball.

My stomach dropped to my toes. I'd managed to shove all thoughts of New York—and what it would mean for Jack and I—far, far from my mind. Because that was the healthy way to deal with big life changes, right?

"Not yet." I gripped the stuffed gator tight. "I *did* get fired, though."

"What?" He stopped, eyes wide. "When? Why?"

I laughed and pulled him forward. "Mrs. Needermyer terminated her contract with us. Not that I blame her. Ron wouldn't budge on that book."

"That sucks." Jack swung our hands back and forth between us. "I know you were excited about it."

"Yeah," I sighed. "But there'll be other books to be excited about."

A memory of the Amish cookbook I'd left sitting on my desk yesterday flashed through my head. *Hopefully.*

Jack smiled. "So, hey. I have to check on my booth," he said as we eased passed the Blue Haired Biddies' booth unnoticed. "And then we'll head to the bumper cars."

I dug my feet into the dirt. "Your booth? That Aunt Bonnie is running? Aunt Bonnie that would impale me with a rolling pin given the chance?"

"Rolling pin?" Jack laughed. "Do you have any idea how much force it would take to impale someone with a rolling pin?"

"Ah, well you underestimate the amount of hatred that woman has for me." I struggled to keep a straight face.

"Of all things in a kitchen," he continued as if I hadn't spoken. "A rolling pin?"

"I'm not a master chef." I glared at him. His lips twitched and I felt a laugh simmering inside me. "I don't know what everything is called."

"But you do know about knives, right? And skewers? And cleavers? And, hell, even a salad fork would be more likely than a rolling pin."

"Shut it."

To my right, a little girl dropped her cotton candy in the dirt and started to cry. *I feel you, kid.* Bonnie was bound to throw dirt on the delicious cotton candy that'd been my day.

"We'll get you an even bigger one," the girl's mom told her as she led her away. I looked up at Jack, my lips lifting.

"If I start crying, are you going to promise me an even bigger one?"

Jack's brows dropped over his eyes. He must not have noticed the cotton candy tragedy. "Never mind. Let's go." Taking his hand, I started through the crowd. "But you owe me. The biggest cotton candy you can get your hands on."

"See. I thought you were talking about something else."

"Oh, no." I shook my head, a grave look on my face. "*That's* not nearly big enough."

Jack put his free hand against his chest. "Ouch. That hurt. You're a mean lady."

"Yeah, but there's a good chance I may put out at some point, so…" I looked back at him, grinning.

"You do make a good case," he said as we reached the rows of vendor booths. Jack's was located at the far end and we started toward it. "You're lucky you're hot. I—"

"See? Look! Right there!" I gestured to Bonnie Nolan, who definitely was attempting to shoot death rays from her eyes. "She's envisioning me dead. Incinerated. Vaporized. Whatever."

Jack put his arm snugly around my waist. "She'll have to whatever both of us, then."

Bonnie's expression did not soften as we neared. If anything, she looked angrier up close. "Hey, Aunt Bon." Jack tossed her an easy grin.

Nothing. How could a person look at that face and *not* smile in return? "Hello, dear," she said, her voice cool, even as her eyes warmed minutely. Okay, so she wasn't *completely* immune to Jack's charms. "How's your dad?"

Jack's smile faltered. "No change." His arm tightened around my waist. "How is it going here?" He gestured toward the booth with his free hand, changing the subject before Bonnie could prod any further.

I took in the display of delectable treats. From cookies to cupcakes to pies, my eyes devoured everything and my mouth nearly watered. How was it I'd been sleeping with the creator of such divine baked goods and I hadn't tried any of them?

"Oh, good. Great," Bonnie said. "This is all we've got left for today."

Jack grinned like a little boy who'd just hit his first home run. "Awesome."

Pride bloomed in my chest. He hadn't said anything, but I knew he was worried about how his booth was faring without him.

Bonnie returned his smile, momentarily melting her ice queen persona. "Yes, it is. People are already asking if there'll be more cherry pie tomorrow."

At that, Jack ran his hand over his face, briefly looking exhausted. It hit me then. He'd stayed up all last night to get everything ready for the fair, after being at the hospital all day. And he'd be doing it again tonight. As the realization sank in, I could see the lines around his eyes and the overall weighed-down look of a person running on fumes.

Concern must have been clear in my eyes, because the exhaustion was quickly replaced with another trademark smile. "Did you want me to take over from here?" he asked Bonnie. "You can meet Uncle George for some canoodling on the carousel." He waggled his brows and Bonnie blushed. *Blushed!* What?

"Oh no." She waved a hand. "I've got this. Go on. Enjoy your day. You need some time away." Warm eyes, kind smile, a voice not sharp with barely-veiled insults. This side of Bonnie was like seeing a polar bear in the Sahara.

"You sure?" Jack's brows hung low over his eyes, guilt etching itself onto his face. "I can—"

"I'm sure. Now, go!"

"All right. If you insist." He looked to me and back to Bonnie. "I'll have everything ready for Uncle George to pick up from Dad's in the morning. For now, though, looks like I'm going to enjoy the rest of the day with my lady." As he said it, his arm tightened around my waist. The giant alligator's snout bopped him in the face, preventing his attempt to pull me closer.

I laughed. "Mr. Chompers is protecting my virtue."

A snort came from Bonnie's direction, followed by mumbled words that sounded an awful lot like, "What virtue?"

I stiffened. Jack tensed, too. We both looked at her, and her head lifted. Heat flooded her face once she realized she'd been heard. "I-I'm sorry, dear," she said.

Jack didn't soften. "You're apologizing to the wrong person."

"But, Jack." Her tone became saccharine. "I'm just looking out for you." She dragged her eyes from him to me, poison oozing from them. "I don't want you to get hurt."

Jack glanced down at me, his arm tightening around me. Our eyes locked and, for half a second, my world tipped right side up. His lips tilted. "No pain, no gain." Then, back to Bonnie, he said, "You were out of line, Aunt Bonnie."

Bonnie blinked and opened her mouth, soundless words coming out. She hadn't expected Jack to stand up to her. I hadn't, either. Reaching between us with my free hand, I linked my fingers with his. He glanced over and gave me a silent nod. *Should've done it sooner*, it said. Tightening is fingers around mine, he turned back to Bonnie.

Finally, she caved. "Okay. I'm sorry, Tierney." She looked at Jack before adding, "That was rude of me."

I nodded, realizing only when my knuckles ached just how tightly I'd been gripping Mr. Chompers. "Thank you."

"All right, then," Jack said. "We're going to get going. Got some bumper cars to ride and some cotton candy to eat." He tossed me a grin and I blushed. "Thank you again for helping out, Aunt Bon." With a quick kiss dropped on her cheek, we were gone, disappearing into the crowd.

***

The drive back into Port Agnes had been quiet. At some point, Cat curled up in the corner of the backseat and fell asleep. Luke remained silent in the other corner. Jack had reached over about halfway home, resting his hand on my knee. I smiled over at him and turned my eyes back to the road just as my favorite radio station cued up an old Journey tune.

As soon as I pulled into the Elliott boys' driveway and killed the engine, Luke jolted to life. "Thanks for a fantastic day, Tierney." He leaned up to smile at me. "I look forward to seeing you again." He gave Jack a pointed look before he opened his door and got out. "Give Cat my regards when she wakes up."

"Will do." Once he was inside the house, I turned to Jack, a shy smile on my lips. "So…"

"So," he repeated. "I'd ask you if you wanted to come inside, but you've got Sleeping Beauty back there, and—"

As if on cue, Cat let out a loud snore and shifted positions. I shook my head. "I guarantee she's just pretending to be asleep, so she could avoid the awkward goodbyes with the dude she just boned."

"You don't know me," she muttered, prompting a laugh from Jack. "Now, either you two get on with the smoochies, or Jack gets out of the car so we can go. I am in desperate need of my bed."

"Hey." Jack craned his neck to see her. "How about *you* get out of the car so we can get on with the smoochies?"

"Nope. Doesn't work that way. Besides, it's not like I'd watch or anything. I'm not a creeper."

I rolled my eyes. "Anyway." I reached over to give Jack's hand a squeeze. "I should get going. Call me if you need anything, or if…well, just call me."

He pulled my hand to his lips and placed a soft kiss on my knuckles. "Okay," he said against my hand. "Have a good night."

My heart fluttered. "You, too." And then he just sat there, giving me that look, that heated, tender look, until Cat groaned from the back seat.

"Oh, for the love of..." She sat up and shoved open her door. "You've got five minutes. Better make the best of 'em." And then she slammed the door shut, leaving us alone.

Jack grinned and reached over, undoing my seatbelt. "Get over here. The clock is ticking."

My body obeyed his order before my mind even registered, and I found myself in his lap within seconds.

"Mmm," he murmured, his hands moving to cup my ass. "I like a girl who takes orders."

I shoved my fingers through his hair and rested my forehead against his, looking into his eyes. "Shut up and kiss me."

"I like a girl who gives orders even more," he murmured before covering my lips with his.

35: To the Rescue

The next morning, Cat and I were squeezed into her tiny kitchen, making pancakes and scrambled eggs before we settled down to a marathon of *My Boyfriend the Vampire*—a very nice Sunday, if you asked me. I had just flipped the final pancake when my phone buzzed from its place on the counter.

Cat glared. "Who dares interrupt our morning?"

I shrugged an apology and crossed the kitchen to grab the offending object. "Why the hell is Bonnie Nolan calling me?" I considered the Ignore button but a thought stopped me. What if something had happened with Jack's dad?

With a halting heart, I answered.

"Tierney? It's Bonnie." She didn't sound pleased. She didn't sound distraught, either. That was a good sign.

"Hi…" I started, raising my eyebrows at Cat. "How are things?"

"Just fine."

"Good." *What the hell?* I mouthed to Cat as we descended into silence. Seconds ticked by. I motioned for Cat to stir the eggs and she spun away. When Bonnie didn't say anything, I prodded. "Is there anything...?"

"Oh, yes. Yes, I'm sorry." What was going on? I'd never known Bonnie to be this speechless. Usually, she had an abundance of words. Especially for me.

"I'm about to sit down to breakfast, so..."

"I need a favor."

Ahh. There it is. "Okay..."

"Jasper Higgins just called. He has to drive into Hope Falls today to pick up his granddaughter. Her visit has been planned for months, but apparently he's getting forgetful in his old age." Her voice was wry as I tried to figure out why she felt the need to call and tell me this. *And who Jasper Higgins was...*

"Anyhoo," she continued, speaking faster, like she was going to change her mind about this favor any second now. "He's not going to be there to run his booth, and he's asked me to do it for him."

"But...you're running Jack's booth."

"Right."

Everything was quiet for a beat or two. "Oh," I finally said. "*Oh.*"

"Yes. I know. It's quite the predicament," she said, instead of actually asking me the question. I leaned against the counter and tore a piece off a pancake. The idea of Bonnie squirming in her sweater set gave me an immense amount of satisfaction.

I thought about putting her out of her misery, but the feeling passed. Cat moved around me, divvying up the cooked eggs between two plates, and I polished off my pancake. Bonnie had yet to finish.

Spit it out, Bon-Bon, I thought as I sprinkled salt and pepper on my eggs.

Finally, Bonnie heaved a huge-ass sigh. "I need you to run Jack's booth for me today. George already picked everything up and he's setting up the booth now, but he's got his weekly golf date with, well, with your father." She paused. "So, you see, Jack needs you."

Well, if that wasn't a challenge, I didn't know what was. *Jack* needed me. And I wouldn't want to let *Jack* down, would I?

We both knew that wasn't what this was about, though. I heard what she was *really* saying. *If you really care about Jack, you would do this.*

Well, Bonnie. If that was how you wanted to play it. Challenge accepted.

"I'll be there by eleven."

Silence. I did a little victory dance. Only on the inside, though. Because I was classy.

"Thank you." She sounded like she'd just eaten a giant helping of crow. "I'll see you then."

***

Cat was bummed about our ruined plans, but she understood. Well, she understood as much as someone who was anti-relationships could understand. She waved me off with a smirk and an, *I hope he at least puts out after this.*

Bonnie was pacing in front of Jack's booth when I arrived in June Lake. Once she caught sight of me, her worried face smoothed out and she strived for nonchalance.

Too late. You've already revealed your human form.

"Thank you again for doing this," she said as she grabbed her purse and a pair of bunny ears. I frowned as she settled them onto her head. "Jasper Higgins?" She said as she caught my look. "Owns the pet store? Lived across the street from your parents for your entire childhood?"

"Oh. Right. Of course. Of *course.* I knew that!" I smiled and waved a hand. "Just slipped my mind, is all." Jasper wore a different animal costume each year for Spring Thing. Once, he'd dressed up as a snake and hadn't been able to do much more than point with his nose the entire weekend. Wes had even helped him back into his chair when he tipped over once.

Wow. How had I forgotten that?

Shaking my head, I rounded the booth and took a seat. "I've got this if you want to head over to Jasper's."

Bonnie gave me a dubious look, like she didn't quite believe I could hold down the fort. I straightened my shoulders and grinned. "I won't even pocket the profits or anything."

Her eyes sharpened and I raised a hand. "Relax. I was kidding."

With one last look, she walked away and left me alone with a table full of treats that looked so delicious they practically glowed with heavenly light. My eyes landed on a particularly tempting cherry pie. It wasn't the profits Bonnie should have worried about...

"Well, good morning, Tierney!" someone said, breaking me from my pastry-induced trance. I looked up to find the Nesbits smiling at me. I'd gone to school with their daughter, Kate. She hadn't liked me much.

Her parents were lovely, though, and so I graced them with a smile. "Hi! How are you two this lovely morning?"

They were "fantastic" and couldn't wait to get their hands on a dozen of Jack's chocolate chip cookies. Before they left, they asked how Jack's dad was doing, genuine concern on their faces. I'd forgotten that about small towns. People actually knew and cared about what was going on with other people.

I told them I hadn't heard anything new, and they told me to send Jack their love. As they walked away, I picked up my phone. I should call Jack. See how he was holding up. I had just pulled up his contact information when another customer arrived.

The afternoon passed in much the same way. Around two, after numerous attempts to call him, I decided to shoot Jack a text instead. *I'm in June Lake,* it said. *Your pies are selling like hotcakes (you see what I did there?). Hope all is well. Thinking of you!*

Just as I hit Send, Winn stopped in front of the booth. "Taking over for Bonnie, huh?" she said with a raised brow. "Does this mean she's forgiven you for the whole 'breaking her baby boy's heart' thing?"

"Ha." I sat my phone on the table. "Not likely. But it's progress." Pausing, I frowned. "I think."

Winn laughed. "It's not exactly the Bonnie Nolan Seal of Approval, but then again, that's harder than winning an Oscar, a Grammy, *and* a freaking Miss America crown in one fell swoop."

I nodded, about to agree when I noticed a mop of blond hair peeping out from behind Winn. "Is this your son?"

She grinned and reached behind her, taking the boy's hand. "Yep. This is Riley." A pair of big blue eyes blinked at me. "He's just here for the cookies."

"Hey, man." I reached for the bin of cookies. "What's your favorite?"

"Oatmeal raisin." He lifted his chin, peering into the bin. "Or chocolate chip. I can't choose."

"Tell you what." I pulled out one of each, glancing at Winn for approval. At her nod, I held out my hands. "You don't have to choose today."

Riley's eyes widened. "I can have both?" He gave me a grin, revealing the empty space where his two front teeth had been.

I smiled back. Cute kid. "Yes, sir."

"Thank you!" He took the cookies and retreated behind his mom again. A few seconds later, he peered around her. "We're gonna go on the bumper cars. Want to come?"

I glanced at Winn, my insides going squishy. "I wish I could, bud. I have to stay here and sell the cookies."

Riley glanced down at his own cookies then back to me. "Do you get to eat them, too?"

"Not even a crumb," I answered with a huge sigh.

"Do you want one of mine?"

Geez, kid. You're killing me with the cute, I thought, giving him a smile. "No, thank you. Those are for you."

He looked down, as if he were considering another offer, then clearly decided he couldn't live without either cookie. "Okay!"

Winn laughed and put a hand on his head. "You ready for those bumper cars, dude?"

"Yeah!" He jumped up and down, like he had springs glued to his shoes.

"Thank you," his mom said, her smile holding steady. "And good luck winning that Miss America crown."

I laughed and waved them off. I never wanted to be Miss America. I'd just settle for falling below the top ten on Bonnie's Most Loathed list.

Somewhere around five, Bonnie stopped in to check on me. She handed me a single key on a keychain shaped like a slice of pie. "Could you stop by and let Mousse out before you head home?" she asked. "George will be by in a bit to help you pack up."

I hadn't even agreed before she flitted away. I looked at the key in my hand just as my phone jolted to life in my lap. Jumping, I answered.

"Hey, darlin'." Jack's voice rushed over me and my eyelids grew heavy. Man, did I love his voice. "What's this about you selling hotcakes?"

"Oh, you know. Just coming to your rescue is all." I smiled at a mother and daughter who approached the booth. The kid went right for the cupcakes, and his mom handed me her payment. Then, I turned my attention back to Jack. "How are you?"

He released a long sigh. "I'm all right. Heading down to the cafeteria for a sandwich while the doctors are running a few more tests. It's looking like he'll need a double bypass, which isn't ideal. But it's better than...well, the alternative."

His voice was heavy and I wished I could be there to wrap my arms around him. As if my censor had vanished, I told him that. A soft chuckle filled my ear. "You and me both." He sounded so wistful my heart squeezed tight.

"Why don't you come home after you talk to the doctors?" An older woman came over and bought a cherry pie. "I'm running on empty here, I've got the key to your place..."

"Whoa, whoa, whoa," Jack interrupted. "Isn't it a little too soon for that step?"

"Simmer down, pal. Your aunt gave me the key to let Mousse out. I don't think she had anything in mind beyond that." I stood and began rearranging the meager remains of Jack's booth. "I'm not even sure I like you that much."

"Oh, is that how you're going to play it?" His voice warmed. "Because as I recall, you seem to like me quite a bit."

"You are mistaken, good sir. I'm quite fond of *parts* of you." I gave a smile to a passing couple and sat back down. "Other parts...meh."

"Meh?" I could hear the clatter of dishes in the background as Jack made his way through the hospital cafeteria. "I'll have to remember that."

I smiled, longing to see his face, to rest my hand against his cheek, to press my lips to his forehead. "Anyway, come home. I'll make you dinner."

"You'll make me dinner?" He sounded skeptical and I laughed.

"Okay, I'll pour some Cap'n Crunch into a bowl and maybe make some toast. Besides." I sold the last dozen cookies to a man and his two daughters and the continued, "When's the last time you slept?"

"There's no rest for the wicked, doll," he replied and I shook my head.

"I don't know why you're trying to resist this. It's going to happen. Get your cute ass back to your house and let me take care of you." I needed to hold him more than I needed that last cherry pie taunting me from the table. "Please?"

A long sigh filled my ears. A long, overly dramatic, supremely put-upon sigh. "Fine. I'll be there around eight."

We ended the call, and I stuck a couple bills in the moneybox, claiming that last pie for myself. Some things were just too tempting to resist.

36: Cherry Pie & Goodbye

A couple hours later, the sun had begun to dip below the horizon, casting a dreamy golden glow over the fairgrounds. People still milled about, laughing and talking, soaking in the magic hour before darkness took over.

I sat back in my chair and surveyed the booth before me. Slim pickin's. Jack's array of delicious treats had sold well. I couldn't wait to tell him all about it. As I had the thought, I reached for my phone. Maybe just a quick text to see how he was doing...

My phone vibrated as my fingers touched it and I jumped, yanking my hand back as if I'd been zapped. It vibrated again and I realized it wasn't a text. Someone was calling me. I read the ID and frowned.

Why would Ron be calling? And on a Sunday?

Maybe he'd made a decision about the promotion.

The thought paralyzed me. I stared at the buzzing phone in my hand. What if I didn't get it? What if I *did*? What if he'd decided I was unfit for any position at Pencil Pushers and he fired me? What if—

"Enough," I muttered. "Just answer it."

Heart in throat, I croaked out a *hello*.

"Tierney, hello," Ron said into my ear. "How has your weekend been?"

"Not too bad." I tossed an apologetic smile to a family passing the booth and seeing it empty. "You?"

"Also not bad."

"Good." Drumming my fingers on the tabletop, I waited for him to continue. He didn't. "Is there...anything I can help you with?"

"Oh, sorry. Right." He cleared his throat. "We've reached a decision about the New York office, and—"

"And?" I straightened in my seat. My body went cold. "What is it?"

I could hear papers shuffling on Ron's end of the call. Then, he cleared his throat...and went back to shuffling papers.

"You're killing me, Ron!" I groaned. "If you're giving the position to Emily, just tell me."

"Emily?" Ron sounded genuinely puzzled. "Why would she get the job? She's only been with the company less than a year."

"Oh." I gripped the phone tighter. "So..."

"Congratulations, Tierney. The job is yours." He fidgeted with something else on his desk before adding, "We've got a lot of things to cover, so I'll need you in the office bright and early tomorrow."

"Right. Of…of course." I shook my head, trying to grasp the words Ron was saying. My limbs had gone numb, and my brain wasn't far behind. "I—I'll be there."

"Myra wants you in New York as soon as possible," he continued. "We can have you on a flight as early as Wednesday morning. Now, of course we'll put you up in a hotel at first. Until you find your own place. And—"

"Wait." I straightened in my seat. "Wednesday? *This* Wednesday?"

"Right."

"Oh. Wow." All thoughts immediately went to Jack, whose father was still in the hospital. And Cat, who I hadn't even *mentioned* the promotion to yet. And my parents, and Stephen and Rory and…

"Is that going to be a problem?"

I blinked, forcing my attention to Ron. "Um. Shouldn't be," I managed around the panic rising in my chest.

"Good, good." More paper shuffling—what was *with* that? "I'll see you in the morning. Then we can go over more details."

"S-see you then."

Once Ron hung up, I sat my phone on the table and stared. Wednesday. Three days from now. Not enough time to...well, *anything*.

But this is your dream, a voice in my head whispered. *What you've been working for your whole life.*

I sank back in my seat and focused my eyes on the Ferris wheel turning in the distance. All those years, dreaming from the top, and now...now, I had my chance.

So why did I want to cry?

"Hey." A voice broke through my jumbled thoughts. I started and turned to find Wes standing in front of me.

He lifted his hand in a wave and I waved back. "Hey."

"How's it going?" He glanced toward the table and its meager contents.

I cleared my throat and stretched a smile onto my lips. As if my entire world wasn't about to flip upside down. "Just about sold out."

"Nice." He came around the booth to take the seat next to me. A heavy sigh whooshed from him.

I peeked over. "Everything all right, man?"

He glanced back, brows furrowed. "Sam wants to get back together."

I shifted in my seat to see him better. Tense shoulders, grim mouth. *Not* the face of a happily reunited man. "You don't seem too thrilled about that."

"That obvious?"

"Only a little." I smiled. "No fairytale wedding. Your mom's going to be so bummed."

He laughed. "You know it's gonna be all your fault, right?"

"Oh, I know." I grinned. "It's all part of my evil scheme, don't you know? I swooped into town with a master plan to get you to break up with your girlfriend and date me."

"Poor Jack. He hasn't got a clue."

"Right?" I rolled my eyes. "Do you know your mother actually thought that was what I was up to?"

"Yep. She told me all about it." Wes leaned forward and dug his wallet out of his back pocket. As he opened it, he continued. "Little does she know, I kind of stole you from Jack in the first place." He handed me a couple bills. "I need that cookie."

"What?" I glanced down at the money in my hand. "Oh. Yeah. Sure." Then, "Wait, you *knew* Jack liked me, and you went for it anyway?"

"Yeah." Wes carefully peeled the plastic wrap away from a chocolate chip cookie. "I was a jerk back then." He broke the cookie and gave me an apologetic look, one half held out to me. "Didn't work out well for any of us in the end, though, huh?"

"Not even a little bit." I took the cookie. "Dumbass."

Wes laughed and took a bite. "I know."

We ate in silence for a few minutes. Once I'd polished off my half, I turned. "What are you going to do now? You're not here to steal me from Jack again, are you?"

This earned a hearty, genuine laugh. "Oh, no. Lesson learned." His eyes found mine. "Besides, you two seem good together."

At that, I warmed from the inside out. "Thanks." For how much longer? Settling back into my seat, I watched the lights from the Tilt-a-Whirl and pushed that thought aside. "What are you going to do? You know, now that you've ruined your white picket fence future?"

Wes sighed. From the corner of my eye, I saw him sit back and rest his ankle on his knee. "I have no idea."

"You know…" I kept my eyes focused on the lights. "Maybe—and don't tell your mom I said this because I need her to not hate me—but maybe you should take a break."

"What do you mean?"

"From dating. The clinic. June Lake. All of it."

"Why, Tierney Chandler." Wes leaned forward and I looked over to find him smiling at me. "Are you telling me to run away?"

"Why not?" I smiled back. "Get out of here and figure out what the hell you want. *You.* Not your mom or dad or the entire damn town."

His eyes searched my face. "How'd that go for you?"

"Ha. Um. Well…" Warm hazel eyes—eyes I'd spent six years looking into, gazed back at me. The memories hiding in them had me talking before I realized what I was saying. "I got a promotion. Today. Actually, like five minutes ago."

Beside me, Wes shifted just enough to bump his knee with mine. "That's awesome! Congratula—"

"It's in New York."

His smile faltered. "Wow." He let out a low whistle. "That's…"

"Huge? Terrifying? Far away?" I shook my head, dropping my gaze to study my hands. "I don't know if I can do it."

"You can." He said the words with so much certainty that I was caught off guard. Looking up, I found his eyes on me. He nodded, resolute and sure. "You've wanted this your whole life. You're not walking away from it now." He reached across the short distance and took my hand, giving it a squeeze. "I won't let you."

The crunch of gravel jarred us apart. "Sorry, don't mean to interrupt."

A familiar silhouette hovered just outside the booth. I stood and wiped my hands on my jeans. "Jack, hey." Closing the distance, I hugged him. He remained stiff. Pulling back, I studied his face, mostly hidden in the shadows. "Everything okay?"

Behind us, Wes stood. "Hey, man. How's your dad?"

Jack's jaw clenched. I took a step back, my own body tensing in response.

"He's fine." He narrowed his eyes in on Wes's face. "Tired of being poked and prodded by the doctors."

"That sounds about right." Wes laughed, but Jack's face remained still. Clearing his throat, Wes gestured toward the booth. "Do you need help packing up?"

Jack pulled his glare from Wes to look at the remains of the day—not much, which should have made him happy, but his face remained passive. "No. I think you've done enough." With that, he brushed passed us, letting their shoulders bump, and reached for a box.

Wes hesitated for a moment, looking to Jack, then to me. I shook my head, indicating that he should go, and he gave a terse nod. "See you guys later."

As Wes disappeared, I turned my attention back to Jack. I knew where his mind was going—me, Wes. Alone. Holding hands. I had to kill that thought before it took root. Giving his arm a squeeze, I said, "So, Wes just stopped by to—"

He cut me off. "How did it go today?" His head tilted toward the table. "With the booth?"

"I...uh, good."

He nodded, his eyes fixed on the Ferris wheel in the distance.

After a couple seconds of silence, I tried again. "So, your dad is doing better?"

His eyes scraped over me. "You know what I did all day?" He squinted, the lines around his eyes deepening. "I sat with my father, filling out paperwork and answering questions while Luke was playing catch up at work." He shoved a hand through his hair, the fairground lights catching the chaos he created. "And with each form I filled out, each doctor I spoke to, every word I said to my father, he would ask, 'Where's Luke? He'd know this.' Or 'Your brother should be here. He'd get it taken care of.'"

"Shit. Jack, I'm sorry. I—"

"I was there," he continued, like I hadn't uttered a syllable, "doing all this work for that bastard, but I still wasn't good enough."

I reached out to lay my hand on his, comfort him, to ease some of the tension out of his body. But he wasn't finished. "So, imagine how much it sucks to realize it's true here, too." He began throwing things into a box, his movements jerky.

"Wait a damn minute." I put a hand on his arm. "This wasn't—"

He shook my hand off and met my eye. "I didn't sign up to compete with Wes, Tierney." He tossed an empty cupcake pan into the box, the clatter making me flinch. "If that's what this is for you, then count me out."

"The only competition here is the one you've created in your head." I put myself between him and the table, forcing his eyes to mine. "Wes and I are *friends*. Nothing more."

"You've wanted this your whole life," Jack shot Wes's words back to me. *"You're not walking away from it now."*

Shit.

"I should have known better after that first weekend." His words were punctuated by the crash of another pan dropping into the box. "That night you kissed me to convince me—convince *yourself*—that you were over him."

"I *am* over him!" I reached out, but he shook my hand off. "That wasn't what it sounded like."

"No?" His eyes burned into mine. "Enlighten me."

Tears stung behind my eyes. This wasn't how I wanted to tell him.

We stood so close I could feel the heat emanating from him. I wanted so badly to lean in, wrap my arms around him. But the ice in his eyes kept my arms tied to my sides.

"I got the job."

The words came out barely above a whisper, but landed as loud as a stampede of elephants.

After a few beats of absolute quiet, Jack spoke. "Congratulations."

The rigid line of his back urged me to leave him alone, but the ragged beat of my heart begged me to stay. I put my hand on his shoulder. "Jack."

"I can't compete with that." The tense lines around his eyes, the torture behind the blue, told me that this wasn't just about the job. Or Wes.

"No one's asking you to." I pleaded silently for him to give a little, just enough to hear what I was saying.

He looked at me, and the conflict in his eyes nearly brought me to my knees. He wanted to believe me. I could tell. But something held him back. His gaze dropped to my hand on his shoulder and lingered, as if he were deciding to pull back or let me in.

For a moment, a brief, hopeful moment, I thought he was going to. I thought he was ready to end this fight and just let me love him, dammit. But then the moment ended. His face settled into a steely mask and he pulled away.

"Probably for the best." He avoided my eye as he tossed a couple more things into the box.

"What do you mean?"

"You. Me." He gestured between us with a pair of tongs. "This whole thing." Dropping the tongs into the box, he shrugged. "I mean, think about it. My aunt is always going to resent you. And you're always going to wonder about Wes. So, what's the point?"

"I don't—"

"We could save ourselves a lot of time and hurt if we just acknowledged it now and moved on." He said it so casually, like he wasn't ripping my heart from my chest with every word. "Don't you agree?"

"No." I blinked, my eyes burning. "I don't."

"Oh, come on." He pulled down the price list and rolled it up. "You don't really want to spend every day trying to convince Aunt Bonnie that you're not the devil, do you?" Putting the roll into the box, he rounded the table and began taking down the other signs. "And I don't want to constantly feel like I'm in some twisted episode of *The Bachelor*."

Something inside me snapped, like a rubber band pulled too far. *Enough.*

"Would you just stop?" I planted my hands on the table in front of me. "We both know what this is really about."

He raised an eyebrow and waited for me to continue. Still so fucking casual. I would strangle him if I didn't love him so much.

And, you know, prison.

"This isn't about Bonnie, or Wes, or even my job." Walking around the table, I stopped in front of him. "This is about you."

He shifted and crossed his arms over his chest. I took advantage of his silence and continued. "You get so caught up in comparing yourself to everyone else—Wes and Luke and, hell, even your father—but dammit, Jack, you're enough." I took a step closer, jabbing a finger in his chest. "You're enough, but I am goddamn tired of trying to convince you of that."

Surprise flickered over his face, but he held his ground. "That's quite a tragic backstory you've created for me, darlin'. But I don't need your pity."

My cheeks burned as if he'd slapped me. "I don't pity you, Jack," I said as I took another step toward him. Reaching out, I laid my hand against his cheek. "I—I love you, you jackass." My heart sputtered as he leaned into my touch. I thought for a second that he was going to give in. Tell me I was right and he didn't mean it. Pull me into his arms and kiss away this entire moment.

Instead, he smiled. "This isn't one of your happy-ever-after movies." Lifting the box he just filled, he took a step backward. "This is real life." With a pause, he glanced backward, the Ferris wheel bright against the dark sky. "And sometimes, real life means a highway straight out of town."

And before I could say another word, he walked away.

37: *Gloom & Body Odor*

Getting dumped and getting your dream job in the same day sucked.

Getting dumped, getting your dream job, and going to work the next day like everything was normal sucked even more.

Getting dumped, getting your dream job, going to work the next day like everything was normal, and attending a meeting in which you found out that your dream job was not everything you'd hoped for...well, *suck* was not a strong enough word.

In fact, I wasn't sure there *was* a strong enough word for this moment.

"So, basically, you're telling me that I get to pack up and move to a whole new city the *day after tomorrow*, and help get the new office off the ground." I leaned forward and put an elbow on Ron's desk. "And there's no raise?"

It'd been a long night, followed by an even longer morning. Ron had spent the first twenty minutes of our meeting trying to get Myra on the phone. After a couple dropped calls, and countless *Can you hear me now's*, he'd given up and started our meeting without her.

After giving me the rundown of how's and when's of getting to New York, he'd started in on my duties and salary. Usually, I had a bit more tact. This morning, however, tact had stayed home in bed.

Lucky bitch.

"Well, we're just opening this office." Ron fidgeted with a folder in front of him as he addressed my concern. "Our funds are limited."

"But New York is expensive." I lifted my brows. "I eat PB&Js for dinner twice a week *here*. There, I might not be able to afford food at all."

Ron shifted uncomfortably. Good. The thought of my starvation *should* make him uncomfortable.

"You can't just toss around the word *promotion* and expect me not to notice it's the same damn job I've been doing for six years." I sat back in my chair. Damn. I kind of liked tactless Tierney. Tactless Tierney was a lot like the girl I used to be. "You gotta give me something here, Ron."

"Well, there are differences." He rifled through the papers in front of him. "You'd be in charge of the nonfiction department. You'd—"

"Nonfiction?" I straightened. "Like, Amish cookbooks, and Army ants and...how-to-build-a-snowman stuff?"

"I'm pretty sure most people know how to build a snowman." He smiled at his attempt at a joke, but it was short-lived when he saw my unsmiling face. "But, yes. Essentially." When I didn't say anything, he scrambled to add, "You've done such great work on these projects in the past. I have no doubt you'll shine with this new opportunity."

"I've done great work on these projects because you haven't given me the chance to do anything else." I gripped the arms of my chair tight, my brain buzzing with snippets of the last six years. Dry how-to's. Boring biographies. An entire series about insects. I knew more about the sex lives of bugs than I did my own sex life.

"I'm not sure that's true," Ron said, and I dragged my attention back to him. "As the years have gone by, we've increased your responsibilities, given you bigger projects. We've—"

"What about Joy Needermyer?"

"That project didn't fit our requirements. It—"

"When you hired me," I interrupted, leaning forward. All my blood rushed to my head. "You said that I'd have the chance to choose my own projects. That I'd be able to work on something I was passionate about." Sitting back, I finished. "I'm not passionate about bugs, Ron. In fact, unless they decide to invade my personal space, I don't give two shits about bugs."

"I'm sorry you feel that way, Tierney, but we had to make decisions that were best for the company. The Needermyer manuscr—"

"The Needermyer manuscript was brilliant." My eyes held his, daring him to deny it. "You know it. I know it. Hell, even Mrs. Needermyer knew it. Which is why she killed her contract. She got tired of being jerked around by a publisher that had no intentions of giving her a shot."

Ron tilted his head. "We shouldn't have strung her along. I agree. But, in the end—"

"That's not the point." I stood, the manic energy rushing through me forcing me into motion. "The point is, this isn't what I signed up for." I paced across the space between my chair and Ron's desk. With every step I took, I could feel the old Tierney coming back. The one that didn't settle. The big dreamer. "I signed up to do work I was excited about. And, dammit, I was excited about that book. It was the first thing I'd been excited about in years. And I fought, Ron. I fought hard to get you to see how good it was."

"I'm sorry, Tierney. I—"

"But you were never going to see it. And now," I stopped pacing and faced him. "Now, you want me to do the same damn thing I've been doing for years. You want me to go back to projects that don't excite me, that I don't care about. *And* you want me to starve!"

"Well, that's a touch dramati—"

"I can't do it."

Ron stopped. His eyebrows lifted high on his shiny forehead. "Can't do what?"

"This." I motioned between us. My heart slammed loud in my chest. *What am I doing?* I thought, immediately followed by, *Damn, this feels right.* "That." I waved a hand toward the window. "I can't spend one more day in an office, pouring over things that don't matter to me. I want to do something that matters."

"What are you saying?"

I wasn't sure if exhaustion, heartbreak, or the mere idea of spending my life in a monotonous haze was to blame, but I had a hard time regretting the words that came out next.

"I quit."

***

The weird blend of liberation and dread I'd felt as I left the office settled firmly into *what the fuck did I do?* territory rather quickly. What followed was a spectacular bout self-pity. For days, the only people I interacted with were the ones delivering food to my door. The best kind of people, if you asked me. They didn't crush your dreams, or break your heart, or anything.

Exactly three seasons of *My Boyfriend the Vampire* later, Cat came knocking on my door.

"Go away," I grumbled, jabbing the volume button on the remote until I couldn't hear her knock anymore.

Cat, of course, didn't listen. She barged right in. Why, oh why, hadn't I gotten that key back?

"Get up," she said as I buried my head beneath my pillow. She thumped her foot against my knee and gripped the blanket in her hands.

"I don't wanna." My hands tightened around the blanket and I held on tight as Cat yanked it from me.

"Too damn bad. You're starting to stink up the place."

I let the blanket go, taking small satisfaction in Cat stumbling backward a few steps. "You're such a good friend. All sensitive and shit." I struggled to sit up.

"Yeah, well I don't want the entire apartment building to smell like gloom and body odor. Besides." She tossed the blanket aside and raked her critical gaze over me. "You've got pizza sauce on your face."

I swiped at my face with my hand and sank back into the couch, taking in the wreckage around me. A half-eaten turkey sandwich, an open pizza box and a smattering of Chinese containers on the coffee table and a couple of embattled teenage vampires on the TV screen. I'd also managed to only get half-undressed, and still wore exactly half my pinstripe pants, a plain tank top and, for some reason unbeknownst to me, a fuzzy pink sock on one foot.

Lifting a shoulder, I dragged my eyes back to Cat. "I quit my job."

"I heard." Cat began cleaning up the debris on the coffee table.

"And Jack and I broke up."

She paused, a pizza box topped with Chinese containers and soda cans balanced in her hands. "Shit, dude."

"Yup."

Putting the mountain of trash on the counter, Cat plopped down next to me. "I'm sorry."

I looked up to find her stare glued to me, like she was watching a car wreck and she couldn't look away. Morbid fascination from someone who didn't believe in love.

Maybe she had a point.

Blinking back new tears, I looked away. "Thanks."

Leaning forward, she grabbed a half-eaten package of cookies. "Here. I'd hug you, but you really do smell terrible."

I took the cookies and laughed. "Again. Best friend ever."

"I know." Leaping to her feet, she held out her hand. "Up. Go bathe thyself and meet me downstairs in half an hour. This calls for a drink."

***

I promised Cat an hour. Sixty minutes of "fun" before I could call it a night. We were at minute forty-nine.

"Would you stop checking the time?" Cat reached across the table and grabbed my phone. "We're here to celebrate you!"

"What, exactly, are we celebrating?" I muttered, stirring my drink with its straw. "My joblessness? My astounding success with relationships?"

"Your joblessness, of course. It's about time you left that job." She clinked her glass with mine. "You've been miserable for years. New York wasn't going to change that."

"I wasn't miserable. Just—"

"Complacent?" Cat cut in and my mouth snapped shut. "Remember when we first met?" She rested her chin in her hand, dark eyes on me. "You had a plan. You were only going to be with Pencil Pushers for a couple years. Get the experience, the confidence, and go back to New York."

I swallowed and looked down at my empty glass. I saw where she was going.

"You let yourself get comfortable. You let yourself get scared." She gave me a kick under the table, forcing me to look at her again. "But now's your time. You can do whatever you want." Her dark eyes drank in my face. "It's a good thing. Stop looking so terrified."

"Here you go, ladies." Our waitress slid fresh drinks toward us. I started to protest, to tell her we didn't order them, but she tilted her head toward the front of the bar. "Courtesy of the hot deejay."

Our eyes followed her motion to find a tall, beautiful dude grinning our way. "All yours," I said as he started across the bar.

Cat glanced over at me, a twinge of un-Cat-like panic in her eyes. "I'm not interested." Color crept over her cheeks.

I sat back in my seat and crossed my arms over my chest. "Catharine Louise Keller. Are you *blushing*?"

"Pssh." She grabbed her fresh drink and took a swig. "I don't blush."

Intrigue pushed passed all the other crap that had been weighing on me all night. I said nothing as Tall Dude reached our table and put his hand on the back of Cat's chair. He graced her with a smile, revealing a killer set of dimples. This wasn't an unusual occurrence on a night out with Cat—men were drawn to her like Winnie the Pooh to honey. Her reaction, though...*that* was different.

"Hey," the guy said. "I was hoping to see you tonight."

"Well, here I am," Cat replied, shaking her long red locks away from her face to meet his eye. Ahh, there was the confident grin. "What are you gonna do about it?"

The switch flipped. Blushing Cat vanished, replaced by the self-assured vixen I knew and loved. Which was my cue to run away. Run far, far away. "And on that note." I pushed away from the table. "You two crazy kids have a good night."

"Wait, Tier. You don't have to go. Jude isn't staying. We've still got..." she paused to look at her phone. "Three minutes!"

I glanced over at Cat's would-be suitor. Amusement sparked in his hazel eyes and his lips tilted at the corner. Clearly, this wasn't a new game for them. I stood up and patted Cat's shoulder, feeling confident she wouldn't be murderized by The Dimpled One.

"I think you can survive three minutes without me. Nice to meet you, Jude. See you later, Cat." I gave them a smile, grabbed my purse from the back of my chair, and headed toward the exit.

The sticky summer air clung to me as soon as I stepped outside. As the door clicked shut, it drowned out the pulsing music and constant hum of chatter and laughter. I sighed, sinking against the brick wall. Why was it so much work, being around all those people? And why did I suddenly feel so alone?

My phone weighed heavy in my hand. Looking down, my thumb hovered over the home button, wanting more than anything to dial a certain number. Inside, Cat would be settling into a flirty banter with Jude, and I was about to head home to contemplate the things I'd lost over the last few days.

At the top of the list, a pair of bright blue eyes and a killer grin...

Pushing out a sigh, I shoved away from the wall and started down the walk. No point in standing out here in the middle of the night, moping like a lovesick teenager. I couldn't dwell on that. Just like I couldn't dwell on the job thing. Onward and upward. I'd be okay. I just...had to figure out where to start.

With squared shoulders and a stiffened spine, I headed toward my apartment. "You got this," I muttered under my breath. "You're gonna be fine."

38: Pizza Epiphany

What did "fine" mean, really?

For me, it meant getting up the next morning, putting my big girl pants on and finding a new job. I couldn't just sit around and mope forever. There were bills to pay, man.

Luckily, the search was short. There was an opening at *Eliza,* and Cat snagged me an interview. The Associate Editor in the health and beauty department moved to Liechtenstein with her fiancé. Not my dream job by any means. But they paid me, and I needed money, so, it was a match made in mediocre heaven.

Time alternated between a slow crawl and warp speed. It was nearly September before I knew it, and life was back to normal.

Except for the dude-shaped hole in my heart, anyway.

With a sigh, I shoved that trail of thoughts aside and unlocked my apartment. I managed life just fine these last three months without that stupid grin of Jack's. I'd manage just fine after it. Besides, being single was cool. I could do whatever I wanted, whenever I wanted. In fact, I was about to settle down for an awesome night in. Just me and *My Boyfriend the Vampire*. Who needed an *actual* boyfriend?

Kicking off my shoes, I refocused my attention on the night ahead of me: frozen pizza and vampires. Did it really get better than that?

"Open up, hermit lady."

I glared at the door. "Go away, Cat," I called, opening the freezer.

"I'm here to rescue you." I rolled my eyes as she let herself in. "There's a big party at Tryst tonight. Lots of cute dudes." She looked me over, from my bare feet to my work-worn skirt and button down. "Go get hot. Meet me downstairs in an hour."

"I'm good." I pulled my pizza from the freezer and turned on the oven. "I've got a date."

"*Ughhhhh!*" Cat groaned, sagging against the counter. "How many times do I have to tell you fictional characters do not count as dates?"

"I know I've told you this before." I paused to look at her. "But you are such a good friend."

"I know!" She widened her eyes, missing my sarcasm. "I'm trying to be, anyway. But you won't let me." Crossing the small space, she put her hand on my arm and gave me a pleading look. "Why won't you let me help you?"

I shook my head and moved away, locating a pizza pan. "I don't need help. I'm fine."

Cat made a strangled sound of disbelief. "That dude broke you. He's lucky I haven't broken his kneecaps in return."

I laughed—mostly to cover up the jab of pain just beneath my ribcage. "Violence is not the answer."

"The hell it isn't. If some jerkwad broke my heart—not that anyone could ever get that close—I'd fully expect you to kick some ass."

I tried for a smile, barely managing halfway. *If some jerkwad broke my heart,* my mind repeated, resulting in a tense, breath-stealing pain. Blinking, I focused on opening the boxed pizza. "The jerkwad wouldn't live to tell the tale if he broke your heart," I told Cat, thankful my voice remained steady.

"Exactly. So, what's stopping me from finding this dude and ripping his spleen out through his nostril?"

"You play too many zombie games." I put the pizza onto the pan and crossed to the fridge, pulling out a bag of shredded cheese. "I appreciate the sentiment, though."

Cat watched as I piled extra cheese onto the pizza. "Are you going to put pineapple on that?"

Raising my brow, I looked at her. "Duh."

I could see the wheels spinning in her head. Turning to hide my smile, I pulled out a can of pineapple and opened it. "You're welcome to stay in. Have some pizza. Watch some TV."

"I...I really think you should come out. It'd be good for you." Her eyes followed my every movement as I layered rings of pineapple onto the pizza.

"Maybe. But pizza is better." The timer went off, signaling that the oven was preheated. I slipped the pan in and closed the door. "There's ice cream in my freezer."

"Dammit." Cat exited the kitchen and kicked off her high heels. "You win. Which season of *Vampire* are we on?"

***

"I'm just saying," Cat said four hours and two bottles of wine later. "If Makayla would have taken the damn antidote, none of the other shit would have happened." She stood up and carried our empty wine glasses into the kitchen. "Poor Ewan had to rescue her for, like, the ten millionth time this month."

I stretched my feet out in front of me and sank into the couch cushions. "Yeah, but he loves her. He'd rescue her a hundred billion times if he had to."

"Which he probably will, because girl has a pretty face, but not so much with the thinking." Cat rinsed our glasses and returned to the living room for our ice cream bowls.

"You don't have to do that." I waved a dismissive hand and closed my eyes, the wine flowing warm through my blood. "It'll be there in the morning."

"Yeah, let's leave the sticky, sugary mess till morning." Cat's voice was dry as she turned on the faucet. "That's how you get ants, Tierney."

"Ants, schmants." I stood up and stretched my arms over my head, then wandered into the kitchen. "We have anymore wine?"

"Nope." Cat finished washing the dishes and started wiping the counter. "You polished off the last bottle somewhere around the time Ewan's long lost brother took his shirt off."

"Mmm...shirtless vampire." I leaned against the counter, envisioning a wicked grin and abs for days. "Why don't real dudes look like that?"

"Oh, some do." Tossing the sponge in the sink, Cat turned to face me, a grin on her face. "Some look better."

I squinted my eyes at her. "I don't believe you."

"True story." She pulled her long ponytail over her shoulder, her eyes landing on a space just behind me. "Isn't that still your stuff from The Big Quitting?" Closing the short space between us, Cat pulled the lid off the box. "You haven't gone through it yet?"

My hand darted out and I smacked the lid back down before I realized what I was doing. "I should really just throw the whole thing out."

Truthfully, I'd been avoiding it since the day I put it there. I didn't throw it away. I didn't open it. I just let it sit there for a month, taunting me like a symbol of my...my what? Failure? Rebellion? Victory? I hadn't decided yet.

"Whatever," Cat grumbled, lifting her hands away from the box. "Who wants two-month-old M&Ms, anyway?"

"How do you know there are M&Ms in there?" I frowned, lifting the lid just enough to peek inside. Sure enough, a half-full jar of colorful candies sat right on top.

"I may have snacked on them when I was over the other night. Anyway, I should get going." Cat sailed around the counter and stuffed her feet into her shoes. "Thanks for the pizza."

I nodded, still staring into the box. "Sure. See ya."

The sound of Cat closing the door behind her jarred me and I dropped the lid. Rounding the counter, I sat on a barstool and rested my chin in my hands, my eyes glued to the box. What was the point of leaving it there, collecting dust? A constant reminder of the weirdest, worst two days of my life, right in my face. No promotion. No Jack. No job. I really *should* throw it away.

Although...

I pulled the lid off and grabbed the jar of M&Ms, unscrewing the top. No point in wasting perfectly good chocolate.

As I munched on a handful of candy-coated heaven, I eyed the remaining contents. Right on top sat a smattering of stuff from my desk drawers. Stapler, paperclips, rubber bands. What kind of person would throw office supplies out? Setting them aside, I continued digging.

A planner, a handful of pens and pencils and a few legal pads later, I found a thick manila envelope. A shiver of recognition skittered over me. I pulled the envelope out and sat it on the counter. Months of my life was inside. Numerous years of Joy Needermyer's life. And for what? Now that I no longer worked for a publishing company, there wasn't a damn thing I could do for the woman.

Grabbing the envelope, I opened it and slid the manuscript out, thumbing through it. This was the most recent revision. A few months ago, Mrs. Needermyer had been so excited to turn this in. She'd really felt like she nailed it this time, and she had. Such a shame that I hadn't been able to get this fantastic book into the hands of the public.

With a sigh, I sat back in my seat. A sense of failure rushed through me. I'd failed her. I should have tried harder at Pencil Pushers. I should have…

Dropping the manuscript to the counter, I stood and grabbed another handful of candy. My thoughts raced as I chewed. I could have stayed at Pencil Pushers, fought harder to get Mrs. Needermyer's book published, been miserable for years. Or I could've done just what I did— walk away from the thing that made me unhappy.

It just sucked that someone else had to get caught in the crossfire.

Dropping the remaining candy in the jar, I began to pace. If only there were something that I could do. Something to make up for running away instead of standing my ground.

But, as I'd proven yet again, the only thing I was good at was running away. I was the least brave person ever.

As I thought the words, something popped into my head. A memory from a few months ago. Me, Jack, an empty field. Words that had reached right through to the core of me.

"It took a lot of courage to know that life here in June Lake wasn't something that you wanted. It was brave to walk away..."

Jack believed I was brave. That I walked away from Wes because I was brave enough to search for a new life. I'd done the same thing with work. Only...brave people didn't play it safe. My new job? Safe. My nights in? Safe.

I needed to be brave. But what did that mean?

Stopping, I stared at the mess on my counter. Six whole years' worth of my life sat there, scattered and messy and...boring. The only thing that had made me feel alive, excited, had been that manuscript. Maybe that meant I shouldn't walk away from it.

I straightened my shoulders, an idea bubbling at the back of my mind. What if...

Scrambling through the mess on the counter, I grabbed a legal pad and a pen. I had some planning to do.

39: Mail Call

The next month flew by in a whir of brainstorms and phone calls and late nights staring at my computer screen. The end result: my very own literary agency.

Well, technically, *agent*. Singular. Just me. Working out of my apartment after getting home from my day job. But I had plans, dammit. Big ones. Ones that involved getting good books by talented writers out in the world. Starting with Joy Needermyer.

She'd been skeptical. Of course she was skeptical. After working with a publisher for over a year, only to be asked time and time again to tweak something, delete something, blah, blah, blah.

"I'm not getting any younger," she'd said the first time I called her, an echo of her words when she'd fired me a couple months back. "This whole thing is a lot more stress than my old heart can take."

It'd taken two more phone calls and the offer of lunch to even chip at her resolve. She was a stubborn lady, which I both admired and abhorred. Sure wasn't making my job any easier.

Finally, on a sunny October afternoon, I found myself standing on the sidewalk outside a building in Port Agnes, waiting for Mrs. Needermyer to arrive. I'd offered to drive out to Handford for our meeting, but she insisted she wasn't too old for a road trip. Besides, Port Agnes had more restaurants to choose from. Handford boasted exactly one eatery, and Mrs. Needermyer had had her fill of Sloppy Joes from The Burger Place.

Stifling a sigh, I watched the sun play on the Hope River and tried to calm the frantic beat of my heart and the wound-tight nervousness radiating throughout my body.

This has to work, dammit, I thought, twisting the strap of my purse. *It has to.*

"Sorry I'm late."

The voice jarred me. I tore my eyes from the river to find Mrs. Needermyer, all five feed nothing of her, standing on the sidewalk.

"Mrs. Needermyer, thank you so much for meeting me—"

"Joy. Please."

"Joy." I took her hand, which was covered in blue. She must've seen the surprise on my face, because she laughed.

"I'm in the middle of a new project and I lost track of time." She held up both hands and smiled. "Refinishing an old dresser."

"Fun." I smiled. This woman could probably run circles around me with all her energy. I could barely juggle a day job and this crazy agency idea. "If you figure out how to bottle that energy of yours, let me know."

Laughing, she pulled open the door. "My energy comes from sugar, sweet girl. Delicious, decadent sugar." As I followed behind her, she continued. "Who needs real food when you can have pie?"

I felt like I'd just met Cat forty years from now. "I'm pretty sure my best friend has said those exact words."

"Your best friend is a smart girl. Now, I don't know how you operate, but I like to start my meals dessert first." I followed her through the smattering of brightly colored tables inside the Kaleidoscope Café. She settled on a seat facing the window—with a slivered view of the river. In the back of my mind, I recalled another soon-to-be restaurant with an amazing panorama of that same river.

Nope.

Plopping down in the seat across from Joy, I cut that off before it fully formed. It'd become habit to veer down another line of thought as soon as a certain jackass popped into my mind. It was like my brain cells had formed an army of bounty hunters, and Jack's picture plastered their Most Wanted bulletin board.

Fine by me. Didn't need to be thinking of him anyway.

"Now, I don't want to talk business until I've had at least one of everything from this column," Joy said as she settled into her seat. She held the menu up for me. "I'm about to have the most amazing foodgasm ever."

Laughter bubbled passed my lips and I momentarily forgot about the whole Jack thing. "It's a deal." I reached for my menu. "Foodgasms first, business later."

"What can I get for you ladies?" Our waiter, the bearer of a fantastic Afro, greeted us with a grin.

"One of everything on your dessert menu, please," I said. "Except the cherry pie. We'll take two of those."

"You got it." Another grin before he bounced away.

I kept my word. Joy devoured her sugary treats—two cookies, a slice of pie and a cupcake—in peace. We chit-chatted about the weather and my new job and the "bitching blue paint" she was using on the dresser earlier this afternoon. Once she'd eaten the last bite of her decadent fudge cupcake, I decided this was my chance. The other woman was sugared up—literally—and there wouldn't be a better time.

Steeling my spine, I pulled a legal pad and folder from my bag, clicked open a pen and got down to business. "So, Mrs. Needermyer, this is why you should let me be your agent..."

***

I didn't walk away with a signed contract. I did, however, get a very strong *maybe*, which I felt good about. Joy was proving to be a hard shell to crack, but I liked the challenge.

When I got home, I tossed my briefcase on the counter and kicked off my shoes. With a sigh, I leaned down and rubbed my feet. Stupid high heels.

As I rubbed, Cat sailed through the door like a tiny tornado. "How'd it go?"

I straightened. "Good, I think. We'll see." Moving into the kitchen, I called, "You hungry?"

"Is that even a question?" Cat followed me. "I'm always hungry. By the way." She tossed something on the counter. "I checked your mail for you."

"*When* did I give you a key to my mailbox?"

"When you gave me the apartment key." Her words were logical, but her tone clearly said *duh*.

I chose to ignore the tone and picked up the stack of mail. As I sifted through it, Cat moved to the fridge. "What are we looking at?"

"Food," I replied, pausing in my perusal as an unfamiliar envelope caught my eye. Slim white envelope, handwritten address...not the usual bill or junk mail. I sat the rest of the mail aside and turned the envelope over in my hand.

"What's that?" Cat peered over my shoulder, her voice jarring me. "Looks fancy."

"Not sure." Sliding my finger under the flap, I opened it. "My psychic abilities are on the fritz."

"Har." Cat continued her search for dinner as I pulled out the contents of the envelope.

A simple logo greeted me, a single name scrawled across the front of a folded card. *Molly's*.

My heart climbed to my throat. Slowly, I opened the card. *Please join us for the grand opening of Molly's*, it read, followed by the details. When, where, what time, all that information blurred before my eyes. I dropped the invitation to the counter and took a deep breath.

So what? I thought. So Jack was opening his restaurant and he'd sent me an invitation. So it was the first time he'd bothered to contact me in months. So he'd finally reached out.

So fucking what?

I turned to Cat, who had given up her search through my fridge to stare at me. "What'd you find?" I asked, motioning behind her.

"You look like you're about to barf." She pushed the fridge shut and reached behind me. "What was it?"

"Nothing." I tried to snatch the invitation from her hand, but she was too quick. "It doesn't matter." I untucked my button-down shirt and began twisting the hem in my hands. "It's not important."

Cat's eyes skimmed over the information, then she looked at me. Concern chased curiosity across her features until her expression settled on something in between. "You're going, right?"

"Um, no." I took the invitation back and dropped it in the trash. "If that jackass really wanted me there, he could have called. Or come over. Or, you know, *not* spent the last three months pretending I didn't exist." I pulled open the fridge and grabbed the first thing I found. "How's cookie dough sound?"

"For dinner? Sure. Why not?" Cat grabbed the invitation from the garbage and studied it. "Maybe he didn't know what to say. Maybe he was scared, or embarrassed, or whatever."

"What does it matter to you?" I opened the tube of dough and bit into it. "You don't even believe in love."

"Not for me, maybe." She pulled herself onto the counter, her feet dangling. "But I believe in it for other people. I believe in it for you."

I chewed, savoring the chocolate chips. Once I swallowed, I shrugged. "Doesn't matter, Cat. Going to this...thing isn't going to make a damn bit of difference. For all I know, he's just trying to fill up space and needed another name for the guest list."

"Do you really believe that?" She crossed her arms over her chest and leveled me with her stare.

I shifted, sat the dough aside and sighed. "I don't know."

"Only one way to find out."

Silence fell over us as I met Cat's eye. The scared little girl inside me screamed to yank that invitation from Cat's hand and shred it to bits. Another part of me, the stupid, in-love-with-a-jackass part of me begged me to say yes. To go to him. To find out if there was a chance.

Wasn't hard to guess which part won.

With one last sigh, I pushed away from the counter. "Fine. But you're coming with me."

40: *Cupcake Carnage*

I had nearly two weeks to chicken out. To convince Cat that there was no need for me to attend the restaurant grand opening. To make her see that being in Jack's presence would do neither of us any good.

I was unsuccessful. Should have known better, really. Once Cat got something in her head, there was no changing her mind.

So, on a rainy day in mid-October, we sat in Cat's car, staring at the warmly lit building filled with people.

"Jack's in there," I whispered, balling my hands together in my lap to keep from twisting the hem of the teal silk dress Cat had loaned me.

"Kind of the point, toots." Cat leaned closer to the window and squinted. "Delicious food, too. Which, really, is all I came for."

"And here I thought you were being a supportive friend."

"Nah, it's the food." Cat unbuckled her seatbelt. "Now, I'm about to get out and risk ruining what may, in fact, be the best hair day I've had in months with this rain. You better be right behind me, or there will be hell to pay. You don't mess with a good hair day." With that, she shoved open the door and squealed as she got out.

I watched her run across the parking lot to stand under the awning. She waved her hand, and I could imagine the look on her face as I continued to sit in the car. Incredulous, impatient, irritated. I almost wanted to scoot over to the driver's seat and get the hell out of here. Probably would have if Cat hadn't taken the keys.

Taking a deep breath, I tried to calm the tremble in my hands, the slam of my heart. Maybe Jack would be so busy with all the other guests that he wouldn't even notice my presence. Maybe we could slip in, stay long enough to appease Cat's sweet tooth, and slip out. All ninja style.

Except Cat wouldn't allow that to happen. In her mind, this was going to lead to Jack and I realizing how much we love each other. We'd throw ourselves into each other's arms and live happy ever after.

Methinks Cat had a warped sense of how that stuff worked.

Regardless, if I didn't get out of this car soon, seeing Jack would be the least of my worries. Cat would skin me alive for jeopardizing her hair.

With one final sigh, I pushed open the door and ran across the lot.

"It's about freaking time," Cat said as I reached her. "I almost went in without you."

"You should have." I glanced through the window, watching people mill around, laughing and talking and eating. Lots of familiar faces, lots of people I didn't know.

Cat peered in. "I think it's safe to say he didn't invite you to fill out his guest list."

Tearing my eyes away, I crossed my arms over my chest and rubbed my arms. "How about you go inside and get your fill of food while I wait in the car? After, we can go to Shrimpy Dick's for shakes and fries and call it a night."

Without responding, she put her hands on my shoulders and steered me to the door. She paused long enough to pull it open, then pushed me through. "Sorry," she said as we entered the building. "But I've watched you be broken and sad for long enough. You deserve a resolution. One way or the other."

I turned my head toward her, ready to deny the broken sadness, but someone called my name before I could speak.

Cat and I both turned to find Luke heading toward us, looking so much like his brother that my heart sputtered, stalled, and restarted when it realized he wasn't Jack.

"I wasn't sure you were coming," he said when he reached us. His eyes flickered over to Cat and he smiled. "Hello, Cat."

Cat gave him a sparkling smile and rested her fingertips on his arm. "Luke." She batted her lashes. "How have you been?"

I rolled my eyes. "Here we go."

"Good," Luke replied, and I eyed the exit. This was about to turn into the Cat Keller Flirt Fest in 5, 4, 3, 2—

"Tierney, I'm sure you remember my father," Luke said, yanking my attention back to him.

I blinked, the older man coming into focus. His trademark Elliott eyes twinkled in the light as he smiled his hello and took my hand. "How are you, Ms. Chandler?"

Relief blended with the anxiety cocktail already rushing through my veins. I'd wondered how Jack's dad was doing. I hadn't heard a whole lot through the June Lake grapevine.

"I'm doing all right," I replied as I pulled my hand back. "Glad to see you looking so well."

"Thank you, dear." He smiled again and looked around. "I must say, I'm rather impressed with my boy. I think this place is going to be a great success."

Well, you could add *surprise* to the list of emotions I was currently wrangling. "I think so, too." I looked to Luke, who was grinning proudly. *Good,* I thought. *I'm glad they're finally getting on board.*

"Why, I don't think we've met." Cat sidled between Mr. Elliott and me, holding her hand out. "I can see where your boys get their good looks. I must say, those are some *spectacular* genes you've got there."

"Cat!" Grabbing her by the arm, I yanked her away from a shocked—and intrigued?—Jack's dad.

"It was good to see the both of you," I continued as I dragged Cat away. "Really glad you're doing well, sir."

Once we were out of earshot, Cat wriggled out of my grasp. "What'd you do that for? I could've snagged me a rich old dude. A *hot*, rich old dude."

"That man just got out of the hospital." I glared. *"You'll put him back in there."*

"Hey, man. I've heard that's how some dudes like to go out." She turned to look out the window and let out a low whistle. "Wow, that's a nice view."

I let her change the subject, mostly because I was afraid she'd keep talking about Jack's hot dad, and, well, no thanks. Turning toward the window, I took it all in.

The rain was starting to let up and the clouds parted to let the moon peek through. I held my breath and braced myself against the memory racing through me. Jack. Me. The moonlight. A night that changed everything.

"Yeah," I agreed, keeping my eyes on the moon so that Cat couldn't see the tears.

"So, about that food," Cat murmured, bumping my shoulder with hers.

"I...I think I'm going to stay here. You go, though." The thought of pushing through the crowd, possibly running into Jack, was more than enough to keep me glued to the floor.

I didn't have to tell Cat twice. She bounded away, on the hunt for all things delicious. The party in full-swing behind me provided a steady buzz of background noise for my one-track thoughts. I wanted to disappear, fade into the wall like a chameleon, guaranteeing that Jack wouldn't find me. Instead, here I was, out in the open, my bright blue dress designed to draw attention to me.

Cat did that on purpose.

Tearing my eyes from the shimmering river, I turned to face the room. I tried not to think about how close Jack was. I hadn't seen him yet, but I knew he was here. We were even be breathing the same air. After months of no contact, that was enough to send my heart pinging around my ribcage.

Pushing that thought from my mind, I let my eyes roam over the space. From the exposed brick behind the counter to the gleaming hardwood floors and smattering of round, wrought iron tables, the place was beautiful.

The piercing, tense fear and nervousness I'd felt standing outside only moments before dissipated. In its place, pride. Warm, unadulterated pride. He'd done it. Amid all the doubt and resentment from his family, Jack had stayed the course. He'd kept reaching for his dream. And I couldn't have been prouder.

The warmth was immediately followed by the hollow realization that I hadn't been there to see it.

My eyes stung. It was his choice. He walked away. He didn't reach out to me. Until now. Three months later. With a pathetic little postcard. I didn't even rate a phone call.

Sadness shifted to anger and I steeled my spine. Screw this. I deserved more than some bullshit piece of mail.

Scanning the room, I tried to find Cat. In theory, it should have been easy. Bright red hair, flashy black dress. I squinted, turned, and stood on my tiptoes. Nothing. Where did she—

"Whoa, watch it!"

The warning came too late. I collided with a waitress, sending her tray flying through the air.

"Shit! Sorry!" I knelt, picking up the dessert disaster before too many people gathered around. Before *all* the people gathered around.

Before the one person I didn't want to see gathered around.

"You still know how to make a scene, don't you?"

Too late.

I froze, my stomach leaping to my throat. Slowly, I lifted my head to find Jack standing over me, trademark grin on his face.

A clusterfuck of emotions rushed through me. I wanted to throw myself into his arms and kiss that ridiculous grin. I wanted to ball my hand into a fist and knock it right off. I wanted to run away and cry. I didn't do any of those, though. I stood and stared.

363

SOMETHING SO SWEET

"You look gorgeous," he continued, his blue eyes flashing over me from head to toe. "Even if you *are* smooshing red velvet cupcake all over my new floor."

I looked down. Sure enough, there was definite cupcake carnage beneath the toe of my borrowed stiletto. "Yeah. Sorry about that." Lifting my foot, I tried to shake the remains away. Nothing happened.

Shit.

People were starting to stare. Well, stare *more*.

I did *not* need witnesses right now. I needed privacy. I needed to somehow maintain a smidge of dignity. I needed this damn cupcake to get. Off. My. Shoe.

"Ugh!" Giving up, I bent and took my shoes off. Barefoot, it was. Real dignified.

"Congrats, man," I said in Jack's general direction as I eased through the crowd. I had to get out of here. "Looks great."

I got about two steps away when Jack stepped in front of me. "Five minutes, Tierney," he said as I slid to a stop. "Just give me five minutes."

I glanced around us. Curious eyes took in my bare feet, the cupcake-covered shoes in my hand, and the star of the evening asking me to stay.

"I don't want to do this, Jack." I met his eye, keeping my voice low. "I shouldn't have come." I stepped forward again.

Jack matched my step. "But you did." His eyes burned into mine. "You're here, and we need to talk." He paused, then added, "I've missed you."

I ignored the little flutter inside me and gripped my shoes tighter. "You didn't miss me enough to pick up the damn phone." I took another step forward, forcing him back.

"Wait. Just..." He took another step backward, just as I made eye contact with a waiter behind him, a tray of dessert shooters in hand.

Ahh, dammit. *Here we go again.* "Jack, stop—" I started, but not in time. His shoulder bumped the waiter's hand and the tray tipped, spilling a delicious mix of creams and puddings all over his fancy suit jacket.

I snorted, then instantly put a hand over my mouth. Jack looked from the mess—on him, the floor, *and* the poor waiter—and met my eye. "Why do I feel like we've been here before?"

The laugh I'd stifled escaped. Around us, the murmurs became chuckles.

"Food *and* entertainment," someone called out, followed by another person yelling, "Encore!"

Jack's lips tilted in an embarrassed smile. "What do you say, darlin'?" he said just so I could hear. "Care to come to the rescue one last time?" He held up his arms to showcase the mess all over his suit. "I think there are towels in the kitchen." The light caught a glimmer of hope in his eyes, and it matched the one I'd been trying to suppress all night.

I rolled my eyes and took his hand. "All right. Let's go."

We bypassed the continued looks and comments from the crowd and made it to the kitchen. I grabbed a towel from the shelf just inside the entrance and sat my shoes down. Without thinking, I started to wipe at the mess on his jacket.

And I waited. For an apology. An explanation. Something that would make those three months of silence understandable. But was there really anything that would do that? Make up for the hurt, the anger, the long nights of wondering if he was okay? If *I* was okay?

That glimmer of hope transformed into a full-blown blaze of rage.

Fuck that.

"I told you I loved you." I thrust the towel into his hands and met his eye. "I told you I loved you and you walked away."

"I know." Jack's eyes darkened. "I'm sorry."

"You're sorry?" I laughed, spinning away from him to pace. "You're sorry. That's awesome. I've spent the last three months hurt, trying to move on, and you're *sorry*." Wrapping my arms tight around me, I shook my head. "Seriously?"

"I know. It's not enough to make up for—"

"No, it's not, Jack. I told you I loved you. And you didn't call, didn't write. Hell, you could have sent smoke signals." I stopped to face him, the nervous energy, the anger and frustration and pain from the last three months, bubbling over. "I got nothing, though. Radio silence. Some great communication skills you got there, buddy."

He winced. Sighed. Nodded. "You're right. I'm an asshole."

"At least we can agree on that." I blinked away the tears threatening to fall and gritted my teeth. "Why didn't you call?"

Ugh. I hated how small I sounded. How sad and insecure and…well, broken.

Cat had been right about that, at least.

Jack didn't say anything. I looked up to find him staring at the towel in his hand. I waited a couple more seconds in silence before I spoke again.

"Right. Well, this has been swell." Leaning down, I slipped my shoes back on. Cupcake be damned. "But I'm gonna go. I—"

"I didn't call because I was ashamed."

I stopped. "What?"

"You were right." He shoved a hand through his hair, creating more chaos. "I've spent my whole life comparing myself to other people. Convincing myself I'd always come in last." His lips twisted into a rueful smile. "I'd been doing it my whole life. With Luke, with Wes. With you."

He looked lost. Broken. Almost as broken as I felt. I swallowed, ignoring the urge to wrap my arms around him. "Go on."

Glancing my way, he shook his head. "It took you calling me on it to make me see. I've been a coward. My whole damn life, I've been a coward." He pushed his hands into his pockets and rocked back and forth on his heels. "I shouldn't have walked away."

"No, you shouldn't have." I lifted my chin and met his eye. "Jackass."

He smiled, and warmth spread through my veins. That smile, man. It was a wondrous thing. My arms dropped to my sides, defenses falling with them. Couldn't hurt to hear him out, right?

"Sorry to interrupt." The waiter Jack had run into slipped into the kitchen, sheepish look on his face. "But my shift is over, so…"

Jack blinked. "Right, uh…" He glanced my way, an embarrassed smile creeping across his face. Slowly, he reached into his pocket and pulled out his wallet. Taking out a couple bills, he handed them to the waiter. "Thank you."

The waiter took the cash. "Never been paid to screw up before. I could get used to it." With a grin, he shoved the money into his pocket and backed away. "Thanks!"

My mouth dropped open. I looked from the waiter's disappearing back to Jack. "Did—did you do that on *purpose?*"

He grinned, then tried and failed to hide it. "What? No. I would never!" Taking my hand, he pulled me forward. "You wouldn't stop leaving! I did what had to be done."

I glanced down at the mess still on his suit. "What a waste of perfectly good desserts."

"Not if it means you'll hear me out." He tilted my chin up with his finger, meeting my eye. "Don't let those desserts die in vain."

I swallowed against the swell of emotion surging to the surface. "I don't..."

"This jackass is at your mercy." His hand rested on my shoulder, his touch gentle. "You tell me to fuck off, and I'm gone. Outta here. You'll never hear from me again." He took a slow step forward. "I hope you won't, because...because I love you, too." Trailing his hand from my shoulder, he linked his fingers with mine. "And I know I should've said it sooner. I shouldn't have waited so long. I shouldn't have left that night. I should have stayed."

Pausing for breath, he squeezed my hand. "But I wanted to prove myself. To convince myself that I deserved you. So, I waited. Until I was ready—until *this* was ready." He gestured toward the restaurant, still buzzing with life. "And I waited too long, didn't I?"

His eyes fell on me, anguish and hope creating an irresistible blend. My heart crashed against my ribs. Was it too late?

"While you think about that," he continued, holding up a hand to halt anything I may have said. "I'm gonna keep talking. You need all the facts before you tell me to eff off."

I gave him a small nod. "Continue."

"All right." He huffed out a breath. "Okay. Here it is." Shifting his weight, he looked at me, his face open. Nervous. "You make me feel like I can have more. I wanted to be what you believed I was. So I..." He sighed, and pushed his hair back. I watched the emotions play across his face, dying to know what he would say next.

"After my father recovered from his surgery, I told him that I was not cut out for Elliott Enterprises. And that he needed to accept that, to accept me for me, and stop comparing me to Luke."

"Wow," I breathed. I saw his dad, of course, but I didn't know the backstory. "That's...how did that go?"

"About as you'd expect." Jack's shoulder lifted. "But we're working on it. That's something."

"That's a big something. I'm proud of you."

A grin, bright and wide, spread over his face. "That means a lot, coming from you."

I smiled, in spite of the tension knotting in my stomach. "You're welcome."

We stood there, face-to-face, hands linked, for countless seconds. My eyes drank in every detail, from his perpetually messy hair to the hopeful glint in his eyes. He wanted an answer. Needed an answer. And I wanted to give him one. Only, something held me back.

I'd needed an answer, too. For months.

As the thought rang loud in my head, I took a step back. "I...I'm sorry."

Disappointment, heavy and hard, settled on Jack's face. He looked down and nodded. "No, no. I get it." Clearing his throat, he took a step back. "I'm gonna, uh, get back out there."

"Jack, wait." The words were out before I could stop them. He turned, his eyes bright. I wanted to tell him I loved him, too. That I wanted him, needed him, forgave him for walking away. But...

"You hurt me."

"I know."

I swallowed, and wrung my hands together. I wanted to reach out and smooth the lines from his face. But I knew one touch would be my undoing. And I couldn't come undone. Not right now. Taking a deep breath, I stepped backward. "I...I'm not ready to—"

"You're not ready to forgive me. I know. I really messed up. I—"

"I'm not ready to let this go."

My words stopped him. Stopped me, too. I blinked, my eyes stinging. Meeting his gaze, I continued. "I don't want to walk out that door and never see you again. But...but I can't go through hurt like that, Jack. I can't—"

Jack closed the distance between us, taking my hands in his. "You won't. I promise you, I won't hurt you like that again. I—"

"I have to go." Brushing at the tears on my cheeks, I squared my shoulders. "I have to go think."

"Okay." Jack nodded and moved aside, clearing the path for my escape. "All right. I'll, uh...see you around?"

I exhaled, one long, slow breath. Shaking my hair away from my face, I met his eye one last time. "I hope so."

And then, it was my turn to walk away.

41: Pour Some Sugar On Me

Two hours later, I found myself parked at a table in the corner of the first bar I found. I didn't stop when I walked away from Jack. I'd pushed through the crowd and right out the door. Took a right and followed the sidewalk until I found this place.

Through the window, the Hope River glittered in the moonlight. All I could focus on, though, was the way the pendant light caught the flashes of green in my drink. What was this? My third drink? Fourth? Not enough, if the way Jack's face kept running through my mind was anything to go by.

"Hey, hot stuff," the most bestest friend in the world said as she approached my table. I must have called her at some point. Either that, or she'd bugged my phone.

I narrowed my eyes on her face, suspicion taking over. "Did you bug my phone?"

"How much have you had to drink?" she asked, plopping down in the seat across from me.

"Jus' a couple." I shrugged and waved a hand at the cluster of empty glasses next to me. Cat slid the half-empty one from my reach before I could take another sip.

"You're cut off," she said as she took a swig for herself and flagged down the waitress. "Can we get some water and all the pretzels you have, please?"

The middle-aged, bleach-blond waitress nodded, her heavily-lined eyes squinting at me. "Bit of a lightweight, huh?"

Cat laughed. "You have no idea." She drained my drink as the waitress walked away, then crossed her arms on the tabletop, leveling me with her no-bullshit stare. "Talk."

"What's there to talk about?" I shredded the napkin my drink had been sitting on, bitter that Cat had cut me off. I wasn't nearly numb enough. I could still feel every bruise and scrape the night had left behind. "I mean, I don't even know where to start." I stared hard at the tendrils of paper in front of me, biting the inside of my cheek.

I knew where to start. It hurt too much, though. So I started somewhere else instead. "I got cupcake on your shoe." I held up the shoe in question, a smear of cream cheese frosting on the toe. "I got cupcake on your shoe and I didn't even get to eat a cupcake." My eyes filled and I dropped the shoe on the table. "I should have eaten a cupcake!"

The waitress delivered our water and pretzels. I shoved two in my mouth and took satisfaction in the crunch.

"The cupcakes weren't that great." Cat grabbed a handful of pretzels and began crunching too. "You didn't miss much."

"Aww, you're such a good friend for lying to me!" I blinked away another bout of tears. "Such a good friend."

"Okay." Cat patted my hand. "How about that water?"

I nodded and took a gulp. Then another. I could feel Cat's eyes on me, wary and concerned. Reaching for another pretzel, I took a deep breath. "He said he loves me."

"That's good, right?" The genuine confusion in Cat's voice would've made me laugh if I weren't on the verge of a breakdown in the middle of this skanky, dank bar. Of course she was confused. It *sounded* like a good thing. Unless you were Cat. Then, it sounded terrifying.

"You love him, too, right?" she continued, still teetering somewhere between bafflement and disgust.

I nodded and wiped the condensation from my glass.

"So, what's the problem? Why are you drowning in a puddle of cheap booze and tears?"

"Because three months." I reached for a pretzel and broke it between my fingers. "That's why!"

"Maybe you should cut him some slack."

I dropped the pretzel to the table. "Wh-what?"

Cat stopped fidgeting and met my eye. "It's scary, what he did back there."

"Yeah?" I lifted my chin. "So was telling him I loved him, you know, three months ago."

"I know." Cat folded her arms over her chest. "And I'm not saying the dude deserves insta-forgiveness. Just…"

"Just?" Was Cat Keller, infamous commitment-phobe, coming to the defense of the Big L? How drunk *was* I?

"Maybe throw him a goodbye bone or something."

Ahh. There's the Cat I know and love. I snorted. "Not really my preferred way to handle things."

"No, you prefer moping and beating yourself up over whether or not you made the right decision."

My eyes flew to Cat's. "What?"

"Just saying." She summoned the waitress and ordered an appetizer platter. How she could possibly be hungry at a time like this, I did not know. "It's what you did with Wes," she continued. "It's what you did with your job. It's your thing."

"It's not—"

"*Oh, maybe I shouldn't have left Wes. We could've been married by now,*" she sang in a lilting voice. "*Sigh. Why haven't I gotten promoted yet at this job I don't like that much anyway. Boo.*"

"Why are you making me sound British?" I sat back in my seat. "Besides, that's not what I do."

"A super hot guy said he loves me, but how about I spend days and months and years thinking *instead of making out with him?"* As she said it, she lifted an eyebrow. "Really?" she continued in her own voice. "You told him you needed to think?"

My mouth fell open. "You talked to him?"

"Well, yeah." The waitress plopped a platter of fried treats between us, momentarily distracting Cat. "I went looking for you, and you were gone. I found Jack instead. All by his lonesome in the kitchen."

"And he told you all about how mean and horrible and—"

"He told me how much he loves you and he knows he screwed up." She broke a mozzarella stick in half, a string of cheese obscuring her face for a moment. "He told me he'd get it if he never heard from you again." Popping half of the cheesy goodness into her mouth, she added, "He better hear from you again."

"Since when are you an advocate for love?" I snarled, sitting back in my seat. "It doesn't suit you."

"Yeah, well, mopey, cranky, and self-pitying doesn't suit you." She swallowed and took another bite. "I mean, do what you want. But just know that if you don't figure out how to stop sucking the life out of every room you enter, I may need to find another wing woman."

I stole a mozzarella stick and bit into it as I mulled over her words.

"Now, I'm all for making the dude suffer," Cat continued, moving on to the chicken wings. "But at what cost, Tierney?" She bit into a wing. "*At. What. Cost?*"

"You're so classy." I held a napkin out. "People are starting to stare."

She ignored me and licked sauce from her fingers. "All I'm saying is, the dude has suffered plenty. So have you." Shrugging, she reached for a second wing. "Do you really want to keep suffering just to prove a point?"

I sat back in my seat and stared at my sauce-covered best friend. "Is it the booze, or did that actually make sense?"

"Probably the booze." Cat swiped at a smear of sauce on her cheek. "I mean, what do *I* know about this stuff?"

***

"Oh, I can't move," Cat groaned as she put her car in park an hour later. "Why did you let me eat so much?"

I snorted. "You and that spinach dip were having a moment." I unbuckled my seatbelt. "I wasn't in the mood to lose an arm."

She looked over, protest on her lips. After reconsidering, she nodded. "Yeah, okay." Pushing her door open, she got out of the car with another long, dramatic groan. "Oh, god."

Rolling my eyes, I joined her outside. "Is that necessary? People are going to think I'm murdering you. I don't need the cops—"

"Shh." Cat waved a hand, cutting me off. "Listen."

"What are you—" And then I heard it. The pulsing, stripper-esque beat of "Pour Some Sugar On Me," echoing through the street. "The hell?"

"Did you leave music on in your place?" Cat looked at me, her face baffled. "Or is someone giving a striptease somewhere?"

"I don't..." I trailed off, my eyes finding the source straight ahead. "Oh, god."

Cat burst into laughter. "That is the cheesiest thing I have ever seen."

She wasn't kidding. Jack, in his white button-down and undone tie, stood on the hood of his truck, his phone held high over his head.

"Why is he here?" I gave Cat's arm a shove. "I told him I needed to think!"

Cat shoved me back, glaring. "I told him you didn't mean it."

"What?" I pushed her again. "Why would you do that?"

"Listen." She raised a finger, her voice sharp. "You push me one more time, and I'll either barf all over you or slug you in the eye. And I don't think you want to be vomit-covered or bruised for the biggest moment of your life."

"Sorry." I twisted my hands together. "Sorry."

"You're forgiven." Then, she gave *me* a shove. "Now, let's go."

I squawked. "I don't know what to say. I—"

"Something tells me you'll figure it out." Cat put her hands on my shoulders and propelled me forward, ignoring my protests.

When Jack saw me, a smile broke over his face. A smile that shot all kinds of good feelings through my veins. I shrugged Cat off of me and ignored the feels. "What are you doing?" I called up to him, trying my damndest to not notice how cute he looked, silhouetted in the moonlight.

"I didn't have a boom box," he answered with another knock-me-to-my-knees smile. "So I improvised."

"You're disturbing the neighbors." I tried hard to look cranky, even as my insides went all gooey. "Get down here."

"What?" He cupped a hand behind his ear. "Can't hear you."

I laughed, my heart rivaling the beat of the song. "Get. Down. Here." I yelled back, holding out my hand.

Jack glanced down at it, understanding lighting his eyes. He took my hand and climbed down. "This is the fourth time I've played the song," he said once his feet were on solid ground. "I'm pretty sure Mrs. Wallace thinks I'm hitting on her."

Cat laughed. I'd forgotten she was there. She patted Jack on the arm and said, "I'll go let her down easy." Giving us a grin and a wink, she added, "You two do...whatever two crazy in love people do when they're making up." Pausing, she added, "Only, you know, maybe not in the street."

"I make no promises," Jack shot back as Cat skipped up the stairs, earning a thumbs-up from her.

Once she was inside, I took Jack's phone from his hand and silenced the music. Tucking it into his shirt pocket, I said, "All right, Mr. Dobler, what are you doing here?"

"I'm not ready to let this go, either." He took my hand, his eyes burning into me. "And I'm not willing to go another second without showing you that I—"

"This is real life, Jack." I pulled my hands from his, echoing his earlier words. "This isn't one of my happy-ever-after movies, remember?"

He winced. "I know." With a grimace, he added, "If it were, I wouldn't have hurt you in the first place."

I blinked, my eyes stinging. "But you did."

Instead of looking away, he faced the pain on my face. "I was a coward. I took the easy way out." He paused, a humorless laugh punctuating the night air. "Turns out, it wasn't so easy."

I lifted my chin, refusing to give. Even just a little. "Good."

His lips tilted, but he cut off the smile before it could take over. Not the time for smiles. "It wasn't easy. But it was necessary."

I frowned. *Hurting me was necessary?* I wanted to say. *Disappearing from my life was necessary?* But before I could speak them aloud, Jack continued.

"In those months, I looked at myself, at my life, and I saw it all through your eyes." His lips twisted. "The fear, the self-doubt. I'd been playing it *so safe.*" He shook his head. "That wasn't who I wanted to be. Not for me. Not for you."

I shifted, Cat's borrowed shoes pinching my toes. "So, instead of telling me all this, you let me wonder. For months."

"Not my best decision," he said, chagrin on his face. "I know. Believe me. I know it was stupid."

"Really stupid."

"Yep."

"Really, really, *really* stupid."

"I know." He tilted his head. "All the stupid." Huffing out a breath, he continued. "I'm sure there were a thousand less stupid things I could've done, but I had to do it this way." Reaching out, he tucked a tendril of hair behind my ear, his eyes drinking me in. "It would have been so easy to lose myself in you. But then I would've never found myself."

He balled his hand into a fist and shoved it into his pocket. "And I had to do that alone. I had to become someone I could be happy with. That way, even if—"

"Even if I didn't forgive you, you'd still be okay."

"Right." He exhaled, long and slow. When his eyes met mine, there was such a stark nakedness in them that I couldn't breathe. "What's the verdict?"

My heart picked up where the song left off, filling the streets with its beat. I knew the answer, of course. I loved this doofus. But the *what ifs* rang loud in my ears. Fear, like a rusty nail, scraped across my heart. "I—"

"Before you decide," Jack cut in. "I have pie."

I glanced behind him, then back to his face. "Is—is it magic potpie? Because that might help your case."

"Well, no..." He turned and opened the passenger door. When he faced me again, he had a pastry box in his hand. "It's *I'm-Sorry-I-Was-An-Asshole-But-I-Really-Really-Really-Love-You-And-I-Hope-You-Can-Forgive-Me* Cherry Pie."

"That's, uh, quite a mouthful." I took the pie from him and opened the lid. "Looks good, though."

"Oh, it's better than good." Reaching back into the truck, he pulled out a plastic fork. "It's impossible to eat this pie and be mad."

"Yeah?" I took the fork and dug in. "We'll see about that." Holding his eye, I lifted the fork to my lips.

Jack watched as I bit into the pie, curiosity and anticipation on his face. My eyelids fluttered as a mixture of sweet and tart exploded on my tongue. Jesus H. this pie was good.

As I chewed, I kept my face impassive. Really, I wanted to slug him for making something so damn delicious. Once I finished the bite, I shrugged. "S'alright." I sat the box in his hands. "Still mad, though."

His eyes clung to my face, amusement tilting his lips. "I guess I'll be leaving, then," he said as he took a step back.

I gripped the pastry box. "Leave the pie."

"Nuh uh." He pulled the box back. "I go, the pie goes."

"Fine," I groaned. "You don't play fair."

"Sorry." He put the box on the hood of his truck. "The pie's all I got right now."

His words caused an ache in my chest. "It's not all you have."

He lifted his eyes to mine, caution glimmering bright. "No?"

I smiled. "Well, the whole Lloyd Dobler thing was pretty cute." I paused before adding, "Song choice could've been better."

"I thought about sticking with the original, but it just didn't suit you."

"But 'Pour Some Sugar On Me' did?"

"Well, yeah." A slow grin spread over his face. "Sexy. Inappropriate. Kind of makes you want to take your clothes off…"

I laughed and gave his shoulder a shove. "Jackass."

His hand circled around my wrist before I could pull completely away, and he tugged me closer. With his other hand, he tilted my chin up so that we were eye-to-eye. "What do you say? Can you give this jackass a chance to un-jackass himself?"

Reaching up, I pushed my fingers through his hair. The air thickened around us. The moonlight caught a flicker of heat in Jack's eyes. Man oh man, did I want to get this make-up good and started.

I started to pull my hand away, but Jack reached out and grabbed my wrist.

I watched in slow motion as he turned my hand so that my palm was toward his face. Without taking his eyes from mine, he pressed my palm to his cheek. My breath hitched, my heartbeat halted. A jolt shot straight to my toes and I stepped forward until my breasts brushed against Jack's chest, until we were breathing the same air, until Jack's other hand splayed across my lower back and pulled me tight against him. All oxygen seeped from my lungs as I lifted my face to his.

Everything else fell away as Jack's lips came crashing down onto mine. The hunger, the desperation, the heat between us caused an inferno that I gladly threw myself into.

Jack pulled his mouth from mine and dropped kisses over my cheeks and chin and down my neck. "God, I've missed you," he murmured, his voice husky in my ear. His arms tightened around me and I pushed his unruly hair away from his face, looking into his absurdly blue eyes.

"I really do love you, you jackass," I murmured, feeling the truth in those words with every beat of my heart. "It's about time you caught up to me, darlin'."

The End

Note from the Author

THANKS for reading Something So Sweet! I hoped you enjoyed Jack & Tierney's story as much as I did. I've been writing this book for over a decade, on and off, and there are no words to express how it feels to get it out into the world. Mostly relief, because I love this book, but if I had to read it one more time, I may have set the whole damn thing aflame!

SOMETHING So Sweet is the first book in the Breakaway series. Book two, Goodnight & Go, will feature Tierney's best friend, Cat, and a certain dimpled deejay. And, guys, these two are a lot of fun!

WANT a sneak peek at Cat's story? Behind-the-scenes goodness? Cute pictures of my pups? Well, then head over to my website to sign up for my newsletter!

THANKS again for reading! I'll love you forever if you wander over to the interwebz and leave me a review!

Acknowledgments

A MILLION thanks to the ladies of Pigasus Pen, for reading no less than 23,000 versions of this book, and making it better each time. You helped me get from baby writer to published author, and I love you for that! Alyssa Alexander—you lit a fire under my ass and wouldn't let it go out. Thank you for setting my deadline for me, and pushing me every step of the way. Can I be you when I grow up? Erin King—you probably read this book more than anyone else, and I appreciate your patience and forever useful insight. Thank you! Louise Knott Ahern, for the hours'-long writing-and-brainstorming sessions, faith, and wisdom. My parents for raising a dreamer, and believing she'd make those dreams come true. My brother, for sharing all my girly posts on his Facebook page. Everyone in the Capital City Writers Association—it really DOES take a village, and I'm glad I found mine.

AND, last but not least, my writing lobster, Christina Mitchell. Your endless support, brilliant advice, and wicked sense of humor got me through the darkest times in my life—both in and outside of my writing. I am forever grateful for the hours upon hours we've spent writing, laughing, and ogling Dean Winchester. You are the Tierney to my Cat, and I love you.

About the Author

MEIKA USHER is a romance author, a puppy mama, and a lover of all things pizza. When she's not writing snarky, sexy, love stories, she can be found binge-watching Supernatural (she's a Dean girl), memorizing all the song lyrics ever (it's her superpower), or planning to see the world, one country at a time (Prague is next on her list). Meika can be found on the interwebz at meikausher.com.